P9-CNI-243

Praise for *Summertime* by J. M. Coetzee

"The novel is a postmodern masterpiece." —*New York Post*

"Reading *Summertime*, you wonder at how artfully this modern master can 'sublime' (his verb) the raw material of life and love in an attempt to grasp the truth about human nature, which may, in the end, be just too elusive for words." —*O, The Oprah Magazine*

"*Summertime* is a challenging but rewarding read, a warts-and-all mosaic of an irascible character. Even though the facts of the fiction are not always in accord with information known about the real Coetzee, the variant perspectives coalesce to form an intriguing likeness of a formidable writer." —*The Seattle Times*

"A compelling testament to the limitations of art, a bracing example of one of our major writers." —*The Boston Globe*

"Intimately rewarding . . . it calls into question the demands we place on art and the people who make it. . . . *Summertime* dares us to ponder." —*TimeOut New York* (four stars)

"Delve[s] deeper into the workings of a writer's mind than we ever could have hoped to go." —*The Nation*

"J. M. Coetzee's magnificent *Summertime* is a work of fiction. Never, though has a genre seemed more ambiguous, more masterfully and provocatively tampered with than in this incredible novel. . . . Genius." —*BookPage*

"There is a highly subtle kind of heroism in the way people in his novels struggle to deal with everyday life and sometimes succeed." —*The San Diego Union-Tribune*

"*Summertime*, with its dark tone softened by surprising dabs of humor, is a rich addition to Coetzee's formidable oeuvre." —*PortlandOregonian.com*

"Intriguingly designed novel . . . with its candor and frank design, and intricate passions on display." —NPR's *All Things Considered*

ABOUT THE AUTHOR

J. M. Coetzee was awarded the Nobel Prize in Literature in 2003. He has won many other literary awards, including the Booker Prize (twice), the Prix Étranger Femina, the Jerusalem Prize, the Lannan Literary Award, the *Irish Times* International Fiction Prize, the Commonwealth Writers Prize, and South Africa's premier literary award, the CNA Prize (three times). He is the author of nineteen books, most recently *Diary of a Bad Year*. A native of South Africa, Coetzee now lives in Adelaide, Australia.

J. M. Coetzee

Summertime

FICTION

PENGUIN BOOKS

PENGUIN BOOKS

Published by the Penguin Group
Penguin Group (USA) Inc., 375 Hudson Street, New York, New York 10014, U.S.A.
Penguin Group (Canada), 90 Eglinton Avenue East, Suite 700, Toronto,
Ontario, Canada M4P 2Y3 (a division of Pearson Penguin Canada Inc.)
Penguin Books Ltd, 80 Strand, London WC2R 0RL, England
Penguin Ireland, 25 St Stephen's Green, Dublin 2, Ireland (a division of Penguin Books Ltd)
Penguin Group (Australia), 250 Camberwell Road, Camberwell,
Victoria 3124, Australia (a division of Pearson Australia Group Pty Ltd)
Penguin Books India Pvt Ltd, 11 Community Centre, Panchsheel Park, New Delhi – 110 017, India
Penguin Group (NZ), 67 Apollo Drive, Rosedale, North Shore 0632,
New Zealand (a division of Pearson New Zealand Ltd)
Penguin Books (South Africa) (Pty) Ltd, 24 Sturdee Avenue,
Rosebank, Johannesburg 2196, South Africa

Penguin Books Ltd, Registered Offices: 80 Strand, London WC2R 0RL, England

First published in Great Britain by Harvill Secker,
an imprint of the Random House Group Limited 2009
Published in the United States of America by Viking Penguin,
a member of Penguin Group (USA) Inc. 2009
Published in Penguin Books 2010

3 5 7 9 10 8 6 4 2

Portions of this work first appeared in *The New York Review of Books*.

Excerpt from *Waiting for Godot* by Samuel Beckett. Copyright © 1954 by Grove Press, Inc.
Copyright © renewed 1982 by Samuel Beckett.
Used by permission of Grove / Atlantic, Inc. This selection has been altered by J. M. Coetzee.

PUBLISHER'S NOTE
This is a work of fiction. Names, characters, places, and incidents are either the product of the author's imagination or are used fictitiously, and any resemblance to actual persons, living or dead, business establishments, events, or locales is entirely coincidental.

THE LIBRARY OF CONGRESS HAS CATALOGED THE HARDCOVER EDITION AS FOLLOWS:
Coetzee, J. M., 1940–
Summertime : fiction / J. M. Coetzee.
p. cm.
Sequel to: Boyhood, and Youth.
ISBN 978-0-670-02138-3 (hc.)
ISBN 978-0-14-311845-9 (pbk.)
1. Authors—Fiction. 2. Autobiographical fiction. I. Title.
PR9369.3.C58S86 2010
823'.914—dc22   2009037527

Printed in the United States of America

Contents

Author's note

My thanks to Marilia Bandeira for assistance with Brazilian Portuguese, and to the estate of Samuel Beckett for permission to quote (in fact to misquote) from *Waiting for Godot*.

Notebooks 1972–75

22 August 1972

IN YESTERDAY'S *Sunday Times*, a report from Francistown in Botswana. Sometime last week, in the middle of the night, a car, a white American model, drove up to a house in a residential area. Men wearing balaclavas jumped out, kicked down the front door, and began shooting. When they had done with shooting they set fire to the house and drove off. From the embers the neighbours dragged seven charred bodies: two men, three women, two children.

The killers appeared to be black, but one of the neighbours heard them speaking Afrikaans among themselves and was convinced they were whites in blackface. The dead were South Africans, refugees who had moved into the house mere weeks ago.

Approached for comment, the South African Minister of Foreign Affairs, through a spokesman, calls the report 'unverified'. Inquiries will be undertaken, he says, to determine whether the deceased were indeed South African citizens. As for the military, an unnamed source denies that the SA Defence Force had anything to do with the matter. The killings are probably an internal ANC matter, he suggests, reflecting 'ongoing tensions' between factions.

So they come out, week after week, these tales from the borderlands, murders followed by bland denials. He reads the reports and feels soiled. So this is what he has come back to! Yet where in the world can one hide where one will not feel soiled? Would he feel any cleaner in the snows of Sweden, reading at a distance about his people and their latest pranks?

How to escape the filth: not a new question. An old rat-question that will not let go, that leaves its nasty, suppurating wound. Agenbite of inwit.

'I see the Defence Force is up to its old tricks again,' he remarks to his father. 'In Botswana this time.' But his father is too wary to rise to the bait. When his father picks up the news-paper, he takes care to skip straight to the sports pages, missing out the politics – the politics and the killings.

His father has nothing but disdain for the continent to the north of them. *Buffoons* is the word he uses to dismiss the leaders of African states: petty tyrants who can barely spell their own names, chauffeured from one banquet to another in their Rolls-Royces, wearing Ruritanian uniforms festooned with medals they have awarded themselves. Africa: a place of starving masses with homicidal buffoons lording it over them.

'They broke into a house in Francistown and killed everyone,' he presses on nonetheless. 'Executed them. Including the chil-dren. Look. Read the report. It's on the front page.'

His father shrugs. His father can find no form of words spacious enough to cover his distaste for, on the one hand, thugs who slaughter defenceless women and children and, on the other, terrorists who wage war from havens across the border.

4

He resolves the problem by immersing himself in the cricket scores. As a response to a moral dilemma it is feeble; yet is his own response – fits of rage and despair – any better?

Once upon a time he used to think that the men who dreamed up the South African version of public order, who brought into being the vast system of labour reserves and internal passports and satellite townships, had based their vision on a tragic misreading of history. They had misread history because, born on farms or in small towns in the hinterland, and isolated within a language spoken nowhere else in the world, they had no appreciation of the scale of the forces that had since 1945 been sweeping away the old colonial world. Yet to say they had misread history was in itself misleading. For they read no history at all. On the contrary, they turned their backs on it, dismissing it as a mass of slanders put together by foreigners who held Afrikaners in contempt and would turn a blind eye if they were massacred by the blacks, down to the last woman and child. Alone and friendless at the remote tip of a hostile continent, they erected their fortress state and retreated behind its walls: there they would keep the flame of Western Christian civilization burning until finally the world came to its senses.

That was the way they spoke, more or less, the men who ran the National Party and the security state, and for a long time he thought they spoke from the heart. But not any more. Their talk of saving civilization, he now tends to think, has never been anything but a bluff. Behind a smokescreen of patriotism they are at this very moment sitting and calculating how long they can keep the show running (the mines, the factories) before they will need to pack their bags, shred any incriminating documents, and fly off to Zürich or Monaco or San Diego, where under the cover of holding companies with names like Algro Trading or Handfast Securities they years ago bought themselves villas and apartments as insurance against the day of reckoning (*dies irae, dies illa*).

According to his new, revised way of thinking, the men who ordered the killer squad into Francistown have no mistaken vision of history, much less a tragic one. Indeed, they most likely laugh up their sleeves at folk so silly as to have visions of any kind. As for the fate of Christian civilization in Africa, they have never given two hoots about it. And these – these! – are the men under whose dirty thumb he lives!

To be expanded on: his father's response to the times as compared to his own; their differences, their (overriding) similarities.

1 September 1972

The house that he shares with his father dates from the 1920s. The walls, built in part of baked brick but in the main of mud-brick, are by now so rotten with damp creeping up from the earth that they have begun to crumble. To insulate them from the damp is an impossible task; the best that can be done is to lay an impermeable concrete apron around the periphery of the house and hope that slowly they will dry out.

From a home improvement guide he learns that for each metre of concrete he will require three bags of sand, five bags of stone, and one bag of cement. If he makes the apron around the house ten centimetres deep, he calculates, he will need thirty bags of sand, fifty bags of stone, and ten bags of cement, which will entail six trips to the builders' yard, six full loads in a one-ton truck.

Halfway through the first day of work it dawns on him that he has made a mistake of a calamitous order. Either he misread the guide or in his calculations he confused cubic metres with square metres. It is going to take many more than ten bags of cement, plus sand and stone, to lay ninety-six square metres of concrete. It is going to take many more than six trips to the builders' yard; he is going to have to sacrifice more than just a few weekends of his life.

Week after week, using a shovel and a wheelbarrow, he mixes sand, stone, cement and water; block after block he pours liquid concrete and levels it. His back hurts, his arms and wrists are so stiff that he can barely hold a pen. Above all the labour bores him. Yet he is not unhappy. What he finds himself doing is what people like him should have been doing ever since 1652, namely, his own dirty work. In fact, once he forgets about the time he is giving up, the work begins to take on its own pleasure. There is such a thing as a well-laid slab whose well-laidness is plain for all to see. The slabs he is laying will outlast his tenancy of the house, may even outlast his spell on earth; in which case he will in a certain sense have cheated death. One might spend the rest of one's life laying slabs, and fall each night into the profoundest sleep, tired with the ache of honest toil.

How many of the ragged workingmen who pass him in the street are secret authors of works that will outlast them: roads, walls, pylons? Immortality of a kind, a limited immortality, is not so hard to achieve after all. Why then does he persist in inscribing marks on paper, in the faint hope that people not yet born will take the trouble to decipher them?

To be expanded on: his readiness to throw himself into half-baked projects; the alacrity with which he retreats from creative work into mindless industry.

16 April 1973

The same *Sunday Times* which, in among exposés of torrid love affairs between teachers and schoolgirls in country towns, in among pictures of pouting starlets in exiguous bikinis, comes out with revelations of atrocities committed by the security forces, reports that the Minister of the Interior has granted a visa allowing Breyten Breytenbach to come back to the land of his birth to visit his ailing parents. A compassionate visa, it is called; it covers both Breytenbach and his wife.

Breytenbach left the country years ago to live in Paris, and soon thereafter queered his pitch by marrying a Vietnamese woman, that is to say, a non-white, an Asiatic. He not only married her but, if one is to believe the poems in which she figures, is passionately in love with her. Despite which, says the *Sunday Times*, the Minister in his compassion will permit the couple a thirty-day visit during which the so-called Mrs Breytenbach will be treated as a white person, a temporary white, an honorary white.

From the moment they arrive in South Africa Breyten and Yolande, he swarthily handsome, she delicately beautiful, are dogged by the press. Zoom lenses capture every intimate moment as they picnic with friends or paddle in a mountain stream.

The Breytenbachs make a public appearance at a literary conference in Cape Town. The hall is packed to the rafters with people come to gape. In his speech Breyten calls Afrikaners a bastard people. It is because they are bastards and ashamed of their bastardy, he says, that they have concocted their cloud-cuckoo scheme of forced separation of the races.

His speech is greeted with huge applause. Soon thereafter he and Yolande fly home to Paris, and the Sunday newspapers return to their menu of naughty nymphets, errant spouses, and state murders.

To be explored: the envy felt by white South Africans (men) for Breytenbach, for his freedom to roam the world and for his unlimited access to a beautiful, exotic sex-companion.

2 September 1973

At the Empire Cinema in Muizenberg last night, an early film of Kurosawa's, *To Live*. A stodgy bureaucrat learns that he has cancer and has only months to live. He is stunned, does not know what to do with himself, where to turn.

He takes his secretary, a bubbly but mindless young woman, out to tea. When she tries to leave he holds her back, gripping her arm. 'I want to be like you!' he says. 'But I don't know how!' She is repelled by the nakedness of his appeal.

Question: How would he react if his father were to grip his arm like that?

13 September 1973

From an employment bureau where he has left his particulars he receives a call. A client seeks expert advice on language matters, will pay by the hour – is he interested? Language matters of what nature, he inquires? The bureau is unable to say.

He calls the number provided, makes an appointment to go to an address in Sea Point. His client is a woman in her sixties, a widow whose husband has departed this world leaving the bulk of his considerable estate in a trust controlled by his brother. Outraged, the widow has resolved to challenge the will. But both firms of lawyers she has consulted have counselled her against trying. The will is, they say, watertight. Nevertheless she refuses to give up. The lawyers, she is convinced, have misread the wording of the will. Giving up on lawyers, she is instead seeking expert support of a linguistic kind.

With a cup of tea at his elbow he peruses the will. Its meaning is perfectly plain. To the widow goes the flat in Sea Point and a sum of money. The remainder of the estate goes into a trust for the benefit of his children by a former marriage.

'I fear I cannot help you,' he says. 'The wording is unambiguous. There is only one way in which it can be read.'

'What about here?' she says. She leans over his shoulder and stabs a finger at the text. Her hand is tiny, her skin mottled; on the third finger is a diamond in an extravagant setting. 'Where it says *Notwithstanding the aforesaid.*'

'It says that if you can demonstrate financial distress you are entitled to apply to the trust for support.'

'What about *notwithstanding*?'

'It means that what is stated in this clause is an exception to what has been stated before and takes precedence over it.'

'But it also means that the trust cannot withstand my claim. What does *withstand* mean if it doesn't mean that?'

'It is not a question of what *withstand* means. It is a question of what *Notwithstanding the aforesaid* means. You must take the phrase as a whole.'

She gives an impatient snort. 'I am hiring you as an expert on English, not as a lawyer,' she says. 'The will is written in English, in English words. What do the words mean? What does *notwithstanding* mean?'

A madwoman, he thinks. *How am I going to get out of this?* But of course she is not mad. She is simply in the grip of rage and greed: rage against the husband who has slipped her grasp, greed for his money.

'The way I understand the clause,' she says, 'if I make a claim then no one, including my brother-in-law, can withstand it. Because that is what *not withstand* means: he can't withstand me. Otherwise what is the point of using the word? Do you see what I mean?'

'I see what you mean,' he says.

He leaves the house with a cheque for ten rands in his pocket. Once he has delivered his report, his expert report, to which he will have attached a copy, attested by a Commissioner of Oaths, of the degree certificate that makes him an expert commentator on the meaning of English words, including the word *notwithstanding*, he will receive the remaining thirty rands of his fee.

He delivers no report. He forgoes the money that is owed him.

When the widow telephones to ask what is up, he quietly puts down the receiver.

Features of his character that emerge from the story: (a) integrity (he declines to read the will as she wants him to); (b) naiveté (he misses a chance to make some money).

31 May 1975

South Africa is not formally in a state of war, but it might as well be. As resistance has grown, the rule of law has step by step been suspended. The police and the people who run the police (as hunters run packs of dogs) are by now more or less unconstrained. In the guise of news, radio and television relay the official lies. Yet over the whole sorry, murderous show there hangs an air of staleness. The old rallying cries – *Uphold white Christian civilization! Honour the sacrifices of the forefathers!* – lack all force. We, or they, or we and they both, have moved into the endgame, and everyone knows it.

Yet while the chess players manoeuvre for advantage, human lives are still being consumed – consumed and shat out. As it is the fate of some generations to be destroyed by war, so it seems the fate of the present one to be ground down by politics.

If Jesus had stooped to play politics he might have become a key man in Roman Judaea, a big operator. It was because he was indifferent to politics, and made his indifference clear, that he was liquidated. How to live one's life outside politics, and one's death too: that was the example he set for his followers.

Odd to find himself contemplating Jesus as a guide. But where should he search for a better one?

Caution: Avoid pushing his interest in Jesus too far and turning this into a conversion narrative.

2 June 1975

The house across the street has new owners, a couple of more or less his own age with young children and a BMW. He pays no attention to them until one day there is a knock at the door. 'Hello, I'm David Truscott, your new neighbour. I've locked myself out. Could I use your telephone?' And then, as an afterthought: 'Don't I know you?'

Recognition dawns. They do indeed know each other. In 1952 David Truscott and he were in the same class, Standard Six, at St Joseph's College. He and David Truscott might have progressed side by side through the rest of high school but for the fact that David failed Standard Six and had to be kept behind. It was not hard to see why he failed: in Standard Six came algebra, and about algebra David could not grasp the first thing, the first thing being that x, y and z were there to liberate one from the tedium of arithmetic. In Latin too, David never quite got the hang of things – of the subjunctive, for example. Even at so early an age it seemed to him clear that David would be better off out of school, away from Latin and algebra, in the real world, counting banknotes in a bank or selling shoes.

But despite being regularly flogged for not grasping things – floggings that he accepted philosophically, though now and again his glasses would cloud with tears – David Truscott persisted in his schooling, pushed no doubt from behind by his parents. Somehow or other he struggled through Standard Six and then Standard Seven and so on to Standard Ten; and now here he is, twenty years later, neat and bright and prosperous and, it emerges, so preoccupied with matters of business that when he set off for the office in the morning he forgot his house key and – since his wife has taken the children to a party – can't get into the family home.

'And what is your line of business?' he inquires of David, more than curious.

'Marketing. I'm with the Woolworths Group. How about you?'

'Oh, I'm in between. I used to teach at a university in the United States, now I'm looking for a position here.'

'Well, we must get together. You must come over for a drink, exchange notes. Do you have children?'

'I am a child. I mean, I live with my father. My father is getting on in years. He needs looking after. But come in. The telephone is over there.'

So David Truscott, who did not understand x and y, is a flourishing marketer or marketeer, while he, who had no trouble understanding x and y and much else besides, is an unemployed intellectual. What does that suggest about the workings of the world? What it seems most obviously to suggest is that the path that leads through Latin and algebra is not the path to material success. But it may suggest much more: that understanding things is a waste of time; that if you want to succeed in the world and have a happy family and a nice home and a BMW you should not try to understand things but just add up the numbers or press the buttons or do whatever else it is that marketers are so richly rewarded for doing.

In the event, David Truscott and he do not get together to have the promised drink and exchange the promised notes. If of an evening it happens that he is in the front garden raking leaves at the time when David Truscott returns from work, the two of them give a neighbourly wave or nod across the street, but no more than that. He sees somewhat more of Mrs Truscott, a pale little creature forever chivvying children into or out of the second car; but he is not introduced to her and has no occasion to speak to her. Tokai Road is a busy thoroughfare, dangerous for children. There is no good reason for the Truscotts to cross to his side, or for him to cross to theirs.

3 June 1975

From where he and the Truscotts live one has only to stroll a kilometre in a southerly direction to come face to face with Pollsmoor. Pollsmoor – no one bothers to call it Pollsmoor Prison – is a place of incarceration ringed around with high walls and barbed wire and watch towers. Once upon a time it stood all alone in a waste of sandy scrubland. But over the years, first hesitantly, then more confidently, the suburban developments have crept closer, until now, hemmed in by neat rows of homes from which model citizens emerge each morning to play their part in the national economy, it is Pollsmoor that has become the anomaly in the landscape.

It is of course an irony that the South African *gulag* should protrude so obscenely into white suburbia, that the same air that he and the Truscotts breathe should have passed through the lungs of miscreants and criminals. But to the barbarians, as Zbigniew Herbert has pointed out, irony is simply like salt: you crunch it between your teeth and enjoy a momentary savour; when the savour is gone, the brute facts are still there. What does one do with the brute fact of Pollsmoor once the irony is used up?

Continuation: the Prisons Service vans that pass along Tokai Road on their way from the courts; flashes of faces, fingers gripping the grated windows; what stories the Truscotts tell their children to explain those hands and faces, some defiant, some forlorn.

Julia

DR FRANKL, YOU have had a chance to read the pages I sent you from John Coetzee's notebooks for the years 1972–75, the years, more or less, when you were friendly with him. As a way of getting into your story, I wonder whether you have any reflections on those entries. Do you recognize in them the man you knew? Do you recognize the country and the times he describes?

Yes, I remember South Africa. I remember Tokai Road, I remember the vans crammed with prisoners on their way to Pollsmoor. I remember it all quite clearly.

Nelson Mandela was of course imprisoned at Pollsmoor. Are you surprised that Coetzee doesn't mention Mandela as a near neighbour?

Mandela wasn't moved to Pollsmoor until later. In 1975 he was still on Robben Island.

Of course, I had forgotten that. And what of Coetzee's relations with his father? He and his father lived together for some while after his mother's death. Did you ever meet his father?

Several times.

Did you see the father in the son?

Do you mean, was John like his father? Physically, no. His father was smaller and slighter: a neat little man, handsome in his way, though plainly not well. He drank on the sly, and smoked, and generally did not look after himself, whereas John was a quite ferocious abstainer.

And in other respects? Were they alike in other respects?

They were both loners. Socially inept. Repressed, in the wider sense of the word.

And how did you come to meet John Coetzee?

I'll tell you in a moment. But first, there was something I didn't understand about those notebook entries: the italicized passages at the end of them – *To be expanded on* and so forth. Who wrote those? Did you?

Coetzee wrote them himself. They are memos to himself, written in 1999 or 2000, when he was thinking of adapting those particular entries for a book.

I see. How I met John. I first bumped into him in a supermarket. This was in the summer of 1972, not long after we had moved to the Cape. I seemed to be spending a lot of time in supermarkets in those days, even though our needs – I mean my needs and my child's – were quite simple. I shopped because I was bored, because I needed to get away from the house, but mainly because the supermarket gave me peace and gave me pleasure: the airiness, the whiteness, the cleanness, the muzak, the quiet hiss of trolley wheels. And then there were all the choices – this spaghetti sauce against that spaghetti sauce, this toothpaste against that toothpaste, and so forth, on and on. I found it calming. It was good for my soul. Other women I knew played tennis or did yoga. I shopped.

This was the heyday of apartheid, the 1970s, so you didn't see many people of colour in a supermarket, except of course the staff. Didn't see many men either. That was part of the pleasure. I didn't have to put on a performance. I could be myself.

You didn't see many men, but in the Tokai branch of Pick n Pay there was one I noticed now and again. I noticed him but he didn't notice me, he was too absorbed in his shopping. I approved of that. In appearance he was not what most people would call attractive. He was scrawny, he had a beard, he wore horn-rimmed glasses and sandals. He looked out of place, like a bird, one of those flightless birds; or like an abstracted scientist who had wandered by mistake out of his laboratory. There was an air of seediness about him too, an air of failure. I guessed there was no woman in his life, and it turned out I was right. What he plainly needed was someone to take care of him, some no-longer-young hippie with beads and hairy armpits and no makeup who would do the shopping and the cooking and cleaning and maybe supply him with dope too. I didn't get close enough to check out his feet, but I was ready to bet the toenails weren't trimmed.

I was always conscious, in those days, of when a man was looking at me. I could feel a pressure on my limbs, on my breasts, the pressure of the male gaze, sometimes subtle, sometimes not so subtle. You won't understand what I am talking about, but any woman will. With this man there was no pressure detectable. None.

Then one day that changed. I was standing in front of the stationery rack. Christmas was around the corner, and I was selecting wrapping paper – you know, paper with jolly Christmas motifs, candles, fir-trees, reindeer. By accident I let a roll slip, and as I bent to pick it up I dropped a second roll. Behind me I heard a man's voice: 'I'll get them.' It was of course your man, John Coetzee. He picked up both rolls, which were quite long, a metre maybe, and returned them to me, and as he did so, whether intentionally or not I still can't say, pressed them into my breast. For a second or two, through the length of the rolls, he could actually be said to have been prodding my breast.

It was outrageous, of course. At the same time it was not important. I tried to show no reaction: did not drop my eyes, did not blush, certainly did not smile. 'Thank you,' I said in a neutral voice, and turned away and went on with my business.

Nevertheless it was a personal act, no use pretending it wasn't. Whether it was going to fade away and be lost among all the other personal moments only time would tell. But not easily ignored, that intimate, unexpected nudge. In fact when I got home I went so far as to lift my bra and examine the breast in question. It was unmarked, of course. Just a breast, a young woman's innocent breast.

Then a couple of days later, driving home along Tokai Road, I spotted him on foot, Mister Prod, carrying his shopping bags. Without thinking twice I stopped and offered him a lift (you are too young to know, but in those days one still offered lifts).

Tokai of the 1970s was what you would call an upwardly mobile suburb. Though land was not cheap, there was a lot of new building going on. But the house where John lived was from an earlier era. It was one of the cottages that had housed farm-workers when Tokai was still farmland. Electricity and plumbing had been added, but as a home it was still fairly basic. I dropped him at the front gate; he did not ask me in.

Time passed. Then, happening one day to drive past the house, which was on Tokai Road, a big road, I caught sight of him. He was standing in the back of a pickup truck, shovelling sand into a wheelbarrow. He wore shorts; he looked pale and not particularly strong, but he seemed to be managing.

What was odd was that it was not customary in those days for a white man to do manual labour, unskilled labour. Kaffir work, it was generally called, work you paid someone else to do. If it was not exactly shameful to be seen shovelling sand, it certainly let the side down, if you know what I mean.

You asked me to give an idea of John as he was in those days, but I can't give you a picture of him alone without any background, otherwise there are things you will fail to understand.

I understand. I mean, I accept that.

I drove past him, as I said, did not slow down, did not wave. The whole story could have ended there and then, the whole connection, and you would not be here listening to me, you would be in some other country listening to the ramblings of some other woman. But, as it happened, I had second thoughts, and turned back.

'Hello, what are you up to?' I called out.

'As you can see: shovelling sand,' he said.

'But to what end?'

'Construction work. Do you want a tour?' And he clambered down from the pickup.

'Not now,' I said. 'Some other day. Is that pickup yours?'

'Yes.'

'So you don't have to walk to the shops. You could drive.'

'Yes.' Then he said: 'Do you live around here?'

'Further out,' I replied. 'Beyond Constantiaberg. In the bush.' It was a joke, the kind of little joke that passed between white South Africans in those days. Because of course it wasn't true that I lived in the bush. The only people who lived in the bush, the real bush, were blacks. What he was meant to understand was that I lived in one of the new developments carved out of the ancestral bush of the Cape Peninsula.

'Well, I won't hold you up any longer,' I said. 'What are you constructing?'

'I'm not constructing, just concreting,' he said. 'I'm not clever enough to construct.' Which I took as a little joke on his part to answer the little joke on mine. Because if he was neither rich nor handsome nor appealing – none of which he was – then, if he was not clever, there was nothing left to be. But of course he had to be clever. He even looked clever, in the way that scientists who spend their lives hunched over microscopes look clever: a narrow, myopic kind of cleverness to go with the horn-rimmed glasses.

You must believe me when I tell you that nothing – nothing! – could have been further from my mind than flirting with this man. For he had no sexual presence whatsoever. It was as though he had been sprayed from head to toe with a neutralizing spray, a neutering spray. Certainly he was guilty of nudging me in the breast with a roll of Christmas paper: I had not forgotten that, my breast retained the memory. But ten to one, I now told myself, it had been nothing but a clumsy accident, the act of a *Schlemiel*.

So why did I have second thoughts? Why did I turn back? Not an easy question to answer. If there is such a thing as taking to a person, I am not sure that I took to John, not for a long time. John was not easy to take to, his whole stance toward the world was too wary, too defensive for that. I presume his mother must have taken to him, when he was little, and loved him, because that is what mothers are there for. But it was hard to imagine anyone else doing so.

You don't mind a little frank talk, do you? So let me fill out the picture. I was twenty-six at the time, and had had carnal relations with only two men. Two. The first was a boy I met when I was fifteen. For years, until he was called up into the army, he and I were as tight as twins. After he went away I moped for a while, kept to myself, then found a new boyfriend. With the new boyfriend I remained as tight as twins throughout my student years; as soon as we graduated he and I were married, with both families' blessing. In each case it was all or nothing. My nature has always been like that: all or nothing. So at the age of twenty-six I was in many respects an innocent. I had not the faintest idea, for instance, how one went about seducing a man.

Don't misunderstand me. It was not that I led a sheltered life. A sheltered life was not possible in the circles in which we, my husband and I, moved. More than once, at cocktail parties, some man or other, usually a business acquaintance of my husband's, had manoeuvred me into a corner and leant close and asked in a low voice whether I didn't feel lonely out in the suburbs, with Mark away so much of the time, whether I wouldn't like to get away one day next week for lunch. Of course I didn't play along, but this, I inferred, was how extra-marital affairs were initiated. A strange man would take you to lunch and after lunch drive you to a beach cottage belonging to a friend to which he happened to have a key, or to a city hotel, and there the sexual part of the transaction would be carried out. Then the next day the man would phone to say how much he had enjoyed his time with you and would you like to meet again next Tuesday? And so it would proceed, Tuesday after Tuesday, the discreet lunches, the episodes in bed, until the man stopped calling or you stopped answering his calls; and the sum of it all was called having an affair.

In the world of business — I'll say more about my husband and his business in a moment — there is pressure on men — or at least there was in those days — to have presentable wives, and therefore on wives to be presentable; to be presentable and to be accommodating too, within bounds. That is why, even though my husband would get upset when I told him about the over-tures his colleagues were making to me, he and they continued to have cordial relations. No displays of outrage, no fisticuffs, no duels at dawn, just now and then a bout of quiet fuming and bad temper in the confines of the home.

The whole question of who in that little enclosed world was sleeping with whom seems to me now, as I look back, darker than anyone was prepared to admit, darker and more sinister. The men both liked and disliked it that their wives were coveted by other men. They felt threatened but they were nevertheless excited. And the women, the wives, were excited too: I would have had to be blind not to see that. Excitement all around, an envelope of libidinous excitement. From which I purposely excised myself. At the parties I mention I was as presentable as one was required to be but I was never accommodating.

As a result I made no friends among the wives, who then put their heads together and decided I was cold and supercilious. What is more, they made certain their judgment got relayed to me. As for me, I would like to be able to say I could not have cared less, but that was not true, I was too young and unsure of myself.

Mark did not want me to sleep with other men. At the same time he wanted other men to see what kind of woman he had married, and to envy him for it. Much the same, I presume, held for his friends and colleagues: they wanted the wives of other men to succumb to their advances but they wanted their own wives to remain chaste − chaste and alluring. Logically it made no sense. As a social microsystem it was unsustainable. Yet these were businessmen, what the French call men of affairs, astute, clever (in another sense of the word *clever*), men who knew about systems, about which systems are sustainable and which are not. That is why I say that the system of the licit illicit in which they all participated was darker than they were prepared to admit. It could continue to operate, in my view, only at considerable psychic cost to them, and only as long as they refused to acknowledge what at some level they must have known.

At the beginning of our marriage, Mark's and mine, when we were so sure of each other that we did not believe anything could shake us, we made a pact that we would have no secrets from each other. As far as I was concerned, that pact still held at the time I am telling you about. I hid nothing from Mark. I hid nothing because I had nothing to hide. Mark, on the other hand, had once transgressed. He had transgressed and had confessed his transgression, and been shaken by the consequences. After that jolt he privately concluded it was more convenient to lie than to tell the truth.

The field Mark was employed in was financial services. His firm identified investment opportunities for clients and managed their investments for them. The clients were for the most part wealthy South Africans trying to get their money out of the country before the country imploded (the word they used) or exploded (the word I preferred). For reasons that were never made clear to me – there were, after all, even in those days, such things as telephones – his job required him to travel once a week to their branch office in Durban for what he called consultations. If you added up the days, it turned out he was spending as much time in Durban as at home.

One of the colleagues Mark consulted with at their branch office was a woman named Yvette. She was older than he, Afrikaans, divorced. At first he used to speak freely of her. She even telephoned him at home, once or twice, on business. Then all mention of her dried up. 'Is there some problem with Yvette?' I asked Mark. 'No,' he said. 'Is she attractive?' 'Not really – just ordinary.'

From that evasiveness on his part I guessed something was brewing. I began to pay attention to odd details: messages that inexplicably didn't reach him, missed flights, things like that.

One day, when he came back from one of his lengthy absences, I confronted him head-on. 'I couldn't get hold of you last night at your hotel,' I said – 'Were you with Yvette?'

'Yes,' he said.

'Did you sleep with her?'

'Yes,' he replied (*I am sorry but I cannot tell a lie*).

'Why?' I said.

He shrugged.

'Why?' I said again.

'Because,' he said.

'Well, bugger you,' I said, and turned my back on him and locked myself in the bathroom, where I did not cry – the thought of crying did not so much as cross my mind – but on the contrary, choking with vengefulness, squeezed a full tube of toothpaste and a full tube of hair-mousse into the hand-basin, flooded the mess with hot water, stirred it with a hairbrush, and flushed it down the sink.

That was the background. After that episode, after his confession did not win him the approval he was expecting, he turned to lying. 'Do you still see Yvette?' I asked after another of his trips.

'I have to see Yvette, I have no choice, we work together,' he replied.

'But do you still see her in *that* way?'

'What you call *that way* is over,' he said. 'It only happened once.'

'Once or twice,' I said.

'Once,' he repeated, cementing the lie.

'In fact, it was just one of those things,' I offered.

'Exactly. Just one of those things.' And therewith words ceased between Mark and me, words and everything else, for the night.

Each time Mark lied he would make sure he looked me straight in the eye. *Levelling with Julia*: that must be how he thought of it. It was from this level look of his that I could tell – infallibly – that he was lying. You won't believe how bad Mark was at lying – how bad men are in general. What a pity I had nothing to lie about, I thought. I could have shown Mark a thing or two, technique-wise.

Chronologically speaking, Mark was older than me, but that was not how I saw it. The way I saw it, I was the oldest in our family, followed by Mark, who was about thirteen, followed by our daughter Christina, who would be two at her next birthday. In respect of maturity my husband was therefore closer to the child than he was to me.

As for Mister Prod, Mister Nudge, the man shovelling sand from the back of the truck – to return to him – I had no idea how old he was. For all I knew, he might be another thirteen-year-old. Or he might actually, *mirabile dictu*, be a grown-up. I was going to have to wait and see.

'I was out by a factor of six,' he was saying (or maybe it was sixteen, I was only half listening). 'Instead of one ton of sand, six (or sixteen) tons of sand. Instead of one and a half tons of gravel, ten tons of gravel. I must have been out of my mind.'

'Out of your mind,' I said, playing for time while I caught up.

'To make a mistake like that.'

'I make mistakes with numbers all the time. I get the decimal point in the wrong place.'

'Yes, but a factor of six isn't like misplacing the decimal point. Not unless you are a Sumerian. Anyway, the answer to your question is, it is going to take for ever.'

What question, I asked myself? And what is this *it* that is going to take for ever?

'I have to go now,' I said. 'I have a child waiting for her lunch.'

'You have children?'

'Yes, I have a child. Why shouldn't I? I am a grown woman with a husband and a child whom I have to feed. Why are you surprised? Why else should I spend so much time in Pick n Pay?'

'For the music?' he offered.

'And you? Don't you have a family?'

'I have a father who lives with me. Or with whom I live. But no family in the conventional sense. My family has flown.'

'No wife? No children?'

'No wife, no children. I am back to being a son.'

They have always interested me, these exchanges between human beings when the words have nothing to do with the traffic of thoughts through the mind. As he and I were speaking, for instance, my memory threw up the visual image of the really quite repulsive stranger, with thick black hair sprouting from his earholes and over the top button of his shirt, who at the most recent barbecue had ever so casually placed a hand on my bottom as I stood dishing up salad for myself: not to stroke me or pinch me, just to cup my buttock in his big hand. If that image was filling my mind, what might be filling the mind of this other, less hirsute man? And how fortunate that most people, even people who are no good at straight-out lying, are at least competent enough at concealment not to reveal what is going on inside them, not by the slightest tremor of the voice or dilation of the pupil!

'Well, goodbye,' I said.

'Goodbye,' he said.

I went home, paid the house-help, gave Chrissie her lunch and put her down for her nap, then baked two sheets of chocolate brownies. While they were still warm I drove back to the house on Tokai Road. It was a beautiful, wind-still day. Your man (remember, I did not know his name at that point) was in the yard doing something with timber and a hammer and nails. He was stripped to the waist; his shoulders were red where the sun had caught them.

'Hello,' I said. 'You should wear a shirt, the sun isn't good for you. Here, I've brought some brownies for you and your father. They are better than the stuff you get at Pick n Pay.'

Looking suspicious, in fact looking quite irritated, he put aside his tools and took the parcel. 'I can't invite you in, too much of a mess,' he said. I was clearly not welcome.

'That's all right,' I said. 'I can't stay anyway, I have to get back to my child. I was just making a neighbourly gesture. Would you and your father like to come over for a meal one evening? A neighbourly meal?'

He gave a smile, the first smile I had had from him. Not an attractive smile, too tight-lipped. He was self-conscious about his teeth, which were in bad shape. 'Thank you,' he said, 'but I'll have to check with my father first. He isn't one for late nights.'

'Tell him it won't be a late night,' I said. 'You can eat and go, I won't be offended. It will just be the three of us. My husband is away.'

You must be getting worried. *What have I let myself in for?* you must be asking yourself. *How can this woman pretend to have total recall of mundane conversations dating back three or four decades? And when is she going to get to the point?* So let me be candid: as far as the dialogue is concerned, I am making it up as I go along. Which I presume is permitted, since we are talking about a writer. What I am telling you may not be true to the letter, but it is true to the spirit, be assured of that. Can I proceed?

[Silence.]

I scribbled my phone number on the box of brownies. 'And let me tell you my name too,' I said, 'in case you were wondering. My name is Julia.'

'Julia. How sweetly flows the liquefaction of her clothes.'

'Really,' I said. What he meant I had no idea.

He arrived as promised the next evening, but without his father. 'My father is not feeling well,' he said. 'He has taken an aspirin and gone to bed.'

We ate at the kitchen table, the two of us, with Chrissie on my lap. 'Say hello to the uncle,' I said to Chrissie. But Chrissie would have nothing to do with the strange man. A child knows when something is up. Feels it in the air.

In fact Christina never took to John, then or later. As a young child she was fair and blue-eyed, like her father and quite unlike me. I'll show you a picture. Sometimes I used to feel that, because she did not take after me in looks, she would never take to me. Strange. I was the one who did all the caring and caring-for in the household, yet compared with Mark I was the intruder, the dark one, the odd one out.

The uncle. That was what I called John in front of the child. Afterwards I regretted it. Something sordid in passing off a lover as one of the family.

Anyway, we ate, we chatted, but the zest, the excitement was beginning to go out of me, leaving me flat. Aside from the wrapping paper incident in the supermarket, which I might or might not have misread, I was the one who had made all the overtures, issued the invitation. *Enough, no more,* I said to myself. *It is up to him now to push the button through the hole or else not push the button through the hole.* So to speak.

The truth is, I was not cut out to be a seductress. I did not even approve of the word, with its overtones of lacy underwear and French perfume. It was precisely in order not to fall into the role of seductress that I had not dressed up for the present

33

occasion. I wore the same white cotton blouse and green Terylene slacks (yes, Terylene) that I had worn to the supermarket that morning. What you see is what you get.

Don't smile. I am perfectly aware how much I was behaving like a character in a book — like one of those high-minded young women in Henry James, say, determined, despite her better instincts, to do the difficult, the modern thing. Particularly when my peers, the wives of Mark's colleagues at the firm, were turning for guidance not to Henry James or George Eliot but to *Vogue* or *Marie Claire* or *Fair Lady*. But then, what are books for if not to change our lives? Would you have come all the way to Kingston to hear what I have to say about John if you did not believe books are important?

No. No, I wouldn't.

Exactly. And John wasn't exactly a snappy dresser himself. One pair of good trousers, three plain white shirts, one pair of shoes: a real child of the Depression. But let me get back to the story.

For supper that night I made a simple lasagne. Pea soup, lasagne, ice cream: that was the menu, bland enough for a two-year-old. The lasagne was sloppier than it should have been because it was made with cottage cheese instead of ricotta. I could have made a second dash to the shops for ricotta, but on principle I did not, just as on principle I did not change my outfit.

What did we talk about over supper? Nothing much. I concentrated on feeding Chrissie — I didn't want her to feel neglected. And John was not a great talker, as you must know.

I don't know. I never met him in the flesh.

34

You never met him? I'm surprised to hear that.

I never sought him out. I never even corresponded with him. I thought it would be better if I had no sense of obligation toward him. It would leave me free to write what I wished.

But you sought me out. Your book is going to be about him yet you chose not to meet him. Your book is not going to be about me yet you asked to meet me. How do you explain that?

Because you were a figure in his life. You were important to him.

How do you know that?

I am just repeating what he said. Not to me, but to lots of people.

He said that I was an important figure in his life? I am surprised. I am gratified. Gratified not that he should have thought so – I agree, I did have quite an impact on his life – but that he should have said so to other people.

Let me make a confession. When you first contacted me, I nearly decided not to speak to you. I thought you were some busybody, some academic newshound who had come upon a list of John's women, his conquests, and was now going down the list, ticking off the names, hoping to get some dirt on him.

You don't have a high opinion of academic researchers.

No, I don't. Which is why I have been trying to make it clear to you that I was not one of his conquests. If anything, he was

35

one of mine. But tell me – I'm curious – to whom did he say that I was important?

To various people. In letters. He doesn't name you, but you are easy enough to identify. Also, he kept a photograph of you. I came across it among his papers.

A photograph! Can I see it? Do you have it with you?

I'll make a copy and send it.

Yes, of course I was important to him. He was in love with me, in his way. But there is an important way of being import-ant, and an unimportant way, and I have my doubts that I made it to the important important level. I mean, he never wrote about me. I never entered his books. Which to me means I never quite flowered within him, never quite came to life.

[Silence.]

No comment? You have read his books. Where in his books do you find traces of me?

I can't answer that. I don't know you well enough to say. Don't you recognize yourself in any of his characters?

No.

Perhaps you are in his books in a more diffuse way, not immediately detectable.

Perhaps. But I would have to be convinced of that. Shall we go on? Where was I?

Supper. Lasagne.

Yes. Lasagne. Conquests. I fed him lasagne and then I completed my conquest of him. How explicit do I need to be? Since he is dead, it can make no difference to him, any indiscreetness on my part. We used the marital bed. If I am going to desecrate my marriage, I thought, I may as well do so thoroughly. And a bed is more comfortable than the sofa or the floor.

As for the experience itself – I mean the experience of infidelity, which is what the experience was, predominantly, for me – it was stranger than I expected, and then over before I could get accustomed to the strangeness. Yet it was exciting, no doubt about that, from start to finish. My heart did not stop hammering. Not something I will forget, ever. Going back to Henry James, there are plenty of betrayals in James, but I recall nothing about the sense of excitement, of heightened self-awareness, during the act itself – the act of betrayal, I mean. Which suggests to me that, though James liked to present himself as a great betrayer, he had never actually done the deed itself, bodily.

My first impressions? I found this new lover of mine bonier than my husband, and lighter. *Doesn't get enough to eat,* I remember thinking. He and his father together in that mean little cottage on Tokai Road, a widower and his celibate son, two incompetents, two of life's failures, supping on polony sausage and biscuits and tea. Since he didn't want to bring his father to me, would I have to start dropping in on them with baskets of nourishing goodies?

The image that has stayed with me is of him leaning over me with his eyes shut, stroking my body, frowning with concentration as if trying to memorize me through touch alone. Up and down his hand roamed, back and forth. I was, at the time, quite proud of my figure. The jogging, the callisthenics, the dieting: if there is no payoff when you undress for a man, when is there ever going to be a payoff? I may not have been a beauty, but at least I must have been a pleasure to handle: nice and trim, a good piece of woman-flesh.

If you find this kind of talk embarrassing, say so and I will shut up. I am in one of the intimate professions, so intimate talk doesn't trouble me as long as it doesn't trouble you. No? No problem? Shall I go on?

That was our first time together. Interesting, an interesting experience, but not earth-shaking. But then, I never expected it to be earth-shaking, not with him.

What I was determined to avoid was emotional entanglement. A passing fling was one thing, an affair of the heart quite another.

Of myself I was fairly sure. I was not about to lose my heart to a man about whom I knew next to nothing. But what of him? Might he be the type to brood on what had passed between us, building it up into something bigger than it really was? Be on your guard, I told myself.

Days went by, however, without any word from him. Each time I drove past the house on Tokai Road I slowed down and peered, but caught no sight of him. Nor was he at the supermarket. There was only one conclusion I could come to: he was avoiding me. In a way that was a good sign; but it annoyed me nevertheless. In fact it hurt me. I wrote him a letter, an old-fashioned letter, and put a stamp on it and dropped it in the mailbox. 'Are you avoiding me?' I wrote. 'What do I have to do to reassure you I want us to be good friends, no more?' No response.

What I did not mention in the letter, and would certainly not mention when next I saw him, was how I passed the weekend immediately after his visit. Mark and I were at each other like rabbits, having sex in the marital bed, on the floor, in the shower, everywhere, even with poor innocent Chrissie wide awake in her cot, crying, calling for me.

Mark had his own ideas about why I was in this inflamed state. Mark thought I could smell his girlfriend from Durban on him and wanted to prove to him how much better a – how shall I put it? – how much better a performer I was than she. On the Monday after the weekend in question he was booked to fly to Durban, but he pulled out – cancelled his flight, called the office to say he was sick. Then he and I went back to bed.

He could not have enough of me. He was positively enraptured with the institution of bourgeois marriage and the opportunities it afforded a man to rut both outside and inside the home.

As for me, I was – I choose my words with deliberation – I was unbearably excited to be having two men so close to each other. To myself I said, in a rather shocked way, *You are behaving like a whore! Is that what you are, by nature?* But beneath it all I was quite proud of myself, of the effect I could have. That weekend I glimpsed for the first time the possibility of growth without end in the realm of the erotic. Until then I had had a rather trite picture of erotic life: you arrive at puberty, you spend a year or two or three hesitating on the brink of the pool, then you plunge in and splash around until you find a mate who satisfies you, and that is the end of it, the end of

39

your quest. What dawned on me that weekend was that at the age of twenty-six my erotic life had barely begun.

Then at last I had a response to my letter. A phone call from John. First some cautious probing: Was I alone, was my husband away? Then the invitation: Would I like to come over for supper, an early supper, and would I like to bring my child?

I arrived at the house with Chrissie in her pram. John was waiting at the door wearing one of those blue-and-white butcher's aprons. 'Come through to the back,' he said, 'we're having a braai.'

That was where I met his father for the first time. His father was sitting hunched over the fire as if he was cold, when in fact the evening was still quite warm. Somewhat creakily he got to his feet to greet me. He looked frail, though it turned out he was only sixty-odd. 'Pleased to meet you,' he said, and gave me a nice smile. He and I got on well from the start. 'And is this Chrissie? Hello, my girl! Come to visit us, eh?'

Unlike his son, he spoke with a heavy Afrikaans accent. But his English was perfectly passable. He had apparently grown up on a farm in the Karoo, with lots of siblings. They had learned their English from a tutor – there was no school nearby – a Miss Jones or Miss Smith, out from the Old Country.

In the walled estate where Mark and I lived each of the units came with a courtyard and a built-in barbecue. Here on Tokai Road there was no such amenity, just an open fire with a few bricks around it. It seemed stupid beyond belief to have an unguarded fire when there was going to be a child around, particularly a child like Chrissie, not yet steady on her feet. I pretended to touch the wire grid, pretended to cry out with pain, whipped my hand away, sucked it. 'Hot!' I said to Chrissie. 'Careful! Don't touch!'

Why do I remember this detail? Because of the sucking. Because I was aware of John's eyes on me, and therefore purposely prolonged the moment. I had – excuse me for boasting – I had a nice mouth in those days, very kissable. My family name was Kiš, which in South Africa, where no one knew about funny diacritics, was spelled K-I-S. *Kiss-kiss,* the girls at school used to hiss when they wanted to provoke me. *Kiss-kiss,* and giggles, and a wet smacking of the lips. I could not have cared less. Nothing wrong with being kissable, I thought. End of digression. I am fully aware it is John you want to hear about, not me and my schooldays.

Grilled sausages and baked potatoes: that was the menu these two men had so imaginatively put together. For the sausages, tomato sauce from a bottle; for the potatoes, margarine. God knows what offal had gone into the making of the sausages. Fortunately I had brought along a couple of those little Heinz jars for the child.

I pleaded a ladylike appetite and took only a single sausage on my plate. With Mark away so much of the time, I found I was eating less and less meat. My diet was mainly fruit and cereal and salads. But for these two men it was meat and potatoes. They ate in the same way, in silence, bolting down their food as if it might be whipped away at any moment. Solitary eaters.

'How is the concreting coming along?' I asked.

'Another month and it will be done, God willing,' said John.

'It's making a real difference to the house,' his father said. 'No doubt about that. Much less damp than there used to be. But it's been a big job, eh, John?'

I recognized the tone at once, the tone of a parent eager to boast about his child. My heart went out to the poor man. A son in his thirties, and nothing to be said for him but that he could lay concrete! And how hard for the son too, the pressure of that longing in the parent, the longing to be proud! If there was one reason above all why I excelled at school, it was to give my parents, who lived such lonely lives in this strange country, something to be proud of.

His English – the father's – was perfectly passable, as I said, but it was clearly not his mother tongue. When he brought out an idiom, like *No doubt about that*, he did so with a little flourish, as if expecting to be applauded.

I asked him what he did. (*Did*: such an inane word; but he knew what I meant.) He told me he was a bookkeeper, that he worked in the city. 'It must be quite a schlep, getting from here to the city,' I said. 'Wouldn't it suit you better if you lived closer in?'

He mumbled some reply that I did not catch. Silence fell. Evidently I had touched on a sore spot. I tried changing the subject, but it did not help.

I had not expected much from the evening, but the flatness of the conversation, the long silences, and something else in the air too, discord or bad temper between the two of them – these were more than I was prepared to stomach. The food had been dreary, the coals were turning grey, I was feeling chilly, darkness had begun to fall, Chrissie was being attacked by mosquitoes. Nothing obliged me to go on sitting in this weed-infested back yard, nothing obliged me to participate in the family tensions of people I barely knew, even if in a technical sense one of them was or had been my lover. So I picked Chrissie up and put her back in her cart.

'Don't leave yet,' said John. 'I'll make coffee.'

'I must go,' I said. 'It's well past the child's bedtime.'

At the gate he tried to kiss me, but I wasn't in the mood for it.

The story I told myself after that evening, the story I settled on, was that my husband's infidelities had provoked me to such an extent that to punish him and salvage my own *amour propre* I had gone out and had a brief infidelity of my own. Now that it was evident what a mistake that infidelity had been, at least in the choice of accomplice, my husband's infidelity appeared in a new light, as probably a mistake too, and thus not worth getting upset about.

Over the marital weekends I think I ought at this point to draw a modest veil. I have said enough. Let me simply remind you that it was against the background of those weekends that my weekday relations with John played themselves out. If John became more than a little intrigued and even infatuated with me, it was because in me he encountered a woman at the peak of her womanly powers, living a heightened sexual life – a life that in fact had little to do with him.

Mr Vincent, I am perfectly aware it is John you want to hear about, not me. But the only story involving John that I can tell, or the only one I am prepared to tell, is this one, namely the story of my life and his part in it, which is quite different, quite another matter, from the story of his life and my part in it. My story, the story of me, began years before John arrived on the scene and went on for years after he made his exit. In the phase I am telling you about today, Mark and I were the protagonists, John and the woman in Durban members of the supporting cast. So you have to choose. Are you going to take what I offer or are you going to leave it? Shall I call off the recital here and now, or shall I go on?

43

Go on.

You are sure? Because there is a further point I wish to make. It is this. You commit a grave error if you think to yourself that the difference between the two stories, the story you wanted to hear and the story you are getting, will be nothing more than a matter of perspective – that while from my point of view the story of John may have been just one episode among many in the long narrative of my marriage, nevertheless, by dint of a quick flip, a quick manipulation of perspective, followed by some clever editing, you can transform it into a story about John and one of the women who passed through his life. Not so. Not so. I warn you most earnestly: if you go away from here and start fiddling with the text, the whole thing will turn to ash in your hands. I *really* was the main character. John *really* was a minor character. I am sorry if I seem to be lecturing you on your own subject, but you will thank me in the end. Do you understand?

I hear what you are saying. I don't necessarily agree, but I hear.

Well, let it not be said I did not warn you.

As I told you, those were great days for me, a second honey-moon, sweeter than the first and longer-lasting too. Why else do you think I remember them so well? *Truly, I am coming into myself!* I said to myself. *This is what a woman can be; this is what a woman can do!*

Do I shock you? Probably not. You belong to an unshockable generation. But it would shock my mother, what I am revealing to you, if she were alive to hear it. My mother would never have dreamed of speaking to a stranger as I am speaking now.

From one of his trips to Singapore Mark had come back with an early-model video camera. Now he set it up in the bedroom to film the two of us making love. *As a record*, he said. *And as a turn-on.* I didn't mind. I let him go ahead. He probably still has the film; he may even watch it when he feels nostalgic about the old days. Or perhaps it is lying forgotten in a box in the attic, and will be found only after his death. The stuff we leave behind! Just imagine his grandchildren, eyes popping as they watch their youthful granddad frolicking in bed with his foreign wife.

Your husband . . .

Mark and I were divorced in 1988. He married again, on the rebound. I never met my successor. They live in the Bahamas, I think, or maybe Bermuda.

Shall we let it rest there? You have heard a lot, and it's been a long day.

But that isn't the end of the story, surely.

On the contrary, it *is* the end of the story. At least of the part that matters.

But you and Coetzee continued to see each other. For years you exchanged letters. So even if that is where the story ends, from your point of view — my apologies, even if that is the end of the part of the story that is of importance to you — there is still a long tail to follow, a long entailment. Can't you give me some idea of the tail?

A short tail, not a long one. I will tell you about it, but not today. I have things to attend to. Come back next week. Fix a date with my receptionist.

Next week I will be gone. Can we meet again tomorrow?

Tomorrow is out of the question. Thursday. I can give you half an hour on Thursday, after my last appointment.

YES, THE TAIL. Where shall I begin? Let me start with John's father. One morning, not long after that dreary barbecue, I was driving down Tokai Road when I noticed someone waiting by himself at a bus stop. It was the elder Coetzee. I was in a hurry, but it would have been too rude to simply drive past, so I stopped and offered him a ride.

He asked how Chrissie was getting on. I said she was missing her father, who was away from home much of the time. I asked about John and the concreting. He gave some vague answer.

Neither of us was really in the mood for talk, but I forced myself. If he didn't mind my asking, I asked, how long was it since his wife passed away? He told me. Of his life with her, whether it had been happy or not, whether he missed her, he volunteered nothing.

'And is John your only child?' I asked.

'No, no, he has a brother, a younger brother.' He seemed surprised I did not know.

'That's curious,' I said, 'because John has the air of an only child.' Which I meant critically. I meant that he was preoccupied with himself, did not seem to make allowances for people around him.

He gave no answer – did not inquire, for instance, what air it was that an only child might have.

I asked about his second son, about where he lived. In England, replied Mr C. He had quit South Africa years ago and never come back. 'You must miss him,' I said. He shrugged. That was his characteristic response: the wordless shrug.

I must tell you, from the very first I found something unbearably sorrowful about this man. Sitting next to me in the car in his dark business suit, giving off a smell of cheap deodorant, he may have seemed the personification of stiff rectitude, but if he had suddenly burst into tears I would not have been surprised, not in the slightest. All alone save for that cold fish his elder son, trudging off each morning to what sounded like a soul-destroying job, coming back at night to a silent house – I felt more than a little pity for him.

'Well, one misses so much,' he said at last, when I thought he was not going to answer at all. He spoke in a whisper, gazing straight ahead.

I dropped him in Wynberg near the train station. 'Thanks for the lift, Julia,' he said, 'very kind of you.'

It was the first time he had actually used my name. I could have replied, *See you soon.* I could have replied, *You and John must come over for a bite.* But I didn't. I just gave a wave and drove off.

How mean! I berated myself. *How hard-hearted!* Why was I so hard on him, on both of them?

And indeed, why was I, why am I, so critical of John? At least he was looking after his father. At least, if something went wrong, his father would have a shoulder to lean on. That was more than could be said for me. My father – you are probably not interested, why should you be?, but let me tell you anyway

– my father was at that very moment in a private sanatorium outside Port Elizabeth. His clothes were locked away, he had nothing to wear, day or night, but pyjamas and a dressing gown and slippers. And he was dosed to the gills with tranquillizers. Why so? Simply for the convenience of the nursing staff, to keep him tractable. Because when he neglected to take his pills he became agitated and started to shout.

[Silence.]

Did John love his father, do you think?

Boys love their mothers, not their fathers. Don't you know your Freud? Boys hate their fathers and want to supplant them in their mothers' affections. No, of course John did not love his father, he did not love anybody, he was not built for love. But he did feel guilty about his father. He felt guilty and therefore behaved dutifully. With certain lapses.

I was telling you about my own father. My father was born in 1905, so at the time we are talking about he was getting on for seventy, and his mind was going. He had forgotten who he was, forgotten the rudimentary English he picked up when he came to South Africa. To the nurses he spoke sometimes German, sometimes Magyar, of which they understood not a word. He was convinced he was in Madagascar, in a prison camp. The Nazis had taken over Madagascar, he thought, and turned it into a *Strafkolonie* for Jews. Nor did he remember who I was. On one of my visits he mistook me for his sister Trudi, my aunt, whom I had never met but who looked a bit like me. He wanted me to go to the prison commandant and

48

plead on his behalf. *'Ich bin der Erstgeborene,'* he kept saying: I am the first-born. If *der Erstgeborene* was not going to be allowed to work (my father was a jeweller and diamond-cutter by trade), how would his family survive?

That's why I am here. That's why I am a therapist. Because of what I saw in that sanatorium. To save people from being treated as my father was treated there.

The money that kept my father in the sanatorium was supplied by my brother, his son. My brother was the one who religiously visited every week, even though my father recognized him only intermittently. In the sole sense that matters, my brother had taken on the burden of his care. In the sole sense that matters, I had abandoned him. And I was his favourite – I, his beloved Julischka, so pretty, so clever, so affectionate!

Do you know what I hope for, above all else? I hope that in the afterlife we will get a chance, each of us, to say our sorries to the people we have wronged. I will have plenty of sorries to say, believe you me.

Enough of fathers. Let me get back to the story of Julia and her adulterous dealings, the story you have travelled so far to hear.

One day my husband announced that he would be going to Hong Kong for discussions with the firm's overseas partners.

'How long will you be away?' I asked.

'A week,' he replied. 'Maybe a day or two longer if the discussions go well.'

I thought no more of it until, shortly before he was due to leave, I got a phone call from the wife of one of his colleagues: was I packing an evening dress for the Hong Kong trip? It's just Mark who is going to Hong Kong, I replied, I am not accompanying him. Oh, she said, I thought all the wives were invited.

When Mark came home I raised the subject. 'June just phoned,' I said. 'She says she is going with Alistair to Hong Kong. She says all the wives are invited.'

'Wives are invited but the firm isn't paying for them,' Mark said. 'Do you really want to come all the way to Hong Kong to sit in a hotel with a bunch of wives from the firm, bitching about the weather? Hong Kong is like a steambath at this time of year. And what will you do with Chrissie? Do you want to take Chrissie along too?'

'I have no desire whatsoever to go to Hong Kong and sit in a hotel with a screaming child,' I said. 'I just want to know what's what. So that I don't have to be humiliated when your friends phone.'

'Well, now you know what's what,' he said.

He was wrong. I didn't know. But I could guess. Specifically I could guess that the girlfriend from Durban was going to be in Hong Kong too. From that moment I was as cold as ice to Mark. *Let this put paid, you bastard, to any idea you may have that your adulteries excite me!* That was what I thought to myself.

'Is this all about Hong Kong?' he said to me, when at last the message began to get through. 'If you want to come to Hong Kong, for God's sake just say the word, instead of stalking around the house like a tiger with indigestion.'

'And what might that word be?' I said. 'Is the word *Please*? No, I don't want to accompany you to Hong Kong of all places. I would only be bored, as you say, sitting and kvetching with the wives while the men are busy elsewhere deciding the future of the world. I will be happier here at home where I belong, looking after your child.'

That was how things stood between us the day Mark left.

Just a minute, I'm confused. Where are we in time? When did this trip to Hong Kong take place?

It must have been sometime in 1973, early 1973, I can't give you a precise date.

So you and John Coetzee had been seeing each other . . .

No. He and I had not been seeing each other. You asked at the beginning how I came to meet John, and I told you. That was the head of the tale. Now we are coming to the tail of the tale, namely, how our relationship drifted on and then came to an end.

But where is the body of the tale, you ask? There is no body. I can't supply a body because there was none. This is a tale without a body.

We return to Mark, to the fateful day he left for Hong Kong. No sooner was he gone than I jumped into the car, drove to Tokai Road, and pushed a note under the front door: 'Drop by this afternoon, if you feel like it, around 2.'

As two o'clock approached I could feel the fever mount in me. The child felt it too. She was restless, she cried, she clung to me, she would not sleep. Fever, but what kind of fever, I wondered to myself? A fever of madness? A fever of rage?

I waited but John did not come, not at two, not at three. He came at five-thirty, by which time I had fallen asleep on the sofa with Chrissie, hot and sticky, on my shoulder. The doorbell woke me; when I opened the door to him I was still groggy and confused.

'Sorry I couldn't come earlier,' he said, 'but I teach in the afternoons.'

It was too late, of course. Chrissie was awake, and jealous in her own way.

Later John returned, by arrangement, and we spent the night together. In fact while Mark was in Hong Kong, John spent every night in my bed, departing at the crack of dawn so as not to bump into the house-help. For the sleep I lost I compensated by napping in the afternoons. What he did to make up for lost sleep I have no idea. Maybe his students, his Portuguese girls — you know about them, about his scatterlings from the ex-Portuguese empire? No? Remind me to tell you — maybe his girls had to suffer for his nocturnal excesses.

My high summer with Mark had given me a new conception of sex: as a contest, a variety of wrestling in which you do your best to subject your opponent to your erotic will. For all his failings, Mark was a more than competent sex wrestler, though not as subtle or as steely as I. Whereas my verdict on John — and here at last, *at last*, comes the moment you have been waiting for, Mr Biographer — my verdict on John Coetzee, after seven nights of testing, was that he was not in my league, not as I was then.

John had what I would call a sexual mode, into which he would switch when he took off his clothes. In sexual mode he could perform the male part perfectly adequately — adequately, competently, but — for my taste — too impersonally. I never had the feeling that he was with *me*, me in all my reality. Rather, it was as if he was engaged with some erotic image of me inside his head; perhaps even with some image of Woman with a capital W.

At the time I was simply disappointed. Now I would go further. In his lovemaking I now think there was an autistic quality. I offer this not as a criticism but as a diagnosis, if it interests you. Characteristically the autistic type treats other people as automata, mysterious automata. In return he expects to be treated as a mysterious automaton too. If you are autistic, falling in love translates as turning some or other chosen other into the inscrutable object of your desire; being loved translates as being treated reciprocally as the inscrutable object of the other's desire. Two inscrutable automata having inscrutable commerce with each other's bodies: that was how it felt to be in bed with John. Two separate enterprises on the go, his and mine. What his enterprise was I can't say, it was .opaque to me. But to sum up: sex with him lacked all thrill.

In my practice I have not had much experience of patients I would classify as clinically autistic. Nevertheless, regarding their sex lives, my guess is that they prefer masturbation to the real thing.

As I think I told you, John was only the third man I had had. Three men, and I left them all behind, sex-wise. A sad story. After those three I lost interest in white South Africans, white South African men. There was some quality they had in common that I found it hard to put a finger on, but that I somehow connected with the evasive flicker I caught in the eyes of Mark's colleagues when they spoke about the future of the country – as if there were some conspiracy they all belonged to that was going to create a fake, trompe-l'oeil future where no future had seemed possible before. Like a camera shutter opening up for an instant to reveal the falseness at their core.

Of course I was a South African too, and as white as white could be. I was born among the whites, was reared among them, lived among them. But I had a second self to fall back on: Julia Kiš, or even better Kiš Julia, of Szombathely. As long as I did not desert Julia Kiš, as long as Julia Kiš did not desert me, I could see things to which other whites were blind.

For instance, white South Africans in those days liked to think of themselves as the Jews of Africa, or at least the Israelis of Africa: cunning, unscrupulous, resilient, running close to the ground, hated and envied by the tribes they ruled over. All false. All nonsense. It takes a Jew to know a Jew, as it takes a woman to know a man. Those people were not tough, they were not even cunning, or cunning enough. And they were certainly not Jews. In fact they were babes in the wood. That is how I think of them now: a tribe of babies looked after by slaves.

John used to twitch in his sleep, so much that it kept me awake. When I couldn't stand it any more I would give him a shake. 'You were having a bad dream,' I would say. 'I never dream,' he would mumble in return, and go straight back to sleep. Soon he would be twitching and jerking again. It reached a point where I began to long to have Mark back in my bed. At least Mark slept like a log.

Enough of that. You get the picture. Not a sensual idyll. Far from it. What else? What else do you want to know?

Let me ask this. You are Jewish and John was not. Was there ever any tension because of that?

Tension? Why should there have been tension? Tension on whose side? I was not planning to marry John, after all. No, John and I got on perfectly well in that respect. It was Northerners he didn't get on with, particularly the English. The English stifled him, he said, with their good manners, their well-bred reserve. He preferred people who were ready to give more of themselves; then sometimes he would pluck up the courage to give a little of himself in return.

Any further questions before I go on?

No.

One morning (I skip ahead, I would like to get this over with) John appeared at the front door. 'I won't stay,' he said, 'but I thought you might like this.' He was holding out a book. On the cover: *Dusklands*, by J M Coetzee.

I was taken completely aback. 'You wrote this?' I said. I knew he wrote, but then, lots of people write; I had no inkling that in his case it was serious.

'It's for you. It's a proof copy. I got two proof copies in the mail today.'

I flipped through the book. Someone complaining about his wife. Someone travelling by ox-cart. 'What is it?' I said. 'Is it fiction?'

'Sort of.'

Sort of. 'Thank you,' I said. 'I look forward to reading it. Is it going to make you a lot of money? Will you be able to give up teaching?'

He found that very funny. He was in a gay mood, because of the book. Not often that I saw that side of him.

'I didn't know your father was an historian,' I remarked the next time we met. I was referring to the preface to his book, in which the author, the writer, this man in front of me, claimed that his father, the little man who went off every morning to his bookkeeping job in the city, was also an historian who haunted the archives and turned up old documents.

'You mean the preface?' he said. 'Oh, that's all made up.'

'And how does your father feel about it,' I said – 'about having false claims made about him, about being turned into a character in a book?'

John looked uncomfortable. What he did not want to reveal, as I found out later, was that his father had not set eyes on *Dusklands*.

'And Jacobus Coetzee?' I said. 'Did you make up your estimable ancestor Jacobus Coetzee too?'

'No, there was a real Jacobus Coetzee,' he said. 'At least, there is a real, paper-and-ink document which claims to be a transcript of an oral deposition made by someone who gave his name as Jacobus Coetzee. At the foot of that document there is an X which the scribe attests was made by the hand of this same Coetzee, an X because he was illiterate. In that sense I did not make him up.'

'For an illiterate, your Jacobus strikes me as being very literary. In one place I see he quotes Nietzsche.'

'Well, they were surprising fellows, those eighteenth-century frontiersmen. You never knew what they would come up with next.'

I can't say I like *Dusklands*. I know it sounds old-fashioned, but I prefer my books to have proper heroes and heroines, characters you can admire. I have never written stories, I have never had ambitions in that direction, but I suspect it is a lot easier to make up bad characters – contemptible characters – than good ones. That is my opinion, for what it is worth.

Did you ever say so to Coetzee?

Did I say I thought he was going for the easy option? No. I was simply surprised that this intermittent lover of mine, this amateur handyman and part-time schoolteacher, had it in him to write a book-length book and, what is more, find a publisher for it, albeit only in Johannesburg. I was surprised, I was gratified for his sake, I was even a little proud. Reflected glory. In my student years I had hung around with numbers of would-be writers, but none had actually published a book.

I've never asked: What did you study? Psychology?

No, far from it. I studied German literature. As a preparation for my life as housewife and mother I read Novalis and Gottfried Benn. I graduated in literature, after which, for two decades, until Christina grew up and left home, I was – how shall I put it? – intellectually dormant. Then I went back to college. This was in Montreal. I started from scratch with basic science, followed by medical studies, followed by training as a therapist. A long road.

Would relations with Coetzee have been any different, do you think, if you had been trained in psychology rather than in literature?

What a curious question! The answer is no. If I had studied psychology in the South Africa of the 1960s I would have had to immerse myself in the neurological processes of rats and octopi, and John wasn't a rat or an octopus.

What kind of animal was he?

What odd questions you ask! He wasn't any kind of animal, and for a very specific reason: his mental capacities, and specifically his ideational faculties, were overdeveloped, at the cost of his animal self. He was *Homo sapiens*, or even *Homo sapiens sapiens*.

Which leads me back to *Dusklands*. As a piece of writing I don't say *Dusklands* is lacking in passion, but the passion behind it is obscure. I read it as a book about cruelty, an exposé of the cruelty involved in various forms of conquest. But what is the actual source of that cruelty? Its locus, it seems to me, lies within the author himself. The best interpretation I can give the book is that writing it was a project in self-administered therapy. Which casts a certain light back over our time together, our conjoint time.

I am not sure I understand. Can you say more?

What don't you understand?

Are you saying he took out his cruelty on you?

No, not at all. John never behaved toward me with anything but the utmost gentleness. He was what I would call a gentle person, a gentleperson. That was part of his problem. His life project was to be gentle. Let me start again. In *Dusklands* you must recall how much killing there is – killing not only of human beings but of animals. Well, at about the time the book appeared, John announced to me he was becoming a vegetarian. I don't know how long he persisted in it, but I interpreted the vegetarian move as part of a larger project of self-reformation. He had decided he was going to block cruel and violent impulses in every arena of his life – including his love life, I might say –

and channel them into his writing, which as a consequence was going to become a sort of unending cathartic exercise.

How much of this was visible to you at the time, and how much do you owe to later insights as a therapist?

I saw it all – it was on the surface, you didn't need to dig – but at that time I did not have the language to describe it. Besides, I was having an affair with the man. You can't be too analytic in the middle of a love affair.

A love affair. You haven't used that expression before.

Then let me correct myself. An erotic entanglement. Because, young and self-centred as I was then, it would have been hard for me to love, really love, someone as radically incomplete as John. So: I was in the midst of an erotic entanglement with two men, in one of whom I had made a deep investment – I had married him, he was the father of my child – and in the other of whom I had made no investment at all.

Why I made no deeper investment in John has much to do, I now suspect, with his project of turning himself into what I described to you, a gentle man, the kind of man who would do no harm, not even to dumb animals, not even to a woman. I should have been clearer with him, I now think: *If for some reason you are holding yourself back, don't, there is no need!* If I had told him that, if he had taken it to heart, if he had allowed himself to be a little more impetuous, a little more imperious, a little less *thoughtful,* then he might actually have yanked me out of a marriage that was bad for me then and would become worse later. He might actually have saved me, or saved the best years of my life for me, which, as it turned out, were wasted.

[Silence.]

I've lost track. What were we talking about?

Dusklands.

Yes, *Dusklands*. A word of caution. That book was actually written before he met me. Check the chronology. So don't be tempted to read it as about the two of us.

The thought did not cross my mind.

I remember asking John, after *Dusklands*, what new project he had on the go. His answer was vague. 'There is always something or other I am working on,' he said. 'If I yielded to the seduction of not working, what would I do with myself? What would there be to live for? I would have to shoot myself.'

That surprised me – his need to write, I mean. I knew hardly anything about his habits, about how he spent his time, but he had never struck me as an obsessive worker.

'Do you mean that?' I said.

'I get depressed if I am not writing,' he replied.

'Then why the endless house repairs?' I said. 'You could pay someone else to do the repairs, and devote the time you saved to writing.'

'You don't understand,' he said. 'Even if I had the money to employ a builder, which I don't, I would still feel the need to spend X hours a day digging in the garden or moving rocks or mixing concrete.' And he launched into another of his speeches about the need to overthrow the taboo on manual labour.

I wondered whether there might not be some criticism of myself hanging in the air: that the paid labour of my black domestic set me free to have idle affairs with strange men, for instance. But I let it pass. 'Well,' I said, 'you certainly don't understand economics. The first principle of economics is that if we all insisted on spinning our own thread and milking our own cows rather than employing other people to do it for us, we would be stuck for ever in the Stone Age. That is why we have invented an economy based on exchange, which has in turn made possible our long history of material progress. You pay someone else to lay the concrete, and in exchange you get the time to write the book that will justify your leisure and give meaning to your life. That may even give meaning to the life of the workman laying the concrete for you. So that we all prosper.'

'Do you really believe that?' he said. 'That books give meaning to our lives?'

'Yes.' I said. 'A book should be an axe to chop open the frozen sea inside us. What else should it be?'

'A gesture of refusal in the face of time. A bid for immortality.'

'No one is immortal. Books are not immortal. The entire globe on which we stand is going to be sucked into the sun and burnt to a cinder. After which the universe itself will implode and disappear down a black hole. Nothing is going to survive, not me, not you, and certainly not minority-interest books about imaginary frontiersmen in eighteenth-century South Africa.'

'I didn't mean immortal in the sense of existing outside time. I mean surviving beyond one's physical demise.'

'You want people to read you after you are dead?'

'It affords me some consolation to cling to that prospect.'

'Even if you won't be around to witness it?'

'Even if I won't be around to witness it.'

'But why should the people of the future bother to read the book you write if it doesn't speak to them, if it doesn't help them find meaning in their lives?'

'Perhaps they will still like to read books that are well written.'

'That's silly. It's like saying that if I build a good enough gram-radio then people will still be using it in the twenty-fifth century. But they won't. Because gram-radios, however well made, will be obsolete by then. They won't speak to twenty-fifth-century people.'

'Perhaps in the twenty-fifth century there will still be a minority curious to hear what a late-twentieth-century gram-radio sounded like.'

'Collectors. Hobbyists. Is that how you intend to spend your life: sitting at your desk handcrafting an object that might or might not be preserved as a curiosity?'

He shrugged. 'Have you a better idea?'

You think I am showing off. I can see that. You think I make up dialogue to show how smart I am. But that is how they were at times, conversations between John and myself. They were fun. I enjoyed them; I missed them afterwards, after I stopped seeing him. In fact our conversations were probably what I missed most. He was the only man I knew who would let me beat him in an honest argument, who wouldn't bluster or obfuscate or go off in a huff when he saw he was losing. And I always beat him, or nearly always.

The reason was simple. It wasn't that he couldn't argue; but he ran his life according to principles, whereas I was a pragmatist. Pragmatism always beats principles; that is just the way things are. The universe moves, the ground changes under our feet; principles are always a step behind. Principles are the stuff of comedy. Comedy is what you get when principles bump into reality. I know he had a reputation for being dour, but John Coetzee was actually quite funny. A figure of comedy. Dour comedy. Which, in an obscure way, he knew, even accepted. That is why I still look back on him with affection. If you want to know.

[Silence.]

I was always good at arguing. At school everyone used to be nervous around me, even my teachers. *A tongue like a knife*, my mother used to say half-reprovingly. *A girl should not argue like that, a girl should learn to be more soft.* But at other times she would say: *A girl like you should be a lawyer.* She was proud of me, of my spirit, of my sharp tongue. She came from a generation when a daughter was still married from the father's home straight into the husband's, or the father-in-law's.

Anyway, 'Have you a better idea,' John said – 'a better idea for how to use one's life than writing books?'

'No. But I have an idea that might shake you up and help give direction to your life.'

'What is that?'

'Find yourself a good woman and marry her.'

He looked at me strangely. 'Are you making me a proposal?' he said.

I laughed. 'No,' I said, 'I am already married, thank you. Find a woman better suited to you, someone who will take you out of yourself.'

I am already married, therefore marriage to you would constitute bigamy: that was the unspoken part. Yet what was wrong with bigamy, come to think of it, aside from it being against the law? What made bigamy a crime when adultery was only a sin, or a recreation? I was already an adulteress; why should I not be a bigamist or *bigamiste* too? This was Africa, after all. If no African man was going to be hauled before a court for having two wives, why should I be forbidden to have two spouses, a public one and a private one?

'This is not, emphatically not, a proposal,' I repeated, 'but – just hypothetically – if I were free, would you marry me?'

It was only an inquiry, an idle inquiry. Nevertheless, without a word, he took me in his arms and held me so tight that I could not breathe. It was the first act of his I could recollect that seemed to come straight from the heart. Certainly I had seen him worked on by animal desire – we did not spend our time in bed discussing Aristotle – but never before had I seen him in the grip of emotion. *So,* I asked myself in some wonderment, *does this cold fish have feelings after all?*

'What's up?' I said, disengaging myself from his grasp. 'Is there something you want to tell me?'

He was silent. Was he crying? I switched on the bedside lamp and inspected him. No tears, but he did wear a look of stricken mournfulness. 'If you can't tell me what's up,' I said, 'I can't help you.'

Later, when he had pulled himself together, we collaborated to make light of the moment. 'For the right woman,' I said, 'you would make a *prima* husband. Responsible. Hard-working. Intelligent. Quite a catch, in fact. Good in bed too,' though that was not strictly true. 'Affectionate,' I added as an afterthought, though that was not true either.

'And an artist to boot,' he said. 'You forgot to mention that.'
'And an artist to boot. An artist in words.'

[Silence.]

And?

That's all. A difficult passage between the two of us, which we successfully negotiated. My first inkling that he cherished deeper feelings for me.

Deeper than what?

Deeper than the feelings any man might cherish for his neighbour's attractive wife. Or his neighbour's ox or ass.

Are you saying he was in love with you?

In love . . . In love with me or with the idea of me? I don't know. What I do know is that he had reason to be thankful to me. I made things easy for him. There are men who find it hard to court a woman. They are afraid to expose their desire, to open themselves to rebuff. Behind their fear there often lies a childhood history. I never forced John to expose himself. I was the one who did the courting. I was the one who did the seducing. I was the one who managed the terms of the affair. I was even the one who decided when it was over. So you ask, Was he in love? and I reply, He was in gratitude.

[Silence.]

I often wondered, afterwards, what would have happened if instead of fending him off I had responded to his surge of feeling with a surge of feeling of my own. If I had had the courage to divorce Mark back then, rather than waiting another thirteen or fourteen years, and hitched up with John. Would I have made more of my life? Perhaps. Perhaps not. But then I would not be the ex-mistress talking to you. I would be the grieving widow.

Chrissie was the problem, the fly in the ointment. Chrissie was very attached to her father, and I was finding it more and more difficult to handle her. She was no longer a baby – she was getting on for two – and although her progress in speech was disturbingly slow (as it turned out, I needn't have worried, she made up for it in a burst later on), she was growing more agile by the day – agile and fearless. She had learned to clamber out of her cot; I had to hire a handyman to put in a gate at the head of the stairs in case she came tumbling down.

I remember one night Chrissie appeared without warning at my bedside, rubbing her eyes, whimpering, confused. I had the presence of mind to gather her up and whisk her back to her room before she registered that it wasn't Daddy in bed beside me; but what if I wasn't so lucky next time?

I was never quite sure what subterranean effect my double life might be having on Chrissie. On the one hand I told myself that as long as I was physically fulfilled and at peace with myself, the beneficial effects ought to seep through to her too. If that strikes you as self-serving, let me remind you that at that time, in the 1970s, the progressive view, the *bien-pensant* view, was that sex was a force for the good, in any guise, with any partner. On the other hand it was clear that Chrissie was finding the alternation between Daddy and Uncle John in the household puzzling. What was going to happen when she began to speak? What if she got the two of them mixed and called her father Uncle John? There would be hell to pay.

I have always regarded Sigmund Freud as, for the most part, bunk, starting with the Oedipus complex and proceeding to his refusal to see that children were being sexually abused in the homes of his middle-class clientele. Nevertheless I do agree that children, even very young ones, spend a lot of time trying to puzzle out their place in the family. In the case of Chrissie, the family had up to then been a simple affair: me, the sun at the centre of the universe, plus Mommy and Daddy, my attendant planets. I had put some effort into making it clear that Maria, who appeared at eight o'clock in the morning and disappeared at noon, was not part of the family setup. 'Maria must go home now,' I would say to her in front of Maria. 'Say ta-ta to Maria. Maria has her own little girl to feed and look after.' (I referred to Maria's one little girl in order not to complicate matters. I knew perfectly well that Maria had seven children to feed and clothe, five of her own and two passed on by a sister dead of tuberculosis.)

As for Chrissie's wider family, her grandmother on my side had passed away before she was born and her grandfather was tucked away in a sanatorium, as I told you. Mark's parents lived in the rural Eastern Cape in a farmhouse ringed by a two-metre-high electrified fence. They never spent a night away from home for fear the farm would be plundered and the livestock driven off, so they might as well have been in jail. Mark's elder sister lived thousands of miles away in Seattle; my own brother never visited the Cape. So Chrissie had the most stripped-down version of a family possible. The sole complication was the uncle who sneaked in through the back door at midnight and into Mommy's bed. Who was the uncle: one of the family or on the contrary a worm eating away at the heart of the family?

And Maria – how much did Maria know? I could never be sure. Migrant labour was the norm in South Africa in those days, so Maria must have been all too familiar with the phenomenon of the husband who says goodbye to his wife and children and goes off to the big city to find work. But whether Maria approved of wives fooling around in their husbands' absence was another matter. Maria never actually laid eyes on my night-time visitor, but it was hardly likely that she was deceived. Visitors leave too many traces behind.

But what is this? Is it really six o'clock? I had no idea it was so late. We must stop for the day. Can you come back tomorrow?

I'm afraid I head home tomorrow. I fly from here to Toronto, from Toronto to London. I'd hate it if . . .

Very well, let's press on. There is not much more. I'll be quick.

One night John arrived in an unusually excited state. He had with him a little cassette player, and put on a tape, the Schubert string quintet. It was not what I would call sexy music, nor was I particularly in the mood, but he wanted to make love, and specifically – excuse the explicitness – wanted us to co-ordinate our activities to the music, to the slow movement.

Well, the slow movement in question may be very beautiful but I found it far from arousing. Added to which I could not shake off the image on the box containing the tape: Franz Schubert looking not like a god of music but like a harried Viennese clerk with a head-cold.

I don't know if you remember the slow movement, but there is a long violin aria with the viola throbbing below, and I could feel John trying to keep time with it. The whole business struck me as forced, ridiculous. Somehow or other my remoteness communicated itself to John. 'Empty your mind!' he hissed at me. 'Feel through the music!'

Well, there can be nothing more irritating than being told what you must feel. I turned away from him, and his little erotic experiment collapsed at once.

Later on he tried to explain himself. He wanted to prove something to me about the history of feeling, he said. Feelings had natural histories of their own. They came into being within time, flourished for a while or failed to flourish, then died or died out. The kinds of feeling that had flourished in Schubert's day were by now, most of them, dead. The sole way left to us to re-experience them was via the music of the times. Because music was the trace, the inscription, of feeling.

Okay, I said, but why do we have to fuck while we listen to the music?

Because the slow movement of the quintet happens to be about fucking, he replied. If, instead of resisting, I had let the music flow into me and animate me, I would have experienced glimmerings of something quite unusual: what it had felt like to make love in post-Bonaparte Austria.

'What it felt like for post-Bonaparte man or what it felt like for post-Bonaparte woman?' I said. 'For Mr Schubert or for Mrs Schubert?'

That really annoyed him. He didn't like his pet theories to be made fun of.

'Music isn't about fucking,' I went on. 'Music is about

foreplay. It's about courtship. You sing to the maiden *before* you go to bed with her, not while you are in bed with her. You sing to her to woo her, to win her heart. You sing to her to get her into bed. If you aren't happy with me in bed, maybe it is because you haven't won my heart.'

I should have called it a day at that point, but I didn't, I went further. 'The mistake the two of us made,' I said, 'was that we skimped the foreplay. I'm not blaming you, it was as much my fault as yours, but it was a fault nonetheless. Sex is better when it is preceded by a good, long courtship. More emotionally satisfying. More erotically satisfying too. If you are trying to improve our sex life, you won't achieve it by making me fuck in time to music.'

I was quite prepared for him to fight back, to argue the case for musical sex. But he did not rise to the bait. Instead he put on a sullen, defeated look and turned his back on me.

I know I am contradicting what I said earlier on, about him being a good sport and a good loser, but this time I really seemed to have touched a sore spot.

Anyway, there we were. I had gone on the offensive, I couldn't turn back. 'Go home and practise your wooing,' I said. 'Go on. Go away. Take your Schubert with you. Come again when you can do better.'

It was cruel; but he deserved it for not fighting back.

'Right – I'll go,' he said in a sulky voice. 'I have things to do anyway.' And he began to put on his clothes.

Things to do! I picked up the nearest object to hand, which happened to be a quite nice little baked-clay plate, brown with a painted yellow border, one of a set of six that Mark and I had bought in Swaziland. For an instant I could still see the comic side of it: the dark-tressed, bare-breasted mistress exhibiting her stormy central-European temperament by shouting abuse and throwing crockery. Then I hurled the plate.

It hit him on the neck and bounced to the floor without breaking. He hunched his shoulders and turned to me with a puzzled stare. Never before in his life, I am sure, had he had a plate thrown at him. 'Go!' I shouted or perhaps even screamed, and waved him away. Chrissie woke up and began crying.

Strange to say, I felt no regret afterwards. On the contrary, I was aroused and excited and proud of myself. *Straight from the heart!* I said to myself. *My first plate!*

[Silence]

Have there been others?

Other plates? Plenty.

[Silence]

Was that how it ended, then, between you and him?
Not quite. There was a coda. I'll tell you the coda, then that will be that.

It was a condom that spelled the real end, a condom tied at the neck, full of dead sperm. Mark fished it out from under the bed. I was flabbergasted. How could I have missed it? It was as if I wanted it to be found, wanted to shout my infidelity from the rooftops.

Mark and I never used condoms, so there was no point in lying. 'How long has this been going on?' he demanded. 'Since last December,' I said. 'You bitch,' he said, 'you filthy, lying bitch! And I trusted you!'

He was about to storm out of the room, but then as if on an afterthought he turned and – I am sorry, I am going to draw a veil over what happened next, it is too shameful to repeat, too shaming. I will simply say it left me surprised, shocked, but above all furious. 'For that, Mark, I will never forgive you,' I said when I recovered myself. 'There is a line, and you've just crossed it. I'm going. You look after Chrissie for a change.'

At the moment I uttered the words *I'm going, you look after Chrissie*, I swear I meant no more than that I was going out and he could look after the child for the afternoon. But in the five paces it took to reach the front door it came to me in a blinding flash that this could actually be the moment of liberation, the moment when I walked out of an unfulfilling marriage and never came back. The clouds over my head, the clouds in my head, lightened, evaporated. *Don't think*, I told myself, *just do it!* Without missing a step I turned, strode upstairs, stuffed some underwear into a carry-bag, and raced downstairs again.

Mark was barring the way. 'Where do you think you are going?' he demanded. 'Are you going to *him*?'

'Go to hell,' I said. I tried to push past, but he grabbed my arm.

'Let me go!' I said.

No screams, no snarls, just a simple, curt command. Without a word he let go. It was as though out of the skies a crown and regal robes had descended upon me. When I drove off he was still standing in the doorway, dumbstruck.

So easy! I exulted. *So easy! Why didn't I do it before?*

What puzzles me about that moment – which was in fact a key moment in my life – what puzzled me then and continues to puzzle me to the present day is the following. Even if some force within me – let us call it the unconscious, to make things easier, though I have my reservations about the classical unconscious – had held me back from checking under the bed – had held me back precisely in order to precipitate this marital crisis – why on earth did Maria leave the incriminating item lying there – Maria who was definitely not part of my unconscious, Maria whose job it was to clean, to clean up, to clean things away? Did Maria deliberately overlook the condom? Did she draw herself up, when she saw it, and say to herself, *This is going too far! Either I defend the sanctity of the marriage bed or I become complicit in an outrageous affair!*

Sometimes I imagine flying back to South Africa, the new, longed-for, democratic South Africa, with the sole purpose of seeking out Maria, if she is still alive, and having it out with her, getting an answer to that vexing question.

Well, I was certainly not running off to join the *him* of Mark's jealous rage, but where exactly was I heading? For I had no friends in Cape Town, none who were not Mark's in the first place and mine only in the second.

There was an establishment I had spotted while driving through Wynberg, a rambling old mansion with a sign outside: *Canterbury Hotel / Residential / Full or part board / Weekly and monthly rates*. I decided to try the Canterbury.

Yes, said the woman at the desk, there happened to be a room available, would I want it for a week or for a longer term? A week, I said, in the first place.

The room in question – be patient, this is not irrelevant – was on the ground floor. It was spacious, with a neat little bathroom en suite and a compact refrigerator and French doors giving onto a shady, vine-covered veranda. 'Very nice,' I said. 'I'll take it.'

'And your baggage?' said the woman.

'My baggage will be coming,' I said, and she understood. I am sure I was not the first runaway wife to pitch up on the doorstep of the Canterbury. I am sure they enjoyed quite a traffic in pissed-off spouses. And a nice little bonus to be made from the ones who paid for a week, spent a night, then, repentant or exhausted or homesick, checked out the next morning.

Well, I was not repentant and I was certainly not homesick. I was quite ready to make the Canterbury my home until the burden of childcare led Mark to sue for peace.

There was a rigmarole about security that I barely followed – keys for doors, keys for gates – plus rules for parking, rules for visitors, rules for this, rules for that. I would not be having visitors, I informed the woman.

That evening I dined in the lugubrious *salle à manger* of the Canterbury and had a first glimpse of my fellow residents, who came straight out of William Trevor or Muriel Spark. But no doubt I appeared much the same to them: another flushed escapee from a sour marriage. I went to bed early and slept well.

I had thought I would enjoy the solitude. I drove in to the city, did some shopping, saw an exhibition at the National Gallery, had lunch in the Gardens. But the second evening, alone in my room after a wretched meal of wilted salad and poached sole with béchamel sauce, I was suddenly overcome with loneliness and, worse than loneliness, self-pity. From the public telephone in the lobby I called John and, in murmurs (the receptionist was eavesdropping), told him of my situation.

'Would you like me to come by?' he said. 'We could go to a late movie.'

'Yes,' I said; 'yes, yes, yes.'

I repeat as emphatically as I can, I did not run away from my husband and child in order to be with John. It was not that kind of affair. In fact, it was hardly an affair at all, more of a friendship, an extramarital friendship with a sexual component whose importance, at least on my side, was symbolic rather than substantial. Sleeping with John was my way of retaining my self-respect. I hope you understand that.

Nevertheless, *nevertheless*, within minutes of his arrival at the Canterbury he and I were in bed, and – what is more – our lovemaking was, for once, something truly to write home about. I even shed tears at its conclusion. 'I don't know why I am crying,' I sobbed, 'I am so happy.'

'It is because you didn't get any sleep last night,' he said, thinking he needed to console me. 'It is because you are overwrought.'

I stared at him. *Because you are overwrought*: he really seemed to believe that. It quite took my breath away, how stupid he could be, how insensitive. Yet in his wrongheaded way perhaps he was right. For my day of freedom had been coloured by a memory that kept creeping back, the memory of that humiliating face-off with Mark, which had left me feeling more like a spanked child than an erring spouse. But for that, I would probably not have telephoned John, and would therefore not be in bed with him. So yes: I was upset, and why not? My world had been turned upside down.

There was another source too for my uneasiness, even harder to confront: shame at having been found out. Because really, if you regarded the situation with a cold eye, I, with my sordid little tit-for-tat affair in Constantiaberg, was behaving no better than Mark, with his sordid little liaison in Durban.

The fact was, I had reached some kind of moral limit. The fit of euphoria at leaving home had evaporated; my sense of outrage was seeping away; as for the solitary life, its allure was fading fast. Yet how could I repair the damage other than by returning to Mark with my tail between my legs, suing for peace, and resuming my duties as chastened wife and mother? And in the midst of all that confusion of spirit, this piercingly sweet lovemaking! What was my body trying to tell me? That when one's defences are down the gateways to pleasure open up? That the marital bed is a bad place to commit adultery, hotels are better? What John felt I had no idea, he was never a forthcoming person; but for myself I knew without a doubt that the half hour I had just been through would endure as a landmark in my erotic life. Which it has. To this day. Why else would I still be talking about it?

[Silence.]

I'm glad I told you that story. Now I feel less guilty about the Schubert business.

[Silence.]

Anyway, I fell asleep in John's arms. When I awoke it was dark and I hadn't the faintest idea where I was. *Chrissie*, I thought – *I have completely forgotten to feed Chrissie!* I even groped in the wrong place for the light switch before it all came back to me. I was alone (no trace of John); it was six in the morning.

From the lobby I called Mark. 'Hello, it's me,' I said in my most neutral, most pacific voice. 'Sorry to call so early, but how is Chrissie?'

For his part, however, Mark was in no mood for conciliation. 'Where are you?' he demanded.

'I'm phoning from Wynberg,' I said. 'I have moved into a hotel. I thought we should take a break from each other until things cool down. How is Chrissie? What are your plans for the week? Are you going to be in Durban?'

'What I do is none of your business,' he said. 'If you want to stay away, stay away.'

Even on the telephone I could hear he was still in a rage. When Mark was cross he would explode his plosives: *none of your business,* with a puff of infuriated air on the *b* that would make your eyeballs shrivel. Memories of everything I disliked about him came flooding back. 'Don't be silly, Mark,' I said, 'you don't know how to look after a child.'

'Nor do you, you filthy bitch!' he said, and slammed down the receiver.

Later that morning, when I went to the shops, I found my bank account had been blocked.

I drove out to Constantiaberg. My latchkey turned the latch, but the door was double-locked. I knocked and knocked. No reply. No sign of Maria either. I circled the house. Mark's car was gone, the windows were closed.

I telephoned his office. 'He's away at our Durban office,' said the girl at the switchboard.

'There's an emergency at his home,' I said. 'Could you contact Durban and leave a message? Ask him to give his wife a call as soon as he can, at the following number. Say it's urgent.' And I gave the hotel number.

For hours I waited. No call.

Where was Chrissie? That was what I needed to know most

of all. It seemed beyond belief that Mark could have taken the child to Durban. But if he hadn't, what had he done with her?

I telephoned Durban direct. No, said the secretary, Mark was not in Durban, was not expected this week. Had I tried the firm's Cape Town office?

Distraught by now, I telephoned John. 'My husband has taken the child and decamped, vanished into thin air,' I said. 'I have no money. I don't know what to do. Do you have any suggestions?'

There was an elderly couple in the lobby, guests, openly listening to me. But I had ceased to care who knew of my troubles. I wanted to cry, but I think I laughed instead. 'He has absconded with my child, and because of what?' I said. 'Is this' – I gestured toward my surroundings, that is, toward the interior of the Canterbury Hotel (Residential) – 'is this what I am being punished for?' Then I really began to cry.

Being miles away, John could not have seen my gesture, therefore (it occurred to me afterwards) must have attached a quite different meaning to the word *this*. I must have seemed to be referring to my affair with him – to have been dismissing it as unworthy of such a fuss.

'Do you want to go to the police?' he said.

'Don't be ridiculous,' I said. 'You can't run away from a man and then accuse him of stealing your child.'

'Would you like me to come over and fetch you?' I could hear the caution in his voice. And I could sympathize. I too would have been cautious in his position, with an hysterical female on the line. But I didn't want caution, I wanted my child back. 'No, I would not like to be fetched,' I snapped.

'Have you at least had something to eat?' he said.

'I don't want anything to eat,' I said. 'That's enough of this stupid conversation. I'm sorry, I don't know why I called. Goodbye.' And I put down the phone.

I didn't want anything to eat, though I wouldn't have minded something to drink: a stiff whisky, for instance, followed by a dead, dreamless sleep.

I had just slumped down in my room and covered my head with a pillow when there was a tapping at the French door. It was John. Words between us, which I won't repeat. To be brief, he took me back to Tokai and bedded me down in his room. He himself slept on the sofa in the living-room. I was half expecting him to come to me during the night, but he didn't.

I was woken by murmured talk. The sun was up. I heard the front door close. A long silence. I was alone in this strange house.

The bathroom was primitive, the toilet not clean. An unpleasant smell of male sweat and damp towels hung in the air. Where John had gone, when he would be back, I had no idea. I made myself coffee and did some exploring. From room to room the ceilings were so low I felt I would suffocate. It was only a farm cottage, I understood that, but why had it been built for midgets?

I peered into the elder Coetzee's room. The light had been left on, a single dim bulb without a shade in the centre of the ceiling. The bed was unmade. On a table by the bedside, a newspaper folded open to the crossword puzzle. On the wall a painting, amateurish, of a whitewashed Cape Dutch farm-house, and a framed photograph of a severe-looking woman. The window, which was small and covered with a lattice of steel bars, looked out onto a stoep empty but for a pair of canvas deckchairs and a row of withered ferns in pots.

John's room, where I had slept, was larger and better lit. A bookshelf: dictionaries, phrasebooks, teach yourself this, teach yourself that. Beckett. Kafka. On the table, a mess of papers. A filing cabinet. Idly I searched through the drawers. In the bottom drawer, a box of photographs, which I burrowed amongst. What was I looking for? I didn't know. For something I would recognize only when I found it. But it was not there. Most of the photographs were from his school years: sports teams, class portraits.

From the front I heard noises, and went outdoors. A beautiful day, the sky a brilliant blue. John was unloading sheets of galvanized iron roofing from his truck. 'I'm sorry if I forsook you,' he said. 'I needed to pick these up, and I didn't want to wake you.'

I drew up a deckchair in a sunny spot, closed my eyes, and indulged in a little day-dreaming. I wasn't about to abandon my child. I wasn't about to walk out on my marriage. Nevertheless, what if I did? What if I forgot about Mark and Chrissie, settled down in this ugly little house, became the third member of the Coetzee family, the adjunct, Snow White to the two dwarves, doing the cooking, the cleaning, the laundering, maybe even helping with roof repairs? How long before my wounds healed? And then how long before my true prince rode by, the prince of my dreams, who would recognize me for who I was, lift me onto his white stallion, and bear me off into the sunset?

Because John Coetzee was not my prince. Finally I come to the point. If that was the question at the back of your mind when you came to Kingston — *Is this going to be another of those women who mistook John Coetzee for their secret prince?* — then you have your answer now. John was not my prince. Not only that: if you have been listening carefully you will see by now how very unlikely it was that he could have been a prince, a satisfactory prince, to any maiden on earth.

You don't agree? You think otherwise? You think the fault

lay with me, not him – the fault, the deficiency? Well, cast your mind back to the books he wrote. What is the one theme that keeps recurring from book to book? It is that the woman doesn't fall in love with the man. The man may or may not love the woman; but the woman never loves the man. What do you think that theme reflects? My guess, my highly informed guess, is that it reflects his life experience. Women didn't fall for him – not women in their right senses. They inspected him, they sniffed him, maybe they even tried him out. Then they moved on.

They moved on as I did. I could have remained in Tokai, as I said, in the Snow White role. As an idea it was not without its seductions. But in the end I did not. John was a friend to me during a rough patch in my life, he was a crutch I sometimes leant on, but he was never going to be my lover, not in the real sense of the word. For real love you need two full human beings, and the two need to fit together, to fit into each other. Like Yin and Yang. Like an electrical plug and an electrical socket. Like male and female. He and I didn't fit.

Believe me, over the course of the years I have given plenty of thought to John and his type. What I am going to tell you now I offer with due consideration, and I hope without animus. Because, as I said, John was important to me. He taught me a lot. He was a friend who remained a friend even after I broke up with him. When I felt low I could always rely on him to joke with me and lift my spirits. He raised me once to un-expected erotic heights – once only, alas! But the fact is, John wasn't made for love, wasn't constructed that way – wasn't constructed to fit into or be fitted into. Like a sphere. Like a glass ball. There was no way to connect with him. That is my conclusion, my mature conclusion.

Which may not come as a surprise to you. You probably think it holds true for artists in general, male artists: that they aren't built for what I am calling love; that they can't or won't give themselves fully for the simple reason that there is a secret essence of themselves they need to preserve for the sake of their art. Am I right? Is that what you think?

Do I think that artists aren't built for love? No. Not necessarily. I try to keep an open mind on the subject.

Well, you can't keep your mind open indefinitely, not if you mean to get your book written. Consider. Here we have a man who, in the most intimate of human relations, cannot connect, or can connect only briefly, intermittently. Yet how does he make his living? He makes his living writing reports, expert reports, on intimate human experience. Because that is what novels are about — isn't it? — intimate experience. Novels as opposed to poetry or painting. Doesn't that strike you as odd?

[Silence.]

I have been very open with you, Mr Vincent. For instance, the Schubert business: I never told anyone about that before you. Why not? Because I thought it would cast John in too ridiculous a light. Because who but a total dummy would order the woman he is supposed to be in love with to take lessons in love-making from some dead composer, some Viennese *Bagatellenmeister*? When a man and a woman are in love they create their own music, it comes instinctively, they don't need lessons. But what does our friend John do? He drags a third presence into the bedroom. Franz Schubert becomes number one, the master of love; John becomes number two, the master's disciple and executant; and I become number three, the instrument on whom the sex-music is going to be played. That – it seems to me – tells you all you need to know about John Coetzee. The man who mistook his mistress for a violin. Who probably did the same with every other woman in his life: mistook her for some instrument or other, violin, bassoon, timpani. Who was so dumb, so cut off from reality, that he could not distinguish between playing on a woman and loving a woman. A man who loved by numbers. One doesn't know whether to laugh or cry!

That is why he was never my Prince Charming. That is why I never let him bear me off on his white steed. Because he was not a prince but a frog. Because he was not human, not fully human.

I said I would be frank with you, and I have kept my promise. I will tell you one more frank thing, just one more, then I will stop, and that will be the end of it.

It is about the night I tried to describe to you, the night at the Canterbury Hotel, when, after all our experimenting, the two of us finally hit on the right chemical combination. How could we have achieved that, you may ask – as I ask too – if John was a frog and not a prince?

Let me tell you how I now see that pivotal night. I was hurt and confused, as I said, and beside myself with worry. John saw or guessed what was going on in me and for once opened his heart, the heart he normally kept wrapped in armour. With open hearts, his and mine, we came together. For him it could and should have marked a sea-change, that first opening of the heart. It could have marked the beginning of a new life for the two of us together. Yet what happened in fact? In the middle of the night John woke up and saw me sleeping beside him with no doubt a look of peace on my face, even of bliss, bliss is not unattainable in this world. He saw me – saw me as I was at that moment – took fright, hurriedly strapped the armour back over his heart, this time with chains and a double padlock, and stole out into the darkness.

Do you think I find it easy to forgive him for that? Do you?

You are being a little hard on him, if I may say so.

No, I am not. I am just telling the truth. Without the truth, no matter how hard, there can be no healing. That's all. That's the end of my offering to your book. Look, it's nearly eight o'clock. Time for you to go. You have a plane – don't you? – to catch in the morning.

Just one question more, one brief question.

No, absolutely not, no more questions. You have had time enough. End. *Fin.* Go.

Interview conducted in Kingston,
Ontario, May 2008.

Margot

LET ME TELL you, Mrs Jonker, what I have been doing since we met last December. After I got back to England I transcribed the tapes of our conversations. I asked a colleague from South Africa to check that I had the Afrikaans words right. Then I did something fairly radical. I cut out my prompts and questions and fixed up the prose to read as an uninterrupted narrative spoken in your voice.

What I would like to do today, if you are agreeable, is to read through the new text with you. How does that sound?

All right.

One further point. Because the story you told was so long I dramatized it here and there, letting people speak in their own voices. You will see what I mean once we get going.

All right.

Here goes then.

In the old days, at Christmas-time, there would be huge

gatherings on the family farm. From far and wide the sons and daughters of Gerrit and Lenie Coetzee would converge on Voëlfontein, bringing with them their spouses and offspring, more and more offspring each year, for a week of laughing and joking and reminiscing and, above all, eating. For the menfolk it was a time for hunting too: game-birds, antelope.

But by now, in the 1970s, those family gatherings are sadly diminished. Gerrit Coetzee is long in the grave, Lenie shuffles around a nursing home in The Strand. Of their twelve sons and daughters, the firstborn has already joined the multitudinous shades; in private moments –

Multitudinous shades?

Too grand-sounding? I'll change it. The firstborn has already departed this life. In private moments the survivors have intimations of their own end, and shudder.

I don't like that.

I'll cut it out. No problem. Has already departed this life. Among the survivors the joking has grown more subdued, the reminiscing sadder, the eating more temperate. As for hunting parties, there are no more of those: old bones are weary, and anyway, after year upon year of drought, there is nothing left in the veld that would count as game.

Of the third generation, the sons and daughters of the sons and daughters, most are by now too absorbed in their own affairs to attend, or too indifferent to the larger family. This year only four of the generation are present: her cousin Michiel, who has inherited the farm; her cousin John from Cape Town; her sister Carol; and herself, Margot. And of the four, she alone, she suspects, looks back to the old days with nostalgia.

I don't understand. Why do you call me she?

Of the four, Margot alone, she – Margot – suspects, looks back with nostalgia . . . You can hear how clumsy it is. It just doesn't work that way. The *she* I use is like *I* but is not *I*. Do you really dislike it so much?

I find it confusing. But go on.

John's presence on the farm is a source of unease. After years spent overseas – so many years it was concluded he was gone for good – he has suddenly reappeared among them under some cloud or other, some disgrace. One story being whispered about is that he has been in an American jail.

The family simply does not know how to behave toward him. Never yet have they had a criminal – if that is what he is, a criminal – in their midst. A bankrupt, yes: the man who married her aunt Marie, a braggart and heavy drinker of whom the family had disapproved from the start, declared himself bankrupt to avoid paying his debts and thereafter did not a stitch of work, loafing at home, living off his wife's earnings. But bankruptcy, while it may leave a bad taste in the mouth, is not a crime; whereas going to jail is going to jail.

Her own feeling is that the Coetzees ought to try harder to make the lost sheep feel welcome. She has a lingering soft spot for John. As children they used to talk quite openly of marrying each other when they grew up. They thought it was allowed – why should it not be? They did not understand why the adults smiled, smiled and would not say why.

Did I really tell you that?

You did. Do you want me to cut it out? I like it.

No, leave it in. [Laughs.] Go on.

Her sister Carol is of quite another mind. Carol is married to a German, an engineer, who has for years been trying to get the two of them out of South Africa and into the United States. Carol has made it plain she does not want it to appear in her dossier that she is related to a man who, whether or not he is technically a criminal, has in some way fallen foul of American law. But Carol's hostility to John goes deeper than that. She finds him affected and supercilious. From the heights of his *engelse* [English] education, says Carol, John looks down on the Coetzees, one and all. Why he has decided to descend upon them at Christmastide she cannot imagine.

She, Margot, is distressed by her sister's attitude. Her sister, she believes, has grown more and more hardhearted ever since she married and began to move in her husband's circle, a circle of German and Swiss expatriates who came to South Africa during the 1960s to make quick money and are preparing to abandon ship now that the country is going through stormy times.

I don't know. I don't know if I can let you say that.

Well, I will abide by your decision. But that is what you told me, word for word. And bear in mind, it is not as if your sister is going to read an obscure book put out by an academic press in England. Where is your sister living now?

She and Klaus are in Florida in a place called St Petersburg. You never know, one of her friends might come across your book and send it to her. But that is not the main point. When I spoke to you, I was under the impression you were simply going to transcribe our interview and leave it at that. I had no idea you were going to rewrite it completely.

That's not entirely fair. I have not rewritten it, I have simply recast it as a narrative. Changing the form should have no effect on the content. If you feel I am taking liberties with the content itself, that is another question. Am I taking too many liberties?

I don't know. Something sounds wrong, but I can't put my finger on it. All I can say is, your version doesn't sound like what I told you. But I am going to shut up now. I will wait until the end to make up my mind. So go on.

All right.

If Carol is too hard, she is too soft, she will admit to that. She is the one who cries when the new kittens have to be drowned, who blocks her ears when the slaughter-lamb bleats in fear, bleats and bleats. She used to mind, when she was younger, being scoffed at for being tenderhearted; but now, in her mid-thirties, she is not so sure she ought to be ashamed.

Carol claims not to understand why John has come to the gathering, but to her the explanation is obvious. To the haunts of his youth he has brought back his father, who though not much over sixty looks like an old man, looks to be on his last legs – has brought him back so that he can be renewed and fortified, or, if he cannot be renewed, so that he can say his farewells. It is, to her mind, an act of filial duty, one that she thoroughly approves of.

She tracks John down behind the packing-shed, where he is working on his car, or pretending to.

'Something wrong?' she asks.

'It's overheating,' he says. 'We had to stop twice on Du Toit's Kloof to let the engine cool.'

'You should ask Michiel to have a look at it. He knows everything about cars.'

'Michiel is busy with his guests. I'll fix it myself.'

Her guess is that Michiel would welcome any excuse to escape his guests, but she does not press her case. She knows men and male stubbornness, knows that a man will wrestle endlessly with a problem rather than ask another man for help.

'Is this what you drive in Cape Town?' she says. By *this* she means this one-ton Datsun pickup, the kind of light truck she associates with farmers and builders. 'What do you need a truck for?'

'It's useful,' he replies curtly, not explaining what its use might be.

She could not help smiling when he made his arrival on the farm behind the wheel of this selfsame truck, he with his beard and his unkempt hair and his owl-glasses, his father beside him like a mummy, stiff and embarrassed. She wishes she had taken a photograph. She wishes, too, she could talk to John about his hair-style. But the ice is not yet broken, intimate talk will have to wait.

'Anyway,' she says, 'I've been instructed to call you for tea, tea and *melktert* that Aunt Joy has baked.'

'I'll come in a minute,' he says.

They speak Afrikaans together. His Afrikaans is halting; she suspects her English is better than his Afrikaans, though, living in the back country, the *platteland*, she seldom has call to speak English. But they have spoken Afrikaans together since they were children; she is not about to humiliate him by offering to switch.

She blames the deterioration in his Afrikaans on the move he made to Cape Town, to 'English' schools and an 'English' university, and then to the world abroad, where not a word of Afrikaans is to be heard. *In 'n minuut*, he says: in a minute. It is the kind of solecism that Carol will latch onto at once and parody. '*In 'n minuut sal meneer sy tee kom geniet*,' Carol will say: in a minute his lordship will come and partake of tea. She must protect him from Carol, or at least beg Carol to have mercy on him for the space of these few days.

At table that evening she makes sure she is seated beside him. On the farm the evening meal is simply a hotchpotch of leftovers from the midday meal, the main meal of the day: cold mutton, warmed-up rice, and what passes here for salad: green beans with vinegar.

She notices that he passes on the meat platter without helping himself.

'Aren't you having mutton, John?' calls out Carol from the other end of the table in a tone of sweet concern.

'Not tonight, thanks,' John replies. '*Ek het my vanmiddag dik gevreet*': I stuffed myself like a pig this afternoon.

'So you are not a vegetarian. You didn't become a vegetarian while you were overseas.'

'Not a strict vegetarian. *Dis nie 'n woord waarvan ek hou nie. As 'n mens verkies om nie so veel vleis te eet nie . . .*' It is not a word he is fond of. If one chooses not to eat so much meat . . .

'*Ja?*' says Carol. '*As 'n mens so verkies, dan . . . ?*' If that is what you choose, then – what?

Everyone is by now staring at him. He has begun to blush. Clearly he has no idea how to deflect the benign curiosity of the gathering. And if he is paler and scrawnier than a good South African ought to be, might the explanation indeed be, not that he has tarried too long amid the snows of North America, but that he has too long been starved of good Karoo mutton? *As 'n mens verkies . . .* – what is he going to say next?

His blush has grown desperate. A grown man, yet he blushes like a girl! Time to intervene. She lays a reassuring hand on his arm. '*Jy wil seker sê, John, ons het almal ons voorkeure,*' we all have our preferences.

'*Ons voorkeure,*' he says; '*ons fiemies.*' Our preferences; our silly little whims. He spears a green bean and pops it into his mouth.

It is December, and in December it does not get dark until well after nine. Even then – so pristinely clear is the air on the high plateau – the moon and stars are bright enough to light one's footsteps. So after supper she and he go for a walk, making a wide loop to avoid the cluster of cabins that house the farm-workers.

'Thank you for saving me,' he says.

'You know Carol,' she says. 'She has always had a sharp eye. A sharp eye and a sharp tongue. How is your father?'

'Depressed. As you must know, he and my mother did not have a happy marriage. Even so, after her death he went into a decline – moped, didn't know what to do with himself. Men of

94

his generation were brought up helpless. If there isn't some woman on hand to cook and care for them, they simply fade away. If I hadn't offered my father a home he would have starved to death.'

'Is he still working?'

'Yes, he still has his job with the motor-parts dealer, though I think they have been hinting it may be time for him to retire. And his enthusiasm for sport is undimmed.'

'Isn't he a cricket umpire?'

'He was, but not any more. His eyesight has been deteriorating.'

'And you? Didn't you play cricket too?'

'Yes. In fact I still play in the Sunday league. The standard is fairly amateurish, which suits me. Curious: he and I, two Afrikaners devoted to an English game that we aren't much good at. I wonder what that says about us.'

Two Afrikaners. Does he really think of himself as an Afrikaner? She doesn't know many real [egte] Afrikaners who would accept him as one of the tribe. Even his father might not pass scrutiny. To pass as an Afrikaner nowadays you need at the very least to vote National and attend church on Sundays. She can't imagine her cousin putting on a suit and tie and going off to church. Or indeed his father.

They have arrived at the dam. The dam used to be filled by a wind-pump, but during the boom years Michiel installed a diesel-driven pump and left the old wind-pump to rust, because that was what everyone was doing. Now that the oil price has gone through the roof, Michiel may have to think again. He may have to go back to God's wind after all.

'Do you remember,' she says, 'When we used to come here as children . . .'

'And catch tadpoles in a sieve,' he picks up the story, 'and take them back to the house in a bucket of water and the next morning they all would be dead and we could never figure out why.'

'And locusts. We caught locusts too.'

Having mentioned the locusts, she wishes she hadn't. For she has remembered the fate of the locusts, or of one of them. Out of the bottle in which they had trapped it John took the insect and, while she watched, pulled steadily at a long rear leg until it came off the body, dryly, without blood or whatever counts as blood among locusts. Then he released it and they watched. Each time it tried to launch itself into flight it toppled to one side, its wings scrabbling in the dust, the remaining rear leg jerking ineffectually. *Kill it!* she screamed at him. But he did not kill it, just walked away, looking disgusted.

'Do you remember,' she says, 'how once you pulled the leg off a locust and left me to kill it? I was so cross with you.'

'I remember it every day of my life,' he says. 'Every day I ask the poor thing's forgiveness. I was just a child, I say to it, just an ignorant child who did not know better. *Kaggen*, I say, forgive me.'

'*Kaggen*?'

'*Kaggen*. The name of mantis, the mantis god. But the locust will understand. In the afterworld there are no language problems. It's like Eden all over again.'

The mantis god. He has lost her.

A night wind moans through the vanes of the dead wind-pump. She shivers. 'We must go back,' she says.

'In a minute. Have you read the book by Eugène Marais about the year he spent observing a baboon troop? He writes that at nightfall, when the troop stopped foraging and watched the sun go down, he could detect in the eyes of the older

baboons the stirrings of melancholy, the birth of a first aware-
ness of their own mortality.'

'Is that what the sunset makes you think of – mortality?'

'No. But I can't help remembering the first conversation you
and I had, the first meaningful conversation. We must have been
six years old. What the actual words were I don't recall, but I
know I was unburdening my heart to you, telling you everything about myself, all my hopes and longings. And all the time
I was thinking, *So this is what it means to be in love!* Because –
let me confess it – I was in love with you. And ever since that
day, being in love with a woman has meant being free to say
everything on my heart.'

'Everything on your heart . . . What has that to do with
Eugène Marais?'

'Simply that I understand what the old male baboon was
thinking as he watched the sun go down, the troop leader, the
one Marais was closest to. *Never again*, he was thinking: *Just one
life and then never again. Never, never, never.* That is what the Karoo
does to me too. It fills me with melancholy. It spoils me for life.'

She still does not see what baboons have to do with the
Karoo or their childhood years, but she is not going to let on.

'This place wrenches my heart,' he says. 'It wrenched my
heart when I was a child, and I have never been right since.'

His heart is wrenched. She had no inkling of that. It used
to be, she thinks to herself, that she knew without being told
what was going on in other people's hearts. Her own special
talent: *meegevoel*, feeling-with. But not any more, not any more!
She grew up; and as she grew up she grew stiff, like a woman
who never gets asked to dance, who spends her Saturday evenings
waiting in vain on a bench in the church hall, who by the time

some man remembers his manners and offers his hand has lost all pleasure, wants only to go home. What a shock! What a revelation! This cousin of hers carries within him memories of how he loved her! Has carried them all these years!

[Groans.] Did I really say all that?

[Laughs.] You did.

How indiscreet of me! [Laughs.] Never mind, go on.

'Don't reveal that to Carol,' he – John, her cousin – says. 'Don't tell her, with her satirical tongue, how I feel about the Karoo. If you do, I'll never hear the end of it.'

'You and the baboons,' she says. 'Carol has a heart too, believe it or not. But no, I won't tell her your secret. It's getting chilly. Can we go back?'

They circle past the farm-workers' quarters, keeping a decent distance. Through the dark the coals of a cooking-fire glow in fierce points of red.

'How long will you be staying?' she asks. 'Will you still be here for New Year's Day?' *Nuwejaar:* for the *volk,* the people, a red letter day, quite overshadowing Christmas.

'No, I can't stay so long. I have things to attend to in Cape Town.'

'Then can't you leave your father behind and come back later to fetch him? Give him time to relax and build up his strength. He doesn't look well.'

'He won't stay behind. My father has a restless nature. Wherever he is, he wants to be somewhere else. The older he grows, the worse it gets. It's like an itch. He can't keep still. Besides, he has his job to get back to. He takes his job very seriously.'

The farmhouse is quiet. They slip in through the back door. 'Good night,' she says, 'sleep tight.'

In her room she hurries to get into bed. She would like to be asleep by the time her sister and brother-in-law come indoors, or at least to be able to pretend she is asleep. She is not keen to be interrogated on what passed during her ramble with John. Given half a chance, Carol will prise the story out of her. *I was in love with you when I was six; you set the pattern of my love for other women.* What a thing to say! Indeed, what a compliment! But what of herself? What was going on in her six-year-old heart when all that premature passion was going on in his? She agreed to marry him, certainly, but did she agree they were in love? If so, she has no recollection of it. And what of now – what does she feel for him now? His declaration has certainly made her heart glow. What an odd character, this cousin of hers! His oddness does not come from the Coetzee side, she is sure of that, she is after all half Coetzee herself, so it must come from his mother's, from the Meyers or whatever the name was, the Meyers from the Eastern Cape. Meyer or Meier or Meiring.

Then she is asleep.

'He is stuck up,' says Carol. 'He thinks too much of himself. He can't bear to lower himself to talk to ordinary people. When he isn't messing around with his car he is sitting in a corner with a book. And why doesn't he get a haircut? Every time I lay eyes on him I have an urge to tie him down and slap a pudding-bowl over his head and snip off those hideous greasy locks of his.'

'His hair isn't greasy,' she protests, 'it's just too long. I think he washes it with hand-soap. That's why it is all over the place. And he is shy, not stuck up. That's why he keeps to himself. Give him a chance, he's an interesting person.'

'He is flirting with you. Anyone can see it. And you are flirting back. You, his cousin! You should be ashamed of yourself. Why isn't he married? Is he homosexual, do you think? Is he a *moffie*?'

She never knows whether Carol means what she says or is simply out to provoke her. Even here on the farm Carol goes about in modish white slacks and low-cut blouses, high-heeled sandals, heavy bracelets. She buys her clothes in Frankfurt, she says, on business trips with her husband. She certainly makes the rest of them look very dowdy, very staid, very country-cousin. She and Klaus live in Sandton in a twelve-room mansion owned by Anglo-American, for which they pay no rent, with stables and polo-ponies and a groom, though neither of them knows how to ride. They have no children yet; they will have children, Carol informs her, when they are properly settled. Properly settled means settled in America.

In the Sandton set in which she and Klaus move, she confides, quite advanced things go on. She does not spell out what these advanced things may be, and she, Margot, does not want to ask, but they seem to have to do with sex.

I won't let you write that. You can't write that about Carol.

It's what you told me.

Yes, but you can't write down every word I say and broadcast it to the world. I never agreed to that. Carol will never speak to me again.

All right, I'll cut it out or tone it down, I promise. Just hear me to the end. Can I go on?

Go on.

Carol has broken completely from her roots. She bears no resemblance to the *plattelandse meisie,* the country girl, she once used to be. She looks, if anything, German, with her bronzed skin and coiffeured blonde hair and emphatic eyeliner. Stately, big-busted, and barely thirty. Frau Dr Müller. If Frau Dr Müller decided to flirt in the Sandton manner with cousin John, how long would it be before cousin John succumbed? Love means being able to open your heart to the beloved, says John. What would Carol say to that? About love Carol could teach her cousin a thing or two, she is sure − at least about love in its advanced version.

John is not a *moffie*: she knows enough about men to know that. But there is something cool or cold about him, something that if not neuter is at least neutral, as a young child is neutral in matters of sex. There must have been women in his life, if not in South Africa then in America, though he has said not a word about them. Did his American women get to see his heart? If he makes a practice of it, of opening his heart, then he is unusual: men, in her experience, find nothing harder.

She herself has been married for ten years. Ten years ago she said goodbye to Carnarvon, where she had a job as a secretary in a lawyer's office, and moved to her bridegroom's farm east of Middelpos in the Roggeveld where, if she is lucky, if God smiles on her, she will live out the rest of her days.

The farm is home to the two of them, home and *Heim,* but she cannot be at home as much as she wishes. There is no money in sheep-farming any more, not in the barren, drought-ridden Roggeveld. To help make ends meet she has had to go back to work, as a bookkeeper this time, at the one hotel in Calvinia. Four nights of the week, Monday through Thursday, she spends at the hotel; on Fridays her husband drives in from the farm to fetch her, delivering her back in Calvinia at the crack of dawn the next Monday.

Despite this weekly separation – it makes her heart ache, she hates her dreary hotel room, sometimes she cannot hold back her tears, but lays her head on her arms and sobs – she and Lukas have what she would call a happy marriage. More than happy: fortunate, blessed. A good husband, a happy marriage, but no children. Not by design but by fate: her fate, her fault. Of the two sisters, one barren, the other *not yet settled*.

A good husband but close with his feelings. Is a guarded heart an affliction of men in general or just of South African men? Are Germans – Carol's husband, for instance – any better? At this moment Klaus is seated on the stoep with the troop of Coetzee kinsfolk he has acquired by marriage, smoking a cheroot (he freely offers his cheroots around, but his *rookgoed* is too strange, too foreign for the Coetzees), regaling them in his loud baby-Afrikaans, of which he is not in the slightest ashamed, with stories of the times he and Carol have gone skiing in Zermatt. Does Klaus, in the privacy of their Sandton home, now and then open up his heart to Carol in his slick, easy, confident European manner? She doubts it. She doubts that Klaus has much of a heart to show. She has seen little evidence of one. Whereas of the Coetzees it can at least be said that they have hearts, to a man and to a woman. Too much heart, in fact, sometimes, some of them.

'No, he's not a *moffie*,' she says. 'Talk to him and you will see for yourself.'

'WOULD YOU LIKE to go for a drive this afternoon?' John offers. 'We could do a grand tour of the farm, just you and I.'

'In what?' she says. 'In your Datsun?'

'Yes, in my Datsun. It's fixed.'

'Fixed so that it won't break down in the middle of nowhere?'

It is of course a joke. Voëlfontein is already the middle of nowhere. But it is not just a joke. She has no idea how big the farm is, measured in square miles, but she does know you cannot walk from one end of it to the other in a single day, not unless you take your walking seriously.

'It won't break down,' he says. 'But I'll bring spare water along just in case.'

Voëlfontein lies in the Koup region, and in the Koup it has rained not a drop in the past two years. What on earth inspired Grandpa Coetzee to buy land here, where every single farmer is struggling to keep his stock alive?

'What sort of word is *Koup*?' she says. 'Is it English? The place where no one can cope?'

'It's Khoi,' he says. 'Hottentot. *Koup*: dry place. It's a noun, not a verb. You can tell by the final *–p*.'

'Where did you learn that?'

'From books. From grammars put together by missionaries in the old days. There are no speakers of Khoi languages left, not in South Africa. The languages are, for all practical purposes, dead. In South-West Africa there are still a handful of old people speaking Nama. That's the sum of it. The sum of what is left.'

'And Xhosa? Do you speak Xhosa?'

He shakes his head. 'I am interested in the things we have lost, not the things we have kept. Why should I speak Xhosa? There are millions of people who can do that already. They don't need me.'

'I thought languages exist so that we can communicate with each other,' she says. 'What is the point of speaking Hottentot if no one else does?'

He presents her with what she is coming to think of as his secret little smile, betokening that he has an answer to her question, but since she will be too stupid to understand, he will not waste his breath revealing it to her. It is this Mister Know-All smile, above all, that sends Carol into a rage.

'Once you have learned Hottentot out of your old grammar books, who can you speak to?' she repeats.

'Do you want me to tell you?' he says. The little smile has turned into something else, something tight and not very nice.

'Yes, tell me. Answer me.'

'The dead. You can speak with the dead. Who otherwise' – he hesitates, as if the words might be too much for her and even for him – 'who otherwise are cast out into everlasting silence.'

She wanted an answer and now she has one. It is more than enough to shut her up.

They drive for half an hour, to the westernmost boundary of the farm. There, to her surprise, he opens the gate, drives through, closes the gate behind them, and without a word drives on along the rough dirt road. By four-thirty they have arrived at the town of Merweville, where she has not set foot in years.

Outside the Apollo Café he draws to a halt. 'Would you like a cup of coffee?' he says.

They enter the café with half a dozen barefoot children

tagging along behind them, the youngest a mere toddler. Mevrou the proprietess has the radio on, playing Afrikaans pop tunes. They sit down, wave the flies away. The children cluster around their table, staring with unabashed curiosity. '*Middag, jongens,*' says John. '*Middag, meneer,*' says the eldest.

They order coffee and get a version of coffee: pale Nescafé with long-life milk. She takes a sip of hers and pushes it aside. He drinks his abstractedly.

A tiny hand reaches up and filches the cube of sugar from her saucer. '*Toe, loop!*' she says: Run off! The child smiles merrily at her, unwraps the sugar, licks it.

It is by no means the first hint she has had of how far the old barriers between white and Coloured have come down. The signs are more obvious here than in Calvinia. Merweville is a smaller town and in decline, in such decline that it must be in danger of falling off the map. There can be no more than a few hundred people left. Half the houses they drove past seemed unoccupied. The building with the legend *Volkskas* [People's Bank] in white pebbles studded in the mortar over the door houses not a bank but a welding works. Though the worst of the afternoon heat is past, the sole living presence on the main street is provided by two men and a woman stretched out, along with a scrawny dog, in the shade of a flowering jacaranda.

Did I say all that? I don't remember.

I added a detail or two to bring the scene to life. I didn't tell you, but since Merweville figures so largely in your story, I actually visited the town to check it out.

You went to Merweville? How did it seem to you?

Much as you described it. But there is no Apollo Café any more. No café at all. Shall I go on?

John speaks. 'Are you aware that, among his other accomplishments, our grandfather used to be mayor of Merweville?'

'Yes, I am aware of that.' Their mutual grandfather had his finger in all too many pies. He was – the English word occurs to her – a *go-getter* in a land with few go-getters, a man with plenty of – another English word – *spunk,* more spunk probably than all his children put together. But perhaps that is the fate of the children of strong fathers: to be left with less than a full share of spunk. As with the sons, so with the daughters too: a little too self-effacing, the Coetzee women, blessed with too little of whatever the female equivalent of spunk might be.

She has only tenuous memories of their grandfather, who died when she was still a child: of a stooped, grouchy old man with a bristly chin. After the midday meal, she remembers, the whole house would freeze into silence: Grandpa was having his nap. Even at that age she was surprised to see how fear of the old man could make grown people creep about like mice. Yet without that old man she would not be here, nor would John: not just here on earth but here in the Karoo, on Voëlfontein or in Merweville. If her own life, from cradle to grave, has been and is still being determined by the ups and downs of the market in wool and mutton, then that is her grandfather's doing: a man who started out as a *smous*, a hawker peddling cotton prints and pots and pans and patent medicines to countryfolk, then when he had saved up enough money bought a share in a hotel, then sold the hotel and bought land and settled down as of all things a gentleman horse-breeder and sheep-farmer.

'You haven't asked what we are doing here in Merweville,' says John.

'Very well: what are we doing in Merweville?'

'I want to show you something. I am thinking of buying property here.'

She cannot believe her ears. 'You want to buy property? You want to live in Merweville? In *Merweville*? Do you want to be mayor too?'

'No, not live here, just spend time here. Live in Cape Town, come here for weekends and holidays. It's not impossible. Merweville is seven hours from Cape Town if you drive without stopping. You can buy a house for a thousand rand – a four-room house and half a morgen of land with peach trees and apricot trees and orange trees. Where else in the world will you get such a bargain?'

'And your father? What does your father think of this plan of yours?'

'It's better than an old-age home.'

'I don't understand. What is better than an old-age home?'

'Living in Merweville. My father can stay here, take up residence; I will be based in Cape Town but I will come up regularly to see that he is okay.'

'And what will your father do during the time he is here all by himself? Sit on the stoep and wait for the one car a day to drive past? There is a simple reason why you can buy a house in Merweville for peanuts, John: because no one wants to live here. I don't understand you. Why this sudden enthusiasm for Merweville?'

'It's in the Karoo.'

Die Karoo is vir skape geskape! The Karoo was made for sheep! She has to bite back the words. *He means it! He speaks of the Karoo as if it were paradise!* And all of a sudden memories of those Christmastides of yore come flooding back, when they were children roaming the veld as free as wild animals. 'Where do you want to be buried?' he asked her one day, then without waiting for her answer whispered: 'I want to be buried here.' 'For ever?' she said, she, her child self – 'Do you want to be buried for ever?' 'Just till I come out again,' he replied.

Till I come out again. She remembers it all, remembers the very words.

As a child one can do without explanations. One does not demand that everything make sense. But would she be recalling those words of his if they had not puzzled her then and, deep down, continued to puzzle her all these years? *Come out again*: did her cousin really believe, does he really believe, that one comes back from the grave? Who does he think he is: Jesus? And what does he think this place is, this Karoo: the Holy Land?

'If you mean to take up residence in Merweville you will need to get a haircut first,' she says. 'The good folk of the town won't allow a wild man to settle in their midst and corrupt their sons and daughters.'

From Mevrou behind the counter come unmistakable hints that she would like to close up shop. He pays, and they drive off. On the way out of the town he slows down before a house with a *TE KOOP* sign at the gate: For Sale. 'That's the house I had in mind,' he says. 'A thousand rand plus the legal paperwork. Can you believe it?'

The house is a nondescript cube with a corrugated-iron roof, a shaded veranda running the length of the front, and a steep wooden staircase up the side leading to a loft. The paintwork is in a sorry state. In front of the house, in a bedraggled rockery, a couple of aloes struggle to stay alive. Does he really mean to dump his father here, in this dull house in this exhausted hamlet? An old man, trembly, eating out of tins, sleeping between dirty sheets?

'Would you like to take a look?' he says. 'The house is locked, but we can walk around the back.'

She shivers. 'Another time,' she says. 'I'm not in the mood today.'

What she is in the mood for today she does not know. But her mood ceases to matter twenty kilometres out of Merweville, when the engine begins to cough and John frowns and switches it off and coasts to a stop. A smell of burning rubber invades the cab. 'It's overheating again,' he says. 'I won't be a minute.'

From the back he fetches a jerrycan of water. He unscrews the radiator cap, dodging a whoosh of steam, and refills the radiator. 'That should be enough to get us home,' he says. He tries to restart the engine. It turns over dryly without catching.

She knows enough about men never to question their competence with machines. She offers no advice, is careful not to seem impatient, not even to sigh. For an hour, while he fiddles with hoses and clamps and filthies his clothes and tries again and again to get the engine going, she maintains a strict, benign silence.

The sun begins to dip below the horizon; he continues to toil in what might as well be darkness.

'Do you have a torch?' she asks. 'Perhaps I can hold a torch for you.'

But no, he has not brought a torch. Furthermore, since he does not smoke, he does not even have matches. Not a Boy Scout, just a city boy, an unprepared city boy.

'I'll walk back to Merweville and get help,' he says at last. 'Or we can both walk.'

She is wearing light sandals. She is not going to stumble in sandals twenty kilometres across the veld in the dark.

'By the time you get to Merweville it will be midnight,' she says. 'You know no one there. There isn't even a service station. Who are you going to persuade to come out and fix your truck?'

'Then what do you suggest we do?'

'We wait here. If we are lucky, someone will drive past. Otherwise Michiel will come looking for us in the morning.'

'Michiel doesn't know we went to Merweville. I didn't tell him.'

He tries one last time to start the engine. When he turns the key there is a dull click. The battery is flat.

She gets out and, at a decent distance, relieves her bladder. A thin wind has come up. It is cold and is going to be colder. There is nothing in the truck with which to cover themselves, not even a tarpaulin. If they are going to wait out the night, they are going to have to do so huddled in the cab. And then, when they get back to the farm, they are going to have to explain themselves.

She is not yet miserable; she is still removed enough from their situation to find it grimly amusing. But that will soon change. They have nothing to eat, nothing even to drink save water from the can, which smells of petrol. Cold and hunger are going to gnaw away at her fragile good humour. Sleeplessness too, in due course.

She winds the window shut. 'Shall we just forget,' she says, 'that we are a man and a woman, and not be too embarrassed to keep each other warm? Because otherwise we are going to freeze.'

In the thirty-odd years they have known each other they have now and then kissed, in the way that cousins kiss, that is to say, on the cheek. They have embraced too. But tonight an intimacy of quite another order is on the cards. Somehow, on this hard seat, with the gear lever uncomfortably in the way, they are going to have to lie together, or slump together, give warmth to each other. If God is kind and they manage to fall asleep, they may in addition have to suffer the humiliation of snoring or being snored upon. What a test! What a trial!

'And tomorrow,' she says, allowing herself a single acid moment, 'when we get back to civilization, maybe you can arrange to have this truck fixed properly. There is a good mechanic at Leeuw Gamka. Michiel uses him. Just a friendly suggestion.'

'I am sorry. The fault is mine. I try to do things myself when I ought really to leave them to more competent hands. It's because of the country we live in.'

'The country we live in? Why is it the country's fault that your truck keeps breaking down?'

'Because of our long history of making other people do our work for us while we sit in the shade and watch.'

So that is the reason why they are here in the cold and the dark waiting for some passer-by to rescue them. To make a point, namely that white folk should do their own car repairs. How comical.

'The mechanic in Leeuw Gamka is white,' she says. 'I am not suggesting that you take your car to a Native.' She would like to add: *If you want to do your own repairs, for God's sake take a course in auto maintenance first.* But she holds her tongue. 'What other kind of work do you insist on doing,' she says instead, 'besides fixing cars?' *Besides fixing cars and writing poems.*

'I do garden work. I do repairs around the house. I am at present re-laying the drainage. It may seem funny to you but to me it is not a joke. I am making a gesture. I am trying to break the taboo on manual labour.'

'The taboo?'

'Yes. Just as in India it is taboo for upper-caste people to clean up – what shall we call it? – human waste, so, in this country, if a white man touches a pickaxe or a spade he at once becomes unclean.'

'What nonsense you talk! That is simply not true! It's just anti-white prejudice!'

She regrets the words as soon as she has spoken them. She has gone too far, driven him into a corner. Now she is going to have this man's resentment to cope with, on top of the boredom and the cold.

'But I can see your point,' she goes on, helping him out, since he doesn't seem able to help himself. 'You are right in one sense: we have become too used to keeping our hands clean, our white hands. We should be more ready to dirty our hands. I couldn't agree more. End of subject. Are you sleepy yet? I'm not. I have a suggestion. To pass the time, why don't we tell each other stories.'

'You tell a story,' he says stiffly. 'I don't know any stories.'

'Tell me a story from America,' she says. 'You can make it up, it doesn't have to be true. Any story.'

'Given the existence of a personal God,' he says, 'with a white beard quaquaquaqua outside time without extension who from the heights of divine apathia loves us deeply quaquaquaqua with some exceptions.'

He stops. She has not the faintest idea what he is talking about.

'Quaquaquaqua,' he says.

'I give up,' she says. He is silent. 'My turn,' she says. 'Here follows the story of the princess and the pea. Once upon a time there is a princess so delicate that even when she sleeps on ten piled-up feather mattresses she is convinced she can feel a pea, one of those hard little dried peas, underneath the last mattress. She frets and frets all night – *Who put a pea there? Why?* – and as a result doesn't get a wink of sleep. She comes down to break-fast looking haggard. To her parents the king and queen she complains: "I couldn't sleep, and it's all the fault of that accursed pea!" The king sends a serving-woman to remove the pea. The woman searches and searches but can find nothing.

'"Let me hear no more of peas," says the king to his daughter. "There is no pea. The pea is just in your imagination."

'That night the princess reascends her mountain of feather mattresses. She tries to sleep but cannot, because of the pea, the pea that is either underneath the bottom-most mattress or else in her imagination, it does not matter which, the effect is the same. By daybreak she is so exhausted that she cannot even eat breakfast. "It's all the pea's fault!" she laments.

'Exasperated, the king sends an entire troop of serving-women to hunt for the pea, and when they return, reporting that there is no pea, has them all beheaded. "Now are you satisfied?" he bellows at his daughter. "Now will you sleep?"'

She pauses for breath. She has no idea what is going to happen next in this bedtime story, whether the princess will at last manage to fall asleep or not; yet, strangely, she is convinced that, when she opens her lips, the right words will come.

But there is no need for more words. He is asleep. Like a child, this prickly, opinionated, incompetent, ridiculous cousin of hers has fallen asleep with his head on her shoulder. Fast asleep, undoubtedly: she can feel him twitching. No peas under him.

And what of her? Who is going to tell her stories to send her off to the land of nod? Never has she felt more awake. Is this how she is going to have to spend the night: bored, fretting, bearing the weight of a somnolent male?

He claims there is a taboo on whites doing manual labour, but what of the taboo on cousins of opposite sexes spending the night together? What are the Coetzees back on the farm going to say? Truly, she has no feeling toward John that could be called physical, not the faintest quiver of womanly response. Will that be enough to absolve her? Why is there no male aura about him? Does the fault lie with him; or on the contrary does it lie with her, who has so wholeheartedly absorbed the taboo that she cannot think of him as a man? If he has no woman, is that because he has no feeling for women, and therefore women, herself included, respond by having no feeling for him? Is her cousin, if not a *moffie*, then a eunuch?

The air in the cab is becoming stale. Taking care not to wake him, she opens the window a crack. What presences surround them — bushes or trees or perhaps even animals — she senses on her skin rather than sees. From somewhere comes the chirping of a lone cricket. *Stay with me tonight*, she whispers to the cricket.

But perhaps there is a type of woman who is attracted to a man like this, who is happy to listen without contradicting while he airs his opinions, and then to take them on as her own, even the self-evidently silly ones. A woman indifferent to male silliness, indifferent even to sex, simply in search of a man to attach to herself and take care of and protect against the world. A woman who will put up with shoddy work around the house because what matters is not that the windows close and the locks work but that her man have the space in which to live out his idea of himself. And who will afterwards quietly call in hired help, someone good with his hands, to fix up the mess.

For a woman like that, marriage might well be passionless but it need not be childless. Then the whole brood could sit around the table of an evening, the lord and master at the head, his help-meet at the foot, their healthy, well-behaved offspring down the two sides; and over the soup course the master could expatiate on the sanctity of labour. *What a man is my mate!* the wife will whisper to herself. *And what a developed conscience he has!*

Why does she feel so bitter toward John, and even bitterer toward this wife she has conjured up for him out of thin air? The simple answer: because due to his vanity and clumsiness she is stranded on the Merweville road. But the night is long, there is plenty of time to unfold a grander hypothesis and then inspect it to see if it has any virtue. The grander answer: she feels bitter because she had hoped for much from John, and he has failed her.

What had she hoped for from her cousin?

That he would redeem the Coetzee men.

Why did she want the redemption of the Coetzee men?

Because the Coetzee men are so *slapgat*.

Why had she placed her hopes in John in particular?

Because of the Coetzee men he was the one blessed with the best chance. He was blessed with the chance and he did not make use of it.

Slapgat is a word she and her sister throw around rather easily, perhaps because it was thrown around rather easily in their hearing while they were children. It was only after she left home that she noticed the disquiet the word evoked and began to use it more cautiously. A *slap gat*: a rectum, an anus, over which one has less than complete control. Hence *slapgat*: slack, spineless.

Her uncles have turned out *slapgat* because their parents, her grandparents, brought them up that way. While their father thundered and roared and made them quake in their boots, their mother tiptoed around like a mouse. The result was that when they went out into the world they lacked all fibre, lacked backbone, lacked belief in themselves, lacked courage. The life-paths they chose for themselves were without exception easy paths, paths of least resistance. Gingerly they tested the tide, then swam with it.

What made the Coetzees so easygoing and therefore so *gesellig*, such good company, was precisely their preference for the easiest available path; and their *geselligheid* was precisely what made the Christmas get-togethers such fun. They never quarrelled, never squabbled among themselves. They got along famously, all of them. It was the next generation, her generation, who had to pay for their easygoingness. For their children went out into the world expecting the world to be just another *slap, gesellige* place, Voëlfontein writ large. And behold, it was not!

She herself has no children. She cannot conceive. But if, blessedly, she had children, she would take it as her first duty to work the Coetzee blood out of them. How you work *slap* blood out of people she does not know offhand, short of taking them to a hospital and having their blood pumped out and replaced with the blood of some vigorous donor; but perhaps rigorous training in self-assertion, starting at the earliest possible age, would do the trick. Because if there is one thing she knows about the world in which the child of the future will have to grow up, it is that there will be no room for the *slap*.

Even Voëlfontein and the Karoo are no longer Voëlfontein and the Karoo as they used to be. Look at those children in the Apollo Café. Look at cousin Michiel's work gang, who are certainly not the *plaasvolk* of yore. In the attitude of Coloured people in general toward whites there is a new and unsettling hardness. The younger ones regard one with a cold eye, refuse to call one *Baas* or *Miesies*. Strange men flit across the land from one settlement to another, *lokasie* to *lokasie*, and no one will report them as in the old days. The police are finding it harder and harder to come up with information they can trust. People no longer want to be seen talking to the police; sources have dried up. For the farmers, summons for commando duty come more often and for longer. Lukas complains about it all the time. If that is the way things are in the Roggeveld, it must certainly be the way things are here in the Koup.

Business is changing character too. To get on in business it is no longer enough to be friends with all and sundry, to do favours and be owed favours in return. No, nowadays you have to be as hard as nails and ruthless as well. What chance do *slapgat* men stand in such a world? No wonder her Coetzee uncles are not prospering: bank managers idling away the years in dying *platteland* towns, civil servants stalled on the ladder of promotion, penurious farmers, even in the case of John's father a disgraced, disbarred attorney.

If she had children, she would not only do her utmost to purge them of their Coetzee inheritance, she would think seriously of doing what Carol is doing: taking them out of the country, giving them a fresh start in America or Australia or New Zealand, places where they can look forward to a decent future. But as a childless woman she is spared having to make that decision. She has another role prepared for her: to devote herself to her husband and to the farm; to live as good a life as the times allow, as good and as fair and as just.

The barrenness of the future that yawns before Lukas and herself – this is not a new source of pain, no, it returns again and again like a toothache, to the extent that it has by now begun to bore her. She wishes she could dismiss it and get some sleep. How is it that this cousin of hers, whose body manages to be both scrawny and soft at the same time, does not feel the cold, while she, who is undeniably more than a few kilos over her best weight, has begun to shiver? On cold nights she and her husband sleep tight and warm against each other. Why does her cousin's body fail to warm her? Not only does he not warm her, he seems to suck her own body heat away. Is he by nature as heatless as he is sexless?

A ripple of true anger runs through her; and, as if sensing it, this male being beside her stirs. 'Sorry,' he mumbles, sitting upright.

'Sorry for what?'

'I lost track.'

She has no idea what he is talking about and is not going to inquire. He slumps down and in a moment is asleep again.

Where is God in all of this? With God the Father she finds it harder and harder to have dealings. What faith she once had in Him and His providence she has by now lost. Godlessness: her inheritance from the godless Coetzees, no doubt. When she thinks of God, all she can picture is a bearded figure with a booming voice and a grand manner who inhabits a mansion on top of a hill with hosts of servants rushing around anxiously, doing things for Him. Like a good Coetzee, she prefers to steer clear of people like that. The Coetzees look askance at self-important folk, crack jokes about them sotto voce. She may not be as good at jokes as the rest of the family, but she does find God a bit of a trial, a bit of a bore.

Now I must protest. You are really going too far. I said nothing remotely like that. You are putting words of your own in my mouth.

I'm sorry, I must have got carried away. I'll fix it. I'll tone it down.

Cracking jokes sotto voce. Nevertheless, does God in His infinite wisdom have a plan for her and for Lukas? For the Roggeveld? For South Africa? Will things that look merely chaotic today, chaotic and purposeless, reveal themselves at some future date as part of some vast, benign design? For instance: Is there a larger explanation for why a woman in the prime of her life must spend four nights of the week sleeping alone in a dismal second-floor room in the Grand Hotel in Calvinia, month after month, perhaps even year after year, with no end in sight; and for why her husband, a born farmer, must spend most of his time trucking other people's livestock to the abattoirs in Paarl and Maitland – an explanation larger than that the farm would go under without the income these soul-destroying jobs bring in? And is there a larger explanation for why the farm that the two of them are slaving to keep afloat will in the full-ness of time pass into the care not of a son of their loins but of some ignoramus nephew of her husband's, if it is not swallowed down by the bank first? If, in God's vast, benign design, it was never intended that this part of the world – the Roggeveld, the Karoo – should be profitably farmed, then what exactly is His intention for it? Is it meant to fall back into the hands of the *volk*, who will proceed, as in the old, old days, to roam from district to district with their ragged flocks in search of grazing, trampling the fences flat, while people like herself and her husband expire in some forgotten corner, disinherited?

Useless to put questions like that to the Coetzees. *Die boer saai, God maai, maar waar skuil die papegaai?* say the Coetzees, and cackle. Nonsense words. A nonsense family, flighty, without substance; clowns. *'n Hand vol vere*: a handful of feathers. Even the one member for whom she had had some slight hopes, the one beside her who has tumbled straight back into dreamland, turns out to be a lightweight. Who ran away to the big world and now comes creeping back to the little world with his tail between his legs. Failed runaway, failed car mechanic too, for whose failure she is at this moment having to suffer. Failed son. Sitting in that dusty old house in Merweville looking out on the empty, sunstruck street, rattling a pencil between his teeth, trying to think up verses. *O droë land, o barre kranse* . . . O parched land, o barren cliffs . . . What next? Something about *weemoed* for sure, melancholy.

She wakes as first streaks of mauve and orange begin to extend across the sky. In her sleep she has somehow twisted her body and slumped down further in the seat, so that her cousin, still dormant, reclines not against her shoulder but against her rump. Irritably she frees herself. Her eyes are gummy, her bones creak, she has a raging thirst. Opening the door, she slides out.

The air is cold and still. Even as she watches, thornbushes and tufts of grass, touched by the first light, emerge out of nothing. It is as if she were present at the first day of creation. *My God*, she murmurs; she has an urge to sink to her knees.

There is a rustle nearby. She is looking straight into the dark eyes of an antelope, a little steenbok not twenty paces off, and it is looking straight back at her, wary but not afraid, not yet. *My kleintjie!* she says, my little one. More than anything she wants to embrace it, to pour out upon its brow this sudden love; but before she can take a first step the little one has whirled about and raced off with drumming hooves. A hundred yards away it halts, turns, inspects her again, then trots at less urgent pace across the flats and into a dry river bed.

'What's that?' comes her cousin's voice. He has at last awoken; he clambers out of the truck, yawning, stretching.

'A steenbokkie,' she says curtly. 'What are we going to do now?'

'I'll head back to Merweville,' he says. 'You wait here. I should be back by ten o'clock, eleven at the latest.'

'If a car passes and I can get a lift, I'm taking it,' she says. 'Either direction, I'm taking it.'

He looks a mess, with his unkempt hair and beard sticking out at all angles. *Thank God I don't have to wake up with you in my bed every morning*, she thinks. *Not enough of a man. A real man would do better than this*, sowaar!

The sun is showing above the horizon; already she can feel the warmth on her skin. The world may be God's world, but the Karoo belongs first of all to the sun. 'You had better get going,' she says. 'It's going to be a hot day.' And watches as he trudges off, the empty jerrycan slung over his shoulder.

An adventure: perhaps that is the best way to think of it. Here in the back of beyond she and John are having an adventure. For years to come the Coetzees will be reminiscing about it. *Remember the time when Margot and John broke down on that godforsaken Merweville road?* In the meantime, while she waits for her adventure to end, what has she for diversion? The tattered instruction manual for the Datsun; nothing else. No poems. Tyre rotation. Battery maintenance. Tips for fuel economy.

The truck, facing into the rising sun, grows stiflingly hot. She takes shelter in its lee.

On the crest of the road, an apparition: out of the heat-haze emerges first the torso of a man, then by degrees a donkey and donkey-cart. On the wind she can even hear the neat clip-clop of the donkey's hooves.

The figure grows clearer. It is Hendrik from Voëlfontein, and behind him, sitting on the cart, is her cousin.

Laughter and greetings. 'Hendrik has been visiting his daughter in Merweville,' John explains. 'He will give us a ride back to the farm, that is, if his donkey agrees. He says we can hitch the Datsun to the cart and he will tow it.'

Hendrik is alarmed. '*Nee, meneer!*' he says.

'*Ek jok maar net,*' says her cousin. Just joking.

Hendrik is a man of middle age. As the result of a botched operation for a cataract he has lost the sight of one eye. There is something wrong with his lungs too, such that the slightest physical effort makes him wheeze. As a labourer he is not of much use on the farm, but her cousin Michiel keeps him on because that is how things are done here.

Hendrik has a daughter who lives with her husband and children outside Merweville. The husband used to have a job in the town but seems to have lost it; the daughter does domestic work. Hendrik must have set off from their place before first light. About him there is a faint smell of sweet wine; when he climbs down from the cart, she notices, he stumbles. Sozzled by mid-morning: what a life!

Her cousin reads her thoughts. 'I have some water here,' he says, and proffers the full jerrycan. 'It's clean. I filled it at a wind-pump.'

So they set off for the farm, John seated beside Hendrik, she in the back holding an old jute bag over her head to keep off the sun. A car passes them in a cloud of dust, heading for Merweville. If she had seen it in time she would have hailed it – got a ride to Merweville and from there telephoned Michiel to come and fetch her. On the other hand, though the road is rutted and the ride uncomfortable, she likes the idea of arriving at the farmhouse in Hendrik's donkey-cart, likes it more and more: the Coetzees assembled on the stoep for afternoon tea, Hendrik doffing his hat to them, bringing back Jack's errant son, dirty and sunburnt and chastened. '*Ons was so bekommerd!*' they will berate the miscreant. '*Waar was julle dan? Michiel wou selfs die polisie bel!*' From him, nothing but mumble-mumble. '*Die arme Margie! En wat het van die bakkie geword?*' We were so worried! Where were you? Michiel was on the point of phoning the police! Poor Margie! And where is the truck?

There are stretches of road where the incline is so steep that they have to get down and walk. For the rest the little donkey is up to its task, with no more than a touch of the whiplash to its rump now and again to remind it who is master. How slight its frame, how delicate its hooves, yet what staunchness, what powers of endurance! No wonder Jesus had a fondness for donkeys.

Inside the boundary of Voëlfontein they halt at a dam. While the donkey drinks she chats with Hendrik about the daughter in Merweville, then about the other daughter, the one who works in the kitchen at a home for the aged in Beaufort West. Discreetly she does not ask after Hendrik's most recent wife, whom he married when she was no more than a child and who ran away as soon as she could with a man from the railway camp at Leeuw Gamka.

Hendrik finds it easier to talk to her than to her cousin, she can see that. She and he share a language, whereas the Afrikaans John speaks is stiff and bookish. Half of what John says probably goes over Hendrik's head. *Which is more poetic, do you think, Hendrik: the rising sun or the setting sun? A goat or a sheep?*

'*Het Katryn dan nie vir padkos gesorg nie?*' she teases Hendrik: Hasn't your daughter packed lunch for us?

Hendrik goes through the motions of embarrassment, averting his gaze, shuffling. '*Ja-nee, mies,*' he wheezes. A *plaashotnot* from the old days, a farm Hottentot.

As it turns out, Hendrik's daughter has indeed provided *padkos*. From a jacket pocket Hendrik brings out, wrapped in brown paper, a leg of chicken and two slices of buttered white bread, which shame forbids him to divide with them yet equally forbids him to devour in front of them.

'*In Godsnaam eet, man!*' she commands. '*Ons is glad nie honger nie, ons is ook binnekort tuis*': We aren't hungry, and anyway we'll soon be home. And she draws John away on a circuit of the dam so that Hendrik, with his back to them, can hurriedly down his meal.

Ons is glad nie honger nie: a lie, of course. She is famished. The very smell of the cold chicken makes her salivate.

'Sit up front beside the driver,' John suggests. 'For our triumphal return.' And so she does. As they approach the Coetzees, assembled on the stoep exactly as she had foreseen, she takes care to put on a smile and even to wave in a parody of royalty. In response she is greeted with a light ripple of clapping. She descends,

'*Dankie, Hendrik, eerlik dankie,*' she says: Thank you sincerely. '*Mies,*' says Hendrik. Later in the day she will go over to his house and leave some money: for Katryn, she will say, for clothing for her children, though she knows the money will go on liquor.

'*En toe?*' says Carol, in front of everyone. '*Sê vir ons: waar was julle?*' Where were you?

Just for a second there is silence, and in that second she realizes that the question, on the face of it simply a prompt for her to come up with some flippant, amusing retort, is a real one. The Coetzees really want to know where she and John have been; they want to be reassured that nothing truly scandalous has taken place. It takes her breath away, the cheek of it. That people who have known her and loved her all her life could think her capable of misconduct! '*Vra vir John,*' she replies curtly – ask John – and stalks indoors.

When she rejoins them half an hour later the atmosphere is still uneasy.

'Where has John gone?' she asks.

John and Michiel, it turns out, set off just a moment ago in Michiel's pickup to recover the Datsun. They will tow it to Leeuw Gamka, to the mechanic who will fix it properly.

'We stayed up late last night,' says her aunt Beth. 'We waited and waited. Then we decided you and John must have gone to Beaufort and were spending the night there because the National Road is so dangerous at this time of the year. But you didn't phone, and that worried us. This morning Michiel phoned the hotel at Beaufort and they said they hadn't seen you. He phoned Fraserburg too. We never guessed you had gone to Merweville. What were you doing in Merweville?'

What indeed were they doing in Merweville? She turns to

John's father. 'John says you and he are thinking of buying property in Merweville,' she says. 'Is that true, Uncle Jack?'

A shocked silence falls.

'Is it true, Uncle Jack?' she presses him. 'Is it true you are going to move to Merweville?'

'If you put the question like that,' Jack says – the bantering Coetzee manner is gone, he is all caution – 'no, no one is actually going to move to Merweville. John has the idea – I don't know how realistic it is – of buying one of those abandoned houses and fixing it up as a holiday home. That's as far as we have got in talking about it.'

A holiday home in Merweville! Who has ever heard of such a thing! Merweville of all places, with its snooping neighbours and its *diaken* [deacon] knocking at the door, pestering one to attend church! How can Jack, in his day the liveliest and most irreverent of them all, be planning a move to Merweville?

'You should try Koegenaap first, Jack,' says his brother Alan. 'Or Pofadder. In Pofadder the big day of the year is when the dentist from Upington comes visiting to pull teeth. They call it the *Groot Trek,* the Great Trek.'

As soon as their ease is threatened, the Coetzees rush in with jokes. A family drawn up in a tight little *laager* to keep the world and its woes at bay. But how long will the jokes go on doing their magic? One of these days the great foe himself will come knocking at the door, the Grim Reaper, whetting his scythe-blade, calling them out one by one. What power will their jokes have then?

'According to John, you are going to move to Merweville while he stays on in Cape Town,' she persists. 'Are you sure you will be able to cope by yourself, Uncle Jack, without a car?'

A serious question. The Coetzees don't like serious questions. '*Margie word 'n bietjie* grim,' they will say among themselves: Margie is becoming a bit grim. *Is your son planning to shunt you off to the Karoo and abandon you*, she is asking, *and if that is what is afoot, how come you don't raise your voice in protest?*

'No, no,' replies Jack. 'It won't be like you say. Merweville will just be somewhere quiet to take a break. If it goes through. It's just an idea, you know, an idea of John's. It's nothing definite.'

'IT'S A SCHEME to get rid of his father,' says her sister Carol. 'He wants to dump him in the middle of the Karoo and wash his hands of him. Then it will be up to Michiel to take care of him. Because Michiel will be closest.'

'Poor old John!' she replies. 'You always believe the worst of him. What if he is telling the truth? He promises he will visit his father in Merweville every weekend, and spend the school holidays there as well. Why not give him the benefit of the doubt?'

'Because I don't believe a word he says. The whole plan sounds fishy to me. He has never got on with his father.'

'He looks after his father in Cape Town.'

'He lives with his father, but only because he has no money. He is thirty-something years old with no prospects. He ran away from South Africa to escape the army. Then he was thrown out of America because he broke the law. Now he can't find a proper job because he is too stuck-up. The two of them live on the pathetic salary his father gets from the scrapyard where he works.'

'But that's not true!' she protests. Carol is younger than she. Once Carol used to be the follower and she, Margot, the leader.

Now it is Carol who strides ahead, she who tails anxiously behind. How did it happen? 'John teaches in a high school,' she says. 'He earns his own money.'

'That's not what I hear. What I hear is that he coaches dropouts for their matric exams and is paid by the hour. It's part-time work, the sort of thing students do to earn pocket money. Ask him straight out. Ask him what school he teaches at. Ask him what he earns.'

'A big salary isn't all that counts.'

'It isn't just a matter of salary. It's a matter of telling the truth. Let him tell you the truth about why he wants to buy this house in Merweville. Let him tell you who is going to pay for it, he or his father. Let him tell you his plans for the future.' And then, when she looks blank: 'Hasn't he told you? Hasn't he told you his plans?'

'He doesn't have plans. He is a Coetzee, Coetzees don't have plans, they don't have ambitions, they only have idle longings. He has an idle longing to live in the Karoo.'

'His ambition is to be a poet, a full-time poet. This Merweville scheme has nothing to do with his father's welfare. He wants a place in the Karoo where he can come when it suits him, where he can sit with his chin on his hands and contemplate the sunset and write poems.'

John and his poems again! She can't help it, she snorts with laughter. John sitting on the stoep of that dreary little house making up poems! With a beret on his head, no doubt, and a glass of wine at his elbow. And the little Coloured children clustered around him, pestering him with questions. *Wat maak oom? – Nee, oom maak gedigte. Op sy ou ramkiekie maak oom gedigte. Die wêreld is ons woning nie* . . . What is sir doing? – Sir is making poems. On his old banjo sir is making poems. This world is not our dwelling-place . . .

'I'll ask him,' she says, still laughing. 'I'll ask him to show me his poems.'

SHE CATCHES JOHN the next morning as he is setting off on one of his walks. 'Let me come with you,' she says. 'Give me a minute to put on proper shoes.'

They follow the path that runs eastward from the farmstead along the bank of the overgrown river bed toward the dam whose wall burst in the floods of 1943 and has never been repaired. In the shallow waters of the dam a trio of white geese float peacefully. It is still cool, there is no haze, they can see as far as the Nieuweveld Mountains.

'*God*,' she says, '*dis darem mooi. Dit raak jou siel aan, nè, dié ou wêreld.*' Isn't it beautiful. It touches one's soul, this landscape.

They are in a minority, a tiny minority, the two of them, of souls that are stirred by these great, desolate expanses. If anything has held them together over the years, it is that. This landscape, this *kontrei* – it has taken over her heart. When she dies and is buried, she will dissolve into this earth so naturally it will be as if she never had a human life.

'Carol says you are still writing poems,' she says. 'Is that true? Will you show me?'

'I am sorry to disappoint Carol,' he replies stiffly, 'but I haven't written a poem since I was a teenager.'

She bites her tongue. She forgot: you do not ask a man to show you his poems, not in South Africa, not without reassuring him beforehand that it will be all right, he is not going to be mocked. What a country, where poetry is not a manly activity but the province of children and *oujongnooiens* [spinsters] – *oujongnooiens* of both sexes! How Totius or Louis Leipoldt managed she cannot guess. No wonder Carol chooses John's poem-writing to attack, Carol with her nose for other people's weaknesses.

'If you gave up so long ago, why does Carol think you still write?'

'I have no idea. Perhaps she saw me marking student essays and jumped to the wrong conclusion.'

She does not believe him, but she is not going to press him further. If he wants to evade her, let him. If poetry is a part of his life he is too shy or too ashamed to talk about, then so be it.

She does not think of John as a *moffie*, but it continues to puzzle her that he has no woman. A man alone, particularly one of the Coetzee men, seems to her like a boat without oar or rudder or sail. And now two of them, two Coetzee men, living as a couple! While Jack still had the redoubtable Vera behind him he steered a more or less straight course; but now that she is gone he seems quite lost. As for Jack and Vera's son, he could certainly do with some level-headed guidance. But what woman with any sense would want to devote herself to the hapless John?

Carol is convinced John is a bad bet; and the rest of the Coetzee family, despite their good hearts, would probably agree. What sets her, Margot, apart, what keeps her confidence in John precariously afloat, is, oddly enough, the way in which he and his father behave toward each other: if not with affection, that would be saying too much, then at least with respect.

The pair used to be the worst of enemies. The bad blood between Jack and his elder son was the subject of much head-shaking. When that son disappeared overseas, the parents put on the best front they could. He had gone to pursue a career in science, his mother proclaimed. For years she maintained the story that John was working as a scientist in England, even as it became clear that she had no idea for whom he worked or what work he did. *You know how John is*, his father would say: *always very independent. Independent*: what did that mean? Not without reason, the Coetzees took it to mean he had disowned his country, his family, his very parents.

Then Jack and Vera started putting out a new story: John was not in England after all but in America, pursuing ever higher qualifications. Time passed; in the absence of hard news, interest in John and his doings waned. He and his younger brother became just two among thousands of young white men who had run away to escape military service, leaving an embarrassed family behind. He had almost vanished from their collective memory when the scandal of his expulsion from the United States burst upon them.

That terrible war, said his father: it was all the fault of a war in which American boys were sacrificing their lives for the sake of Asians who seemed to feel no gratitude at all. No wonder ordinary Americans were revolting. No wonder they took to the streets. John had been caught up willy-nilly in a street protest, the story proceeded; what followed had just been a bad misunderstanding.

Was it his son's disgrace, and the untruths he had to tell as a consequence, that had turned Jack into a shaky, prematurely aged man? How can she even ask?

'You must be glad to see the Karoo again,' she says to John. 'Aren't you relieved you decided not to stay in America?'

'I don't know,' he replies. 'Of course, in the midst of this' – he does not gesture, but she knows what he means: this sky, this space, the vast silence enclosing them – 'I feel blessed, one of a lucky few. But practically speaking, what future do I have in this country, where I have never fitted in? Perhaps a clean break would have been better after all. Cut yourself free of what you love and hope that the wound heals.'

A frank answer. Thank heaven for that.

'I had a chat with your father yesterday, John, while you and Michiel were away. Seriously, I don't think he fully grasps what you are planning. I am talking about Merweville. Your father is not young any more, and he is not well. You can't dump him in a strange town and expect him to fend for himself. And you can't expect the rest of the family to step in and take care of him once things go wrong. That's all. That's what I wanted to say.'

He does not respond. In his hand is a length of old fencing-wire that he has picked up. Swinging the wire petulantly left and right, flicking off the heads of the waving grass, he descends the slope of the eroded dam wall.

'Don't behave like this!' she calls out, trotting after him. 'Speak to me, for God's sake! Tell me I am wrong! Tell me I am making a mistake!'

He halts and turns upon her a look of cold hostility. 'Let me fill you in on my father's situation,' he says. 'My father has no savings, not a cent, and no insurance. He has only a state pension to look forward to: forty-three rand a month when I last checked. So despite his age, despite his poor health, he has to go on working. Together the two of us earn in a month what a car salesman earns in a week. My father can give up his job only if he moves to a place where living expenses are lower than in the city.'

'But why does he have to move at all? And why to Merweville, to some rundown old ruin?'

'My father and I can't live together indefinitely, Margie. It makes us too miserable, both of us. It's unnatural. Fathers and sons were never meant to share a house.'

'Your father doesn't strike me as a difficult person to live with.'

'Perhaps; but I am a difficult person to live with. My difficulty consists in not wanting to live with other people.'

'So is that what this Merweville business is all about – about you wanting to live by yourself?'

'Yes. Yes and no. I want to be able to be alone when I choose.'

THEY ARE CONGREGATED on the stoep, all the Coetzees, having their morning tea, chatting, idly watching Michiel's three young sons play cricket on the open *werf*.

On the far horizon a cloud of dust materializes and hangs in the air.

'That must be Lukas,' says Michiel, who has the keenest eyes. 'Margie, it's Lukas!'

Lukas, as it turns out, has been on the road since dawn. He is tired but in good spirits nonetheless, full of vim. Barely has he greeted his wife and her family before he lets himself be roped into the boys' game. He may not be competent at cricket, but he loves being with children, and children adore him. He would be the best of fathers: it breaks her heart that he must be childless.

John joins in the game too. He is better at cricket than Lukas, more practised, one can see that at a glance, but children don't warm to him. Nor do dogs, she has noticed. Unlike Lukas, not a father by nature. An *alleenloper*, as some male animals are: a loner. Perhaps it is as well he has not married.

Unlike Lukas; yet there are things she shares with John that she can never share with Lukas. Why? Because of the childhood times they spent together, the most precious of times, when they opened their hearts to each other as one can never do later, even to a husband, even to a husband whom one loves more than all the treasure in the world.

Best to cut yourself free of what you love, he had said during their walk – *cut yourself free and hope the wound heals*. She understands him exactly. That is what they share above all: not just a love of this farm, this *kontrei*, this Karoo, but an understanding that goes with the love, an understanding that love can be too much. To him and to her it was granted to spend their childhood summers in a sacred space. That glory can never be regained; best not to haunt old sites and come away from them mourning what is for ever gone.

Being wary of loving too much is not something that makes sense to Lukas. For Lukas, love is simple, wholehearted. Lukas gives himself over to her with all his heart, and in return she gives him all of herself: *With this body I thee worship.* Through his love her husband brings out what is best in her: even now, sitting here drinking tea, watching him at play, she can feel her body warming to him. From Lukas she has learned what love can be. Whereas her cousin . . . She cannot imagine her cousin giving himself wholeheartedly to anyone. Always a quantum held back, held in reserve. One does not need to be a dog to see that.

It would be nice if Lukas could take a break, if she and he could spend a night or two here on Voëlfontein. But no, tomorrow is Monday, they must be back at Middelpos by nightfall. So after lunch they say their goodbyes to the aunts and uncles. When John's turn comes she hugs him tight, feeling his body against her tense, resistant. '*Totsiens*,' she says: Goodbye. 'I'm going to write you a letter and I want you to write back.' 'Goodbye,' he says. 'Drive safely.'

She begins the promised letter that same night, sitting in her dressing gown and slippers at the table in her own kitchen, the kitchen she married into and has come to love, with its huge old fireplace and its ever-cool, windowless larder whose shelves still groan with jars of jam and preserves she laid in last autumn.

Dear John, she writes, *I was so cross with you when we broke down on the Merweville road – I hope it didn't show too much, I hope you will forgive me. All that bad temper has now blown away, there is no trace left. They say you don't know a person properly until you have spent a night with him (or her). I am glad I had a chance to spend a night with you. In sleep our masks slip off and we are seen as we truly are.*

The Bible looks forward to the day when the lion shall lie down with the lamb, when we will no longer need to be on our guard since we will have no more cause for fear. (Rest assured, you are not the lion, nor am I the lamb.)

I want to raise one last time the subject of Merweville.

We all grow old one day, and in the way we treat our parents we will surely be treated too. What goes around comes around, as they say. I am sure it is hard for you to live with your father when you have been used to living alone, but Merweville is not the right solution.

You are not alone in your difficulties, John. Carol and I face the same problem with our mother. When Klaus and Carol go off to America, that burden will fall squarely on Lukas and me.

I know you are not a believer, so I won't suggest that you pray for guidance. I am not much of a believer either, but prayer is a good thing. Even if there is no one above to listen, one at least brings out the words, which is better than bottling things up.

I wish we had had more time to talk. Do you remember how we used to talk when we were children? It is so precious to me, the memory of those times. How sad that when our turn comes to die our story, the story of you and me, will die too.

I cannot tell you what tenderness I feel for you at this moment. You were always my favourite cousin, but it is more than that. I long to protect you from the world, even though you probably don't need protecting (I am guessing). It is hard to know what to do with feelings like these. It has become such an old-fashioned relationship, hasn't it, cousinship. Soon all the rules we had to memorize about who is allowed to marry whom, first cousins and second cousins and third cousins, will just be anthropology.

Still, I am glad we did not act on our childhood vows (do you remember?) and marry each other. You are probably glad too. We would have made a hopeless couple.

John, you need someone in your life, someone to look after you. Even if you choose someone who is not necessarily the love of your life, married life will be better than what you have now, with just your father and yourself. It is not good to sleep alone night after night. Excuse me for saying this, but I speak from bitter experience.

I should tear up this letter, it's so embarrassing, but I won't. I say to myself, we have known each other a long time, you will surely forgive me if I tread where I should not tread.

Lukas and I are happy together in every possible way. I go down on my knees every night (so to speak) to give thanks that his path crossed mine. How I wish you could have the same!

As if summoned, Lukas comes into the kitchen, bends down over her, presses his lips to her head, slips his hands under the dressing gown, cups her breasts. *'My skat,'* he says: my treasure.

You can't write that. You can't. You are just making things up.

I'll cut it out. Presses his lips to her head. *'My skat,'* he says, 'when are you coming to bed?' 'Now,' she says, and lays down the pen. 'Now.'

Skat: an endearment she disliked until the day she heard it from his lips. Now, when he whispers the word, she melts. This man's treasure, into which he may dip whenever it pleases him.

They lie in each other's arms. The bed creaks, but she could not care less, they are at home, they can make the bed creak as much as they like.

Again!

I promise, when I have finished I will hand over the text to you, the whole text, and let you cut out whatever you wish.

'Was that a letter to John you were writing?' says Lukas.

'Yes. He is so unhappy.'

'Maybe that's just his nature. A melancholy type.'

'But he used not to be. He used to be so happy in the old days. If he could only find someone to take him out of himself!'

But Lukas is asleep. That is his nature, his type: he falls asleep at once, like an innocent child.

She would like to be able to join him, but sleep is slow in coming. It is as if the ghost of her cousin still lurks, calling her back to the dark kitchen to complete what she was writing to him. *Have faith in me*, she whispers. *I promise I will return.*

But when she wakes it is Monday, there is no time for writing, no time for intimacies, they have to set off at once on the drive to Calvinia, she to the hotel, Lukas to the transport depot. In the windowless little office behind the reception desk she labours over the backlog of invoices; by evening she is too exhausted to pursue the letter she was writing, and anyhow she has lost touch with the feeling. *Am thinking of you,* she writes at the foot of the page. Even that is not true, she has not given John a thought all day, she has had no time. *Much love,* she writes. *Margie*. She addresses the envelope and seals it. So. It is done.

Much love, but exactly how much? Enough to save John, in a pinch? Enough to raise him out of himself, out of the melancholy of his type? She doubts it. And what if he does not want to be raised? If his grand plan is to spend weekends on the stoep of the house in Merweville writing poems with the sun beating down on the tin roof and his father coughing in a back room, he may need all the melancholy he can summon up.

That is her first moment of misgiving. The second moment comes as she is mailing the letter, as the envelope is trembling on the very lip of the slot. Is what she has written, what her cousin will be fated to read if she lets the letter go, truly the best she can offer him? *You need someone in your life.* What kind of help is it to be told that? *Much love.*

But then she thinks, *He is a grown man, why should it be up to me to save him?* and she gives the envelope a nudge.

She has to wait ten days, until the Friday of the next week, for a reply.

Dear Margot,

Thank you for your letter, which was waiting for us when we got back from Voëlfontein, and thank you for the good if impracticable advice re marriage.

The drive back from Voëlfontein was incident-free. Michiel's mechanic friend did a first-class job. I apologize again for the night I made you spend in the open.

You write about Merweville. I agree, our plans were not properly thought through, and now that we are back in Cape Town begin to seem a bit crazy. It is one thing to buy a weekend shack on the coast, but who in his right mind would want to spend his summer vacations in a hot Karoo town?

I trust that all is well on the farm. My father sends his love to you and Lukas, as do I.

John

Is that all? The cold formality of his response shocks her, brings an angry flush to her cheeks.

'What is it?' asks Lukas.

She shrugs, 'It's nothing,' she says, and passes the letter over. 'A letter from John.'

He reads it through swiftly. 'So they are dropping their plans for Merweville,' he says. 'That's a relief. Why are you so upset?'

'It's nothing,' she says. 'Just the tone.'

They are parked, the two of them, in front of the post office. This is what they do on Friday afternoons, it is part of the routine they have created for themselves: last thing, after they have done the shopping and before driving back to the farm, they fetch the week's mail and scan it sitting side by side in the pickup. Though she could fetch the mail herself any day of the week, she does not. She and Lukas do it together, as they do together whatever else they can.

For the moment Lukas is absorbed in a letter from the Land Bank, with a long attachment, pages of figures, more important by far than mere family matters. 'Don't hurry, I'll go for a stroll,' she says, and gets out and crosses the street.

The post office is newly built, squat and heavy, with glass bricks instead of windows and a heavy steel grille over the door. She dislikes it. It looks, to her eye, like a police station. She thinks back with fondness to the old post office that was demolished to make way for it, the building that had once upon a time been the Truter house.

Not half her life-span gone, and already she is hankering for the past!

It was never just a question of Merweville, of John and his father, of who was going to be living where, in the city or in the country. *What are we doing here?*: that had been the unspoken question all the time. He had known it and she had known it. Her own letter, however cowardly, had at least hinted at the question: *What are we doing in this barren part of the world? Why are we spending our lives in dreary toil if it was never meant that people should live here, if the whole project of humanizing the place was misconceived from the start?*

This part of the world. The part she means is not Merweville or Calvinia but the whole Karoo, perhaps the whole country. Whose idea was it to lay down roads and railway lines, build towns, bring in people and then bind them to this place, bind them with rivets through the heart, so that they cannot get away? *Better to cut yourself free and hope the wound heals,* he said when they were out walking in the veld. But how do you cut through rivets like that?

140

It is long past closing time. The post office is closed, the shops are closed, the street is deserted. Meyerowitz Jeweller. Babes in the Wood – Laybyes Accepted. Cosmos Café. Foschini Modes.

Meyerowitz ('Diamonds are Forever') has been here longer than she can remember. Babes in the Wood used to be Jan Harmse Slagter. Cosmos Café used to be Cosmos Milk Bar. Foschini Modes used to be Winterberg Algemene Handelaars. All this change, all this busyness! *O droewige land!* O sorrowful land! Foschini Modes is confident enough to open a new branch in Calvinia. What can her cousin the failed emigrant, the poet of melancholy, claim to know about the future of this land that Foschini does not? Her cousin who believes that even baboons, as they stare out over the veld, are overcome with *weemoed*.

Lukas is convinced there will be a political accommodation. John may claim to be a liberal, but Lukas is a more practical liberal than John will ever be, and a more courageous one too. If they chose to, Lukas and she, *boer* and *boervrou,* man and wife, could scrape together a living on their farm. They might have to tighten their belt a notch or two or three, but they would survive. If Lukas chooses instead to drive trucks for the Co-op, if she keeps the books for the hotel, it is not because the farm is a doomed enterprise but because she and Lukas made up their minds long ago they would house their workers properly and pay them a decent wage and make sure their children went to school and support those same workers later when they grew old and infirm; and because all that decency and support costs money, more money than the farm as a farm brings in or ever will bring in, in the foreseeable future.

A farm is not a business: such was the premise she and Lukas agreed on long ago. The Middelpos farm is home not only to the two of them with the ghosts of their unborn children but to thirteen other souls as well. To bring in the money to maintain the whole little community, Lukas has to spend days at a time on the road and she to pass her nights alone in Calvinia. That is what *she* means when she calls Lukas a liberal: he has a generous heart, a liberal heart; and through him she has learned to have a liberal heart too.

And what is wrong with that, as a way of life? That is the question she would like to ask her clever cousin, the one who first ran away from South Africa and now talks of cutting himself free. From what does he mean to free himself? From love? From duty? *My father sends his love, as do I.* What kind of lukewarm love is that? No, she and John may share the same blood but, whatever it is he feels for her, it is not love. Nor does he love his father, not really. Does not even love himself. And what is the point, anyway, of cutting oneself free of everyone and everything? What is he going to do with his freedom? *Love begins at home* – isn't that an English saying? Instead of forever running away, he should find himself a decent woman and look her straight in the eye and say: *Will you wed me? Will you wed me and welcome my aged parent into our home and care for him faithfully until he dies? If you will take on that burden, I will undertake to love you and be faithful to you and find a proper job and work hard and bring home my money and be cheerful and stop kvetching about the* droewige vlaktes, *the mournful plains.* She wishes he were here this moment, in Kerkstraat, Calvinia, so that she could *raas* with him, give him an earful as the English say: she is in the mood.

A whistle. She turns. It is Lukas, leaning out of the car

window. *Skattie, hoe mompel jy dan nou?* he calls out, laughing. How come you are mumbling to yourself?

NO FURTHER LETTERS pass between herself and her cousin. Before long he and his problems have ceased to have any place in her thoughts. More pressing concerns have arisen. The visas have come through that Klaus and Carol have been waiting for, the visas for the Promised Land. With swift efficiency they are readying themselves for the move. One of their first steps is to bring her mother, who has been staying with them and whom Klaus too calls *Ma* though he has a perfectly good mother of his own in Düsseldorf, back to the farm.

They drive the sixteen hundred kilometres from Johannesburg in twelve hours, taking turns at the wheel of the BMW. This feat affords Klaus much satisfaction. He and Carol have completed advanced driving courses and have certificates to show for it; they are looking forward to driving in America, where the roads are so much better than in South Africa, though not of course as good as the German *Autobahnen*.

Ma is not at all well: she, Margot, can see that as soon as she is helped out of the back seat. Her face is puffy, she is not breathing easily, she complains that her legs are sore. Ultimately, Carol explains, the problem lies with her heart: she has been seeing a specialist in Johannesburg and has a new sequence of pills to take three times a day without fail.

Klaus and Carol stay overnight on the farm, then set off back to the city. 'As soon as Ma improves, you and Lukas must bring her to America for a visit,' says Carol. 'We will help with the air fares.' Klaus embraces her, kissing her on both cheeks ('It is warmer that way'). With Lukas he shakes hands.

Lukas detests his brother-in-law. There is not the faintest chance that Lukas will go and visit them in America. As for Klaus, he has never been shy of expressing his verdict on South Africa. 'Beautiful country,' he says, 'beautiful landscapes, rich resources, but, many, many problems. How you will solve them I cannot see. In my opinion things will get worse before they will get better. But that is just my opinion.'

She would like to spit in his eye, but does not.

Her mother cannot stay alone on the farm during the week while she and Lukas are away, there is no question of that. So she arranges for a second bed to be moved into her room at the hotel. It is inconvenient, it means the end of all privacy for her, but there is no alternative. She is billed full board for her mother, though in fact her mother eats like a bird.

They are into the second week of this new regime when a member of the cleaning staff comes upon her mother slumped on a couch in the empty hotel lounge, unconscious and blue in the face. She is rushed to the district hospital and resuscitated. The doctor on duty shakes his head. Her heartbeat is very weak, he says, she needs more urgent and more expert care than she can get in Calvinia; Upington is closer, but it would be preferable if she went to Cape Town.

Within an hour she, Margot, has shut up her office and is on the way to Cape Town, sitting in the cramped back of the ambulance, holding her mother's hand. With them is a young Coloured nurse named Aletta, whose crisp, starched uniform and cheerful air soon set her at ease.

Aletta, it turns out, was born not far away, in Wuppertal in the Cederberg, where her parents still live. She has made the trip to Cape Town more often than she can count. She tells of how, only last week, they had to rush a man from Loeriesfontein to Groote Schuur Hospital along with three fingers packed in ice in a cool-box, fingers he had lost in a mishap with a bandsaw.

'Your mother will be fine,' says Aletta. 'Groote Schuur — only the best.'

At Clanwilliam they stop for petrol. The ambulance driver, who is even younger than Aletta, has brought along a thermos flask of coffee. He offers her, Margot, a cup, but she declines. 'I'm cutting down on coffee,' she says (a lie), 'it keeps me awake.'

She would have liked to buy the two of them a cup of coffee at the café, would have liked to sit down with them in a normal, friendly way, but of course one could not do that without causing a fuss. *Let the time come soon, O Lord,* she prays to herself, *when all this apartheid nonsense will be buried and forgotten.*

They resume their places in the ambulance. Her mother is sleeping. Her colour is better, she is breathing evenly beneath the oxygen mask.

'I must tell you how much I appreciate what you and Johannes are doing for us,' she says to Aletta. Aletta smiles back in the friendliest of ways, with not the faintest trace of irony. She hopes for her words to be understood in their widest sense, with all the meaning that for very shame she cannot express: *I must tell you how grateful I am for what you and your colleague are doing for an old white woman and her daughter, two strangers who have never done anything for you but on the contrary have participated in your humiliation in the land of your birth, day after day after day. I am grateful for the lesson you teach me through your actions, in which I see only human kindness, and above all through that lovely smile of yours.*

They reach the city of Cape Town at the height of the afternoon rush hour. Though theirs is not, strictly speaking, an emergency, Johannes nevertheless sounds his siren as he coolly threads his way through the traffic. At the hospital she trails behind as her mother is wheeled into the emergency unit. By the time she returns to thank Aletta and Johannes, they have left, taken the long road back to the Northern Cape.

When I get back! she promises herself, meaning *When I get back to Calvinia I will make sure I thank them personally!* but also *When I get back I will become a better person, that I swear!* She also thinks: *Who was the man from Loeriesfontein who lost the three fingers? Is it only we whites who are rushed by ambulance to a hospital – only the best! – where well-trained surgeons will sew our fingers back on or give us a new heart as the case may be, and all at no cost? Let it not be so, O Lord, let it not be so!*

When she sees her again, her mother is in a room by herself, awake, in a clean white bed, wearing the nightdress that she, Margot, had the good sense to pack for her. She has lost her hectic colouring, is even able to push aside the mask and mumble a few words: 'Such a fuss!'

She raises her mother's delicate, in fact rather babyish hand to her lips. 'Nonsense,' she says. 'Now Ma must rest. I'll be right here if Ma needs me.'

Her plan is to spend the night at her mother's bedside, but the doctor in charge dissuades her. Her mother is not in danger, he says; her condition is being monitored by the nursing staff; she will be given a sleeping pill and will sleep until morning. She, Margot, the dutiful daughter, has been through enough, best if she got a good night's sleep herself. Does she have somewhere to stay?

She has a cousin in Cape Town, she replies, she can stay with him.

The doctor is older than her, unshaven, with dark, hooded eyes.

She has been told his name but did not catch it. He may be Jewish, but there are many other things he may be too. He smells of cigarette smoke; there is a blue cigarette pack peeking out of his breast pocket. Does she believe him when he says that her mother is not in danger? Yes, she does; but she has always had a tendency to trust doctors, to believe what they say even when she knows they are just guessing; therefore she mistrusts her trust.

'Are you absolutely sure there is no danger, doctor?' she says.

He gives her a tired nod. Absolutely indeed! What is *absolutely* in human affairs? 'In order to take care of your mother you must take care of yourself,' he says.

She feels a welling-up of tears, a welling-up of self-pity too. *Take care of both of us!* she wants to plead. She would like to fall into the arms of this stranger, to be held and comforted. 'Thank you, doctor,' she says.

Lukas is on the road somewhere in the Northern Cape, uncontactable. She calls her cousin John from a public telephone. 'I'll come and fetch you at once,' says John. 'Stay with us as long as you like.'

Years have passed since she was last in Cape Town. She has never been to Tokai, the suburb where he and his father live. Their house sits behind a high wooden fence smelling strongly of damp-rot and engine oil. The night is dark, the pathway from the gate unlit; he takes her arm to guide her. 'Be warned,' he says, 'it is all a bit of a mess.'

At the front door her uncle awaits her. He greets her distractedly; he is agitated in a way that she is familiar with among the Coetzees, talking rapidly, running his fingers through his hair. 'Ma is fine,' she reassures him, 'it was just an episode.' But he prefers not to be reassured, he is in the mood for drama.

John leads her on a tour of the premises. The house is small, ill lit, stuffy; it smells of wet newspaper and fried bacon. If she were in charge she would tear down the dreary curtains and replace them with something lighter and brighter; but of course in this men's world she is not in charge.

He shows her into the room that is to be hers. Her heart sinks. The carpet is mottled with what look like oil stains. Against the wall is a low single bed, and beside it a desk on which books and papers lie piled higgledy-piggledy. Glaring down from the ceiling is the same kind of neon lamp they used to have in the office in the hotel before she had it removed.

Everything here seems to be of the same hue: a brown verging in one direction on dull yellow and in the other on dingy grey. She wonders whether the house has been cleaned, properly cleaned, in years.

Normally this is his bedroom, John explains. He has changed the sheets on the bed; he will empty two drawers for her use. Across the passage are the necessary facilities.

She explores the necessary facilities. The bathroom is grimy, the toilet stained, smelling of old urine.

Since leaving Calvinia she has had nothing to eat but a chocolate bar. She is famished. John offers her what he calls French toast, white bread soaked in egg and fried, of which she eats three slices. He also gives her tea with milk that turns out to be sour (she drinks it anyway).

Her uncle sidles into the kitchen, wearing a pyjama top over his trousers. 'I'll say good night, Margie,' he says. 'Sleep tight. Don't let the fleas bite.' He does not say good night to his son. Around his son he seems distinctly tentative. Have they been having a fight?

148

'I'm restless,' she says to John. 'Shall we go for a walk? I've been cooped up in the back of an ambulance all day.'

He takes her on a ramble through the well-lit streets of suburban Tokai. The houses they pass are all bigger and better than his. 'This used to be farmland not long ago,' he explains. 'Then it was subdivided and sold in lots. Our house used to be a farm-labourer's cottage. That's why it is so shoddily built. Everything leaks: roof, walls. I spend all my free time doing repairs. I'm like the boy with his finger in the dyke.'

'Yes, I begin to see the attraction of Merweville. At least in Merweville it doesn't rain. But why not buy a better house here in the Cape? Write a book. Write a best-seller. Make lots of money.'

It is only a joke, but he chooses to take it seriously. 'I wouldn't know how to write a best-seller,' he says. 'I don't know enough about people and their fantasy lives. Anyway, I wasn't destined for that fate.'

'What fate?'

'The fate of being a rich and successful writer.'

'Then what is the fate you are destined for?'

'For exactly the present one. For living with an ageing parent in a house in the white suburbs with a leaky roof.'

'That's just silly, *slap* talk. That's the Coetzee in you speaking. You could change your fate tomorrow if you would just put your mind to it.'

The dogs of the neighbourhood do not take kindly to strangers roaming their streets by night, arguing. The chorus of barking grows clamorous.

'I wish you could hear yourself, John,' she plunges on. 'You are so full of nonsense! If you don't take hold of yourself you are going to turn into a sour old prune of a man who wants only to be left alone in his corner. Let's go back. I have to get up early.'

SHE SLEEPS BADLY on the uncomfortable, hard mattress. Before first light she is up, making coffee and toast for the three of them. By seven o'clock they are on their way to Groote Schuur Hospital, crammed together in the cab of the Datsun.

She leaves Jack and his son in the waiting room, but then cannot locate her mother. Her mother had an episode during the night, she is informed at the nurses' station, and is back in intensive care. She, Margot, should return to the waiting room, where a doctor will speak to her.

She rejoins Jack and John. The waiting room is already filling up. A woman, a stranger, is slumped in a chair opposite them. Over her head, covering one eye, she has knotted a woollen pullover caked with blood. She wears a tiny skirt and rubber sandals; she smells of mouldy linen and sweet wine; she is moaning softly to herself.

She does her best not to stare, but the woman is itching for a fight. '*Waarna loer jy?*' she glares: What are you staring at? '*Jou moer!*'

She casts her eyes down, withdraws into silence.

Her mother, if she lives, will be sixty-eight next month. Sixty-eight blameless years, blameless and contented. A good woman, all in all: a good mother, a good wife of the distracted, fluttering variety. The kind of woman men find it easy to love because she so clearly needs to be protected. And now cast into this hell-hole! *Jou moer!* – filthy talk. She must get her mother out as soon as she can, and into a private hospital, no matter what the cost.

My little bird, that is what her father used to call her: *my tortelduifie,* my little turtledove. The kind of little bird that prefers not to leave its cage. Growing up she, Margot, had felt big and ungainly beside her mother. *Who will ever love me?* she had asked herself. *Who will ever call me his little dove?*

Someone is tapping her on the shoulder. 'Mrs Jonker?' A fresh young nurse. 'Your mother is awake, she is asking for you.'

'Come,' she says. Jack and John follow her.

Her mother is conscious, she is calm, so calm as to seem a little remote. The oxygen mask has been replaced with a tube into her nose. Her eyes have lost their colour, turned into flat grey pebbles. 'Margie?' she whispers.

She presses her lips to her mother's brow. 'I'm here, Ma,' she says.

The doctor enters, the same doctor as before, with the dark-rimmed eyes. *Kiristany* says the badge on his coat. On duty yesterday afternoon, still on duty this morning.

Her mother has had a cardiac episode, says Doctor Kiristany, but is now stable. She is very weak. Her heart is being stimulated electrically.

'I would like to move my mother to a private hospital,' she says to him, 'somewhere quieter than this.'

He shakes his head. Impossible, he says. He cannot give his consent. Perhaps in a few days' time, if she rallies.

She stands back. Jack bends over his sister, murmuring words she cannot hear. Her mother's eyes are open, her lips move, she seems to be replying. Two old people, two innocents, born in olden times, out of place in the loud, angry place this country has become.

'John?' she says. 'Do you want to speak to Ma?'

He shakes his head. 'She won't know me,' he says.

[Silence.]

And?

That's the end.

The end? But why stop there?

It seems a good place. *She won't know me*: a good line.

[Silence.]

Well, what is your verdict?

My verdict? I still don't understand: if it is a book about John why are you including so much about me? Who is going to want to read about me — me and Lukas and my mother and Carol and Klaus?

You were part of your cousin. He was part of you. That is plain enough, surely. What I am asking is, can it stand as it is?

Not as it is, no. I want to go over it again, as you promised.

> Interviews conducted in Somerset West, South Africa,
> December 2007 and June 2008.

Adriana

SENHORA NASCIMENTO, YOU are Brazilian by birth, but you spent several years in South Africa. How did that come about?

We went to South Africa from Angola, my husband and I and our two daughters. In Angola my husband worked for a newspaper and I had a job with the National Ballet. But then in 1973 the government declared an emergency and shut down his newspaper. They wanted to call him up into the army too – they were calling up all men under the age of forty-five, even those who were not citizens. We could not go back to Brazil, it was still too dangerous, we saw no future for ourselves in Angola, so we left, we took the boat to South Africa. We were not the first to do that, or the last.

And why Cape Town?

Why Cape Town? No special reason, except that we had a relative there, a cousin of my husband's who owned a fruit and vegetable shop. After we arrived we stayed with him and his family, it was difficult for all of us, nine people in three rooms, while we waited for our residence papers. Then my husband managed to find a job as a security guard and we could move into a flat of our own. That was in a place called Epping. A few months later, just before the disaster that ruined everything, we moved again, to Wynberg, to be nearer the children's school.

What disaster do you refer to?

My husband was working night shifts guarding a warehouse near the docks. He was the only guard. There was a robbery – a gang of men broke in. They attacked him, hit him with an axe. Maybe it was a machete, but more likely it was an axe. One side of his face was smashed in. I still don't find it easy to talk about. An axe. Hitting a man in the face with an axe because he is doing his job. I can't understand it.

What happened to him?

There were injuries to his brain. He died. It took a long time, nearly a year, but he died. It was terrible.

I'm sorry.

Yes. For a while the firm he worked for went on paying his wages. Then the money stopped coming. He was not their responsibility any more, they said, he was the responsibility of Social Welfare. Social Welfare! Social Welfare never gave us a penny. My older daughter had to leave school. She took a job as a packer in a supermarket. That brought in a hundred and twenty rands a week. I looked for work too, but I couldn't find a position in ballet, they weren't interested in my kind of ballet, so I had to teach classes at a dance studio. Latin American. Latin American was popular in South Africa in those days. Maria Regina stayed at school. She still had the rest of that year and the next year before she could matriculate. Maria Regina, my younger daughter. I wanted her to get her certificate, not follow her sister into the supermarket, putting cans on shelves for the rest of her life. She was the clever one. She loved books.

In Luanda my husband and I had made an effort to speak a little English at the dinner table, also a little French, just to remind the girls Angola wasn't the whole world, but they didn't really pick it up. At school in Cape Town English was Maria Regina's weakest subject. So I enrolled her for extra lessons in English. The school ran these extra lessons in the afternoons for children like her, new arrivals. That was when I began to hear about Mr Coetzee, the man you are asking about, who, as it turned out, was not one of the regular teachers, no, not at all, but was hired by the school to teach these extra classes.

This Mr Coetzee sounds like an Afrikaner to me, I said to Maria Regina. Can't your school afford a proper English teacher? I want you to learn proper English, from an English person.

I never liked Afrikaners. We saw lots of Afrikaners in Angola, working for the mines or as mercenaries in the army. They treated the blacks like dirt. I didn't like that. In South Africa my husband picked up a few words of Afrikaans – he had to, the security firm was all Afrikaners – but as for me, I didn't even like to listen to the language. Thank God the school did not make the girls learn Afrikaans, that would have been too much.

Mr Coetzee is not an Afrikaner, said Maria Regina. He has a beard. He writes poetry.

Afrikaners can have beards too, I told her, you don't need a beard to write poetry. I want to see this Mr Coetzee for myself, I don't like the sound of him. Tell him to come here to the flat. Tell him to come and drink tea with us and show he is a proper teacher. What is this poetry he writes?

Maria Regina started to fidget. She was at an age when children don't like you to interfere in their school life. But I told her, as long as I pay for extra lessons I will interfere as much as I want. What kind of poetry does this man write?

I don't know, she said. He makes us recite poetry. He makes us learn it by heart.

What does he make you learn by heart? I said. Tell me.

Keats, she said.

What is Keats? I said (I had never heard of Keats, I knew none of those old English writers, we didn't study them in the days when I was at school).

A drowsy numbness overtakes my sense, Maria Regina recited, as though of hemlock I had drunk. Hemlock is poison. It attacks your nervous system.

That is what this Mr Coetzee makes you learn? I said.

It's in the book, she said. It's one of the poems we have to learn for the exam.

My daughters were always complaining I was too strict with them. But I never yielded. Only by watching over them like a hawk could I keep them out of trouble in this strange country where they were not at home, on a continent where we should never have come. Joana was easier, Joana was the good girl, the quiet one. Maria Regina was more reckless, more ready to challenge me. I had to keep Maria Regina on a tight rein, Maria with her poetry and her romantic dreams.

There was the question of the invitation, the correct way to phrase an invitation to your daughter's teacher to visit her parents' home and drink tea. I spoke to Mario's cousin on the telephone, but he was no help. So in the end I had to ask the receptionist at the dance studio to write the letter for me. 'Dear Mr Coetzee,' she wrote, 'I am the mother of Maria Regina Nascimento, who is in your English class. You are invited to a tea at our residence' – I gave the address – 'on such-and-such a day at such-and-such a time. Transport from the school will be arranged. RSVP Adriana Teixeira Nascimento.'

By transport I meant Manuel, the eldest son of Mario's cousin, who used to give Maria Regina a lift home in his van in the afternoons after he had made his deliveries. It would be easy for him to pick up the teacher too.

Mario was your husband.

Mario. My husband, who died.

Please go on. I just wanted to be sure.

Mr Coetzee was the first person who was invited to our flat – the first one outside Mario's family. He was only a schoolteacher – we met plenty of schoolteachers in Luanda, and before Luanda in São Paulo, I had no special esteem for them – but to Maria Regina and even to Joana schoolteachers were gods and goddesses, and I saw no reason why I should disillusion them. The evening before his visit the girls baked a cake and iced it and even wrote on it (they wanted to write 'Welcome Mr Coetzee' but I made them write 'St Bonaventure 1974'). They also baked trayfuls of the little biscuits that in Brazil we call *brevidades*.

Maria Regina was very excited. *Come home early, please, please!* I heard her urging her sister. *Tell your supervisor you are feeling ill!* But Joana wasn't prepared to do that. It is not so easy to take time off, she said, they dock your pay if you don't complete your shift.

So Manuel brought Mr Coetzee to our flat, and I could see at once he was no god. He was in his early thirties, I estimated, badly dressed, with badly cut hair and a beard when he shouldn't have worn a beard, his beard was too thin. Also he struck me at once, I can't say why, as *célibataire*. I mean not just unmarried but also not suited to marriage, like a man who has spent his life in the priesthood and lost his manhood and become incompetent with women. Also his comportment was not good (I am telling you my first impressions). He seemed ill at ease, itching to get away. He had not learned to hide his feelings, which is the first step toward civilized manners.

'How long are you a teacher, Mr Coetzee?' I asked.

He squirmed in his seat, said something I don't remember any more about America, about being a teacher in America. Then, after more questions, it emerged that in fact he had never taught in a school before this one, and — what is worse — did not even have a teacher's certificate. Of course I was surprised. 'If you don't have a certificate, how come you are Maria Regina's teacher?' I said. 'I don't understand.'

The answer, which again took a long time to squeeze out of him, was that, for subjects like music and ballet and foreign languages, schools were permitted to hire persons who had no qualifications, or at least did not have certificates of competence. These unqualified persons would not be paid salaries like proper teachers, they would instead be paid by the school with money collected from parents like me.

'But you are not English,' I said. It was not a question this time, it was an accusation. Here he was, hired to teach the English language, paid out of my money and Joana's money, yet he was not a teacher, and moreover he was an Afrikaner, not an Englishman.

'I agree I am not of English descent,' he said. 'Nevertheless I have spoken English from an early age and have passed university examinations in English, therefore I believe I can teach English. There is nothing special about English. It is just one language among many.'

That is what he said. English is just one language among many. 'My daughter is not going to be like a parrot that mixes up languages, Mr Coetzee,' I said. 'I want her to learn to speak English properly, and with a proper English accent.'

Fortunately for him, this was the moment when Joana arrived home. Joana was already twenty by then, but in the presence of a man she was still bashful. Compared with her sister she was not a beauty – look, here is a snapshot of her with her husband and their little boys, it was taken some time after we moved back to Brazil, you can see, not a beauty, all the beauty went to her sister – but she was a good girl and I always knew she would make a good wife.

Joana came into the room where we were sitting, still wearing her raincoat (I remember that long raincoat of hers). 'My sister,' said Maria Regina, as if she was explaining who this new person was rather than introducing her. Joana said nothing, just looked shy, and as for Mr Coetzee the teacher, he almost knocked over the coffee-table trying to get to his feet.

Why is Maria Regina besotted with this foolish man? What does she see in him? That was the question I asked myself. It was easy enough to guess what a lonely *célibataire* might see in my daughter, who was turning into a real dark-eyed beauty though she was still only a child, but what made her learn poems by heart for this man, something she had never done for her other teachers? Had he perhaps been whispering words to her that had turned her head? Was that the explanation? Was there something going on between the two of them that she was keeping secret from me?

Now if this man were to become interested in Joana, I thought to myself, it would be a different story. Joana may not have a head for poetry, but at least she has her feet on the ground.

'Joana is working this year at Clicks,' I said. 'To get experience. Next year she will take a management course. To be a manager.'

Mr Coetzee nodded abstractedly. Joana said nothing at all.

'Take off your coat, my child,' I said, 'and drink some tea.' We did not normally drink tea, we drank coffee. Joana brought home some tea the day before for this guest of ours, Earl Grey tea it was called, very English but not very nice, I wondered what we were going to do with the rest of the packet.

'Mr Coetzee is from the school,' I repeated to Joana, as if she did not know. 'He is telling us how he is not English but is nevertheless the English teacher.'

'I am not, properly speaking, the English teacher,' Mr Coetzee interjected, addressing Joana. 'I am the Extra English teacher. That means I have been hired by the school to help students who are having difficulty with English. I try to get them through the examinations. So I am a kind of examination coach. That would be a better description of what I do, a better name for me.'

'Do we have to talk about school?' said Maria Regina. 'It is so boring.'

But what we were talking about was not boring at all. Painful, perhaps, for Mr Coetzee, but not boring. 'Go on,' I said to him, ignoring her.

'I do not intend to be an examination coach for the rest of my life,' he said. 'It is something I am doing for the present, something I happen to be qualified to do, to make a living. But it is not my vocation. It is not what I was called into the world to do.'

Called into the world. More and more strange.

'If you would like me to explain my philosophy of teaching I can do so,' he said. 'It is quite brief, brief and simple.'

'Go on,' I said, 'let us hear your brief philosophy.'

'What I call my philosophy of teaching is in fact a philosophy of learning. It comes out of Plato, modified. Before true learning can occur, I believe, there must be in the student's heart a certain yearning for the truth, a certain fire. The true student burns to know. In the teacher she recognizes, or apprehends, the one who has come closer than herself to the truth. So much does she desire the truth embodied in the teacher that she is prepared to burn her old self up to attain it. For his part, the teacher recognizes and encourages the fire in the student, and responds to it by burning with an intenser light. Thus together the two of them rise to a higher realm. So to speak.'

He paused, smiling. Now that he had had his say he seemed more relaxed. *What a strange, vain man!* I thought. *Burn herself up! What nonsense he talks! Dangerous nonsense too! Out of Plato! Is he making fun of us?* But Maria Regina, I noticed, was leaning forward, devouring his face with her eyes. Maria Regina did not think he was joking. *This is not good!* I said to myself.

'That does not sound like philosophy to me, Mr Coetzee,' I said, 'it sounds like something else, I will not say what, since you are our guest. Maria, you can fetch the cake now. Joana, help her; and take off that raincoat. My daughters baked a cake last night in honour of your visit.'

The moment the girls were out of the room I went to the heart of the matter, speaking softly so that they would not hear. 'Maria is still a child, Mr Coetzee. I am paying for her to learn English and get a good certificate. I am not paying for you to play with her feelings. Do you understand?' The girls came back, bearing their cake. 'Do you understand?' I repeated.

'We learn what we most deeply want to learn,' he replied. 'Maria wants to learn – do you not, Maria?'

Maria flushed and sat down.

'Maria wants to learn,' he repeated, 'and she is making good progress. She has a feeling for language. Maybe she will become a writer one day. What a magnificent cake!'

'It is good when a girl can bake,' I said, 'but it is even better when she can speak good English and get good marks in her English examination.'

'Good elocution, good marks,' he said. 'I understand your wishes perfectly.'

When he had left, when the girls had gone to bed, I sat down and wrote him a letter in my bad English, I could not help that, it was not the kind of letter my friend at the studio should see.

Respected Mr Coetzee, I wrote, *I repeat what I told you during your visit. You are employed to teach my daughter English, not to play with her feelings. She is a child, you are a grown man. If you wish to expose your feelings, expose them outside the classroom. Yours faithfully, ATN.*

That is what I said. It may not be how you speak in English, but it is how we speak in Portuguese – your translator will understand. *Expose your feelings outside the classroom* – that was not an invitation to him to pursue me, it was a warning to him not to pursue my daughter.

I sealed up the letter in an envelope and wrote his name on it, *Mr Coetzee / Saint Bonaventure*, and on the Monday morning I put it in Maria Regina's bag. 'Give it to Mr Coetzee,' I said, 'put it in his hand.'

'What is it?' said Maria Regina.

'It is a note from a parent to her daughter's teacher, it is not for your eyes. Now go, or you will miss your bus.'

Of course I made a mistake, I should not have said, *It is not for your eyes.* Maria Regina was beyond the age where, if your mother gives you a command, you obey. She was beyond that age but I did not yet know it yet. I was living in the past.

'Did you give the note to Mr Coetzee?' I asked when she came home.

'Yes,' she said, and nothing more. I did not think I had to ask, *Did you open it in secret and read it before you gave it to him?*

The next day, to my surprise, Maria Regina brought back a note from this teacher of hers, not an answer to mine but an invitation: would we all like to come on a picnic with him and his father? At first I was going to refuse. 'Think,' I said to Maria Regina: 'Do you really want your friends at school to get the impression you are the teacher's favourite? Do you really want them to gossip behind your back?' But that weighed nothing with her, she *wanted* to be the teacher's favourite. She pressed me and pressed me to accept, and Joana backed her up, so in the end I said yes.

There was lots of excitement at home, and lots of baking, and Joana brought things from the shop too, so when Mr Coetzee came to fetch us on the Sunday morning we had a whole basket of cakes and biscuits and sweets with us, enough to feed an army.

He did not fetch us in a car, he did not have a car, no, he came in a truck, the kind that is open at the back, that in Brazil we call a *caminhonete*. So the girls, in their nice clothes, had to sit in the back with the firewood while I sat in the front with him and his father.

That was the only time I met his father. His father was quite old already, and unsteady, with hands that trembled. I thought he might be trembling because he found himself sitting next to a strange woman, but later I saw his hands trembled all the time. When he was introduced to us he said 'How do you do?' very nicely, very courteously, but after that he shut up. All the time we drove he did not speak, not to me, not to his son either. A very quiet man, very humble, or perhaps just frightened of everything.

We drove up into the mountains – we had to stop to let the girls put on their coats, they were getting cold – to a park, I don't remember the name now, where there were pine trees and places in between where people could have picnics, white people only, of course – a nice place, almost empty because it was winter. As soon as we chose our place Mr Coetzee made himself busy unloading the truck and building a fire. I expected Maria Regina to help him, but she slipped away, she said she wanted to explore. That was not a good sign. Because if relations had been *comme il faut* between them, just a teacher and a student, she would not have been embarrassed to help. But it was Joana who came forward instead, Joana was very good that way, very practical and efficient.

So there I was, left behind with his father as if we were the two old people, the grandparents! I found it hard talking to him, as I said, he could not understand my English and was shy too, with a woman; or maybe he just didn't understand who I was.

And then, even before the fire was burning properly, clouds came over and it grew dark and started to rain. 'It is just a shower, it will soon pass,' said Mr Coetzee. 'Why don't the three of you get into the truck.' So the girls and I took shelter in the truck, and he and his father huddled under a tree, and we waited for the rain to pass. But of course it did not, it went on raining and gradually the girls lost their good spirits. 'Why does it have to rain *today* of all days?' whined Maria Regina, just like a baby. 'Because it is winter,' I told her: 'because it is winter and intelligent people, people with their feet on the ground, don't go out on picnics in the middle of winter.'

The fire that Mr Coetzee and Joana had built went out. All the wood was wet by now, so we would never be able to cook our meat. 'Why don't you offer them some of the biscuits you baked?' I said to Maria Regina. Because I had never seen a more miserable sight than those two Dutchmen, the father and the son, sitting together side by side under a tree trying to pretend they were not cold and wet. A miserable sight, but funny too. 'Offer them some biscuits and ask them what we are going to do next. Ask them if they would like to take us to the beach for a swim.'

I said this to make Maria Regina smile, but all I did was make her more cross; so in the end it was Joana who went out in the rain and talked to them and came back with the message that we would leave as soon as it stopped raining, we would go back to their house and they would make tea for us. 'No,' I said to Joana. 'Go back and tell Mr Coetzee no, we cannot come to tea, he must take us straight back to the flat, tomorrow is Monday and Maria Regina has homework that she hasn't even started on.'

Of course it was an unhappy day for Mr Coetzee. He had hoped to make a good impression on me; maybe he also wanted to show off to his father the three attractive Brazilian ladies who were his friends; and instead all he got was a truck full of wet people driving through the rain. But to me it was good that Maria Regina should see what her hero was like in real life, this poet who could not even make a fire.

So that is the story of our expedition into the mountains with Mr Coetzee. When at last we got back in Wynberg, I said to him, in front of his father, in front of the girls, what I had been waiting to say all day. 'It was very kind of you to invite us out, Mr Coetzee, very gentlemanly,' I said, 'but maybe it is not a good idea for a teacher to be favouring one girl in his class above all others just because she is pretty. I am not admonishing you, just asking you to reflect.'

Those were the words I used: *just because she is pretty*. Maria Regina was furious with me for speaking like that, but as for me, I did not care as long as I was understood.

Later that night, when Maria Regina had already gone to bed, Joana came to my room. '*Mamãe*, must you be so hard on Maria?' she said. 'Truly, there is nothing bad going on.'

'Nothing bad?' I said. 'What do you know of the world? What do you know of badness? What do you know of what men will do?'

'He is not a bad man, *mamãe*,' she said. 'Surely you can see that.'

'He is a weak man,' I said. 'A weak man is worse than a bad man. A weak man does not know where to stop. A weak man is helpless before his impulses, he follows wherever they lead.'

'*Mamãe*, we are all weak,' said Joana.

'No, you are wrong, I am not weak,' I said. 'Where would we be, you and Maria Regina and I, if I allowed myself to be weak? Now go to bed. And don't repeat any of this to Maria Regina. Not a word. She will not understand.'

I hoped that would be the end of Mr Coetzee. But no, a day or two later there arrived a letter from him, not via Maria Regina this time but through the mail, a formal letter, typed, the envelope typed too. In it he first apologized for the picnic that had been a failure. He had hoped to speak to me in private, he said, but had had no chance. Could he come and see me? Could he come to the flat, or would I prefer to meet him elsewhere, perhaps have lunch with him? The matter that weighed on him was not Maria Regina, he wanted to stress. Maria was an intelligent young woman, with a good heart; it was a privilege to teach her; I could be assured he would never, *never* betray the trust I had put in him. Intelligent and beautiful too – he hoped I would not mind if he said that. For beauty, true beauty, was more than skin-deep, it was the soul showing through the flesh; and where could Maria Regina have got her beauty but from me?

[Silence.]

And?

That was all. That was the substance. Could he meet me alone.

Of course I asked myself where he had got the idea that I would want to meet him, even want to receive a letter from him. Because I never said a word to encourage him.

So what did you do? Did you meet him?

What did I do? I did nothing and hoped he would leave me alone. I was a woman in mourning, though my husband was not dead, I did not want the attentions of other men, particularly of a man who was my daughter's teacher.

Do you still have that letter?

I don't have any of his letters. I did not keep them. When we left South Africa I did a clean-out of the flat and threw away all the old letters and bills.

And you did not reply?

No.

You did not reply and you did not allow relations to develop any further – relations between yourself and Coetzee?

What is this? Why these questions? You come all the way from England to talk to me, you tell me you are writing a biography of a man who happened many years ago to be my daughter's English teacher, and now suddenly you feel you are permitted to interrogate me about my 'relations'? What kind of biography are you writing? Is it like Hollywood gossip, like secrets of the rich and famous? If I refuse to discuss my so-called relations with this man, will you say I am keeping them secret? No, I did not have, to use your word, *relations* with Mr Coetzee. I will say more. For me it was not natural to have feelings for a man like that, a man who was so soft. Yes, soft.

Are you suggesting he was homosexual?

I am not suggesting anything. But there was a quality he did not have that a woman looks for in a man, a quality of strength, of manliness. My husband had that quality. He always had it, but his time in prison here in Brazil, under the *militares*, brought it out, even though he was not in prison a long time, only six months. After those six months, he used to say, nothing that human beings did to other human beings could come as a surprise to him. Coetzee had no such experience behind him to test his manhood and teach him about life. That is why I say he was soft. He was not a man, he was still a boy.

[Silence.]

As for homosexual, no, I do not say he was homosexual, but he was, as I told you, *célibataire* – I don't know the word for that in English.

A bachelor type? Sexless? Asexual?

No, not sexless. Solitary. Not made for conjugal life. Not made for the company of women.

[Silence.]

You mentioned that there were further letters.

Yes, when I did not reply he wrote again. He wrote many times. Perhaps he thought that if he wrote enough the words would eventually wear me down, like the waves of the sea wear down a rock. I put his letters away in the bureau; some I did not even read. But I thought to myself, *Among the many things this man lacks, the many. many things, one is a tutor to give him lessons in love.* Because if you have fallen in love with a woman you do not sit down and type her one long letter after another, pages and pages, each one ending 'Yours sincerely'. No, you write a letter in your own hand, a proper love-letter, and have it delivered to her with a bouquet of red roses. But then I thought, perhaps this is how these Dutch Protestants behave when they fall in love: prudently, long-windedly, without fire, without grace. And no doubt that is how his lovemaking would be too, if he ever got a chance.

I put his letters away and said nothing of them to the children. That was a mistake. I could easily have said to Maria Regina, *That Mr Coetzee of yours has written me a note to apologize for Sunday. He mentions that he is pleased with your progress in English.* But I was silent, which in the end led to much trouble. Even today, I think, Maria Regina has not forgotten or forgiven.

Do you understand such things, Mr Vincent? Are you married? Do you have children?

Yes, I am married. We have one child, a boy. He will be four next month.

Boys are different. I don't know about boys. But I will tell you one thing, *entre nous*, which you must not repeat in your book. I love both my daughters, but I loved Maria in a different way from Joana. I loved her but I was also very critical of her as she grew up. Joana I was never critical of. Joana was always very simple, very straightforward. But Maria was a charmer. She could – do you use the expression? – twist a man around her finger. If you could have seen her, you would know what I mean.

What has become of her?

She is in her second marriage now. She is living in North America, in Chicago, with her American husband. He is a lawyer in a law firm. I think she is happy with him. I think she has made her peace with the world. Before that she had personal problems, which I will not go into.

Do you have a picture of her that I could perhaps use in the book?

I don't know. I will look. I will see. But it is getting late. Your colleague must be exhausted. Yes, I know how it is, being a translator. It looks easy from the outside, but the truth is you have to pay attention all the time, you cannot relax, the brain gets fatigued. So we stop here. Switch off your machine.

Can we speak again tomorrow?

Tomorrow is not convenient. Wednesday, yes. It is not such a long story, the story of myself and Mr Coetzee. I am sorry if it is a disappointment to you. You come all this way, and now you find there was no grand love affair with a dancer, just a brief infatuation, that is the word I would use, a brief, one-sided infatuation that never grew into anything. Come again on Wednesday at the same hour. I will give you tea.

YOU ASKED, LAST TIME, about pictures. I searched, but it is as I thought, I have none from those years in Cape Town. However, let me show you this one. It was taken at the airport the day we arrived back in São Paulo, by my sister, who came to meet us. See, there we are, the three of us. That is Maria Regina. The date was 1977, she was eighteen, getting on for nineteen. As you can see, a very pretty girl with a nice figure. And that is Joana, and that is me.

They are quite tall, your daughters. Was their father tall?

Yes, Mario was a big man. The girls are not so tall, it is just that they look tall when they are standing next to me.

Well, thank you for showing me. Can I take it away and have a copy made?

For your book? No, I cannot allow that. If you want Maria Regina in your book you must ask her yourself, I cannot speak for her.

I would like to include it as a picture of the three of you together.

No. If you want pictures of the girls you must ask them. As for me, no, I have decided no. It will be taken the wrong way. People will assume I was one of the women in his life, and it was never so.

Yet you were important to him. He was in love with you.

That is what you say. But the truth is, if he was in love, it was not with me, it was with some fantasy that he dreamed up in his own brain and gave my name to. You think I should feel flattered that you want to put me in your book as his lover? You are wrong. To me this man was not a famous writer, he was just a schoolteacher, a schoolteacher who didn't even have a diploma. Therefore no. No picture. What else? What else do you want me to tell you?

You were telling me last time about the letters he wrote you. I know you said you did not always read them; nevertheless, do you by any chance recall more of what he said in them?

One letter was about Franz Schubert – you know Schubert, the musician. He said that listening to Schubert had taught him one of the great secrets of love: how we can sublime love as chemists in the old days sublimed base substances. I remember the letter because of the word *sublime*. Sublime base substances: it made no sense to me. I looked up *sublime* in the big English dictionary I bought for the girls. To sublime: to heat something and extract its essence. We have the same word in Portuguese, *sublimar*, though it is not common. But what did it all mean? That he sat with his eyes closed listening to the music of Schubert while in his mind he heated his love for me, his *base substance*, into something higher, something more spiritual? It was nonsense, worse than nonsense. It did not make me love him, on the contrary it made me recoil.

It was from Schubert that he had learned to sublime love, he said. Not until he met me did he understand why in music movements are called movements. *Movement in stillness, stillness in movement.* That was another phrase I puzzled my head over. What did he mean, and why was he writing these things to me?

You have a good memory.

Yes, there is nothing wrong with my memory. My body is another story. I have arthritis of the hips, that is why I use a stick. The dancer's curse, they call it. And the pain — you will not believe the pain! But I remember South Africa very well. I remember the flat where we lived in Wynberg, where Mr Coetzee came to drink tea. I remember the mountain, Table Mountain. The flat was right under the mountain, so it got no sun in the afternoons. I hated Wynberg. I hated the whole time we spent there, first when my husband was in hospital and then after he died. It was very lonely for me, I cannot tell you how lonely. Worse than Luanda, because of the loneliness. If your Mr Coetzee had offered us his friendship I would not have been so hard on him, so cold. But I was not interested in love, I was still too close to my husband, still grieving for him. And he was just a boy, this Mr Coetzee. I was a woman and he was a boy. He was a boy as a priest is always a boy until suddenly one day he is an old man. The sublimation of love! He was offering to teach me about love, yet what could a boy like him teach me, a boy who knew nothing about life? I could have taught him, perhaps, but I was not interested in him. I just wanted him to keep his hands off Maria Regina.

You say, if he had offered you friendship it would have been different. What kind of friendship did you have in mind?

What kind of friendship? I will tell you. For a long time after the disaster that came over us, the disaster I told you about, I had to struggle with the bureaucracy, first over compensation, then over Joana's papers — Joana was born before we were married, so legally she was not my husband's daughter, she was not even his step-daughter, I will not bore you with the details. I know, in every country the bureaucracy is a labyrinth, I am not saying South Africa was the worst in the world, but whole days I would spend waiting in a line to get a rubber stamp — a rubber stamp for this, a rubber stamp for that — and always, *always* it would be the wrong office or the wrong department or the wrong line.

If we had been Portuguese it would have been different. There were many Portuguese who came to South Africa in those days, from Moçambique and Angola and even Madeira, there were organizations to help the Portuguese. But we were from Brazil, and there were no regulations for Brazilians, no precedents, to the bureaucrats it was as if we arrived in their country from Mars.

And there was the problem of my husband. You cannot sign for this, your husband must come and sign, they would say to me. My husband cannot sign, he is in hospital, I would say. Then take it to him in the hospital and get him to sign it and bring it back, they would say. My husband cannot sign anything, I would say, he is in Stikland, don't you know Stikland? Then let him make his mark, they would say. He cannot make his mark, sometimes he cannot even breathe, I would say. Then I cannot help you, they would say: go to such-and-such an office and tell them your story — perhaps they can help you there.

And all of this pleading and petitioning I had to do alone, unaided, with my bad English that I had learned in school out of books. In Brazil it would have been easy, in Brazil we have these people, we call them *despachantes,* facilitators: they have contacts in the government offices, they know how to steer your papers through the maze, you pay them a fee and they do all the unpleasant business for you one-two-three. That was what

I needed in Cape Town: a facilitator, someone to make things easier for me. Mr Coetzee could have offered to be my facilitator. A facilitator for me and a protector for my girls. Then, just for a minute, just for a day, I could have allowed myself to be weak, an ordinary, weak woman. But no, I dared not relax, or what would have become of us, my daughters and me?

Sometimes, you know, I would be trudging the streets of that ugly, windy city from one government office to another and I would hear this little cry come from my throat, *γi-γi-γi*, so soft that no one around me could hear. I was in distress. I was like an animal calling out in distress.

Let me tell you about my poor husband. When they opened the warehouse the morning after the attack and found him lying there in his blood, they were sure he was dead. They wanted to take him straight to the morgue. But he was not dead. He was a strong man, he fought and fought against death and held death at bay. In the city hospital, I forget its name, the famous one, they did one operation after another on his brain. Then they moved him from there to the hospital I mentioned, the one called Stikland, which was outside the city, an hour by train. Sunday was the only day you were allowed to visit Stikland. So every Sunday morning I would catch the train from Cape Town, and then the train back in the afternoon. That is another thing I remember as if it were yesterday: those sad journeys back and forth.

There was no improvement in my husband, no change. Week after week I would arrive and he would be lying in exactly the same position as before, with his eyes closed and his arms at his sides. They kept his head shaved, so you could see the stitch marks in his scalp. Also for a long time his face was covered with a wire mask where they had done a skin graft.

In all that time in Stikland my husband never opened his eyes, never saw me, never heard me. He was alive, he was breathing, though in a coma so deep he might as well have been dead. Formally I may not have been a widow, yet as far as I was concerned I was already in mourning, for him and for all of us, stranded and helpless in this cruel land.

I asked to bring him back to the flat in Wynberg, so that I could look after him myself, but they would not release him. They had not given up yet, they said. They were hoping that the electric currents they ran through his brain would all of a sudden *do the trick* (those were the words they used).

So they kept him in Stikland, those doctors, to do their tricks on him. Otherwise they cared nothing for him, a stranger, a man from Mars who should have died yet did not.

I promised myself, when they gave up on their electric currents I would bring him home. Then he could die properly, if that was what he wanted. Because though he was unconscious, I knew that deep inside him he felt the humiliation of what was happening to him. And if he could be allowed to die properly, in peace, then we would be released too, I and my daughters. Then we could spit on this atrocious earth of South Africa and be gone. But they never let him go, to the end.

So I sat by his bedside, Sunday after Sunday. *Never again will a woman look with love on this mutilated face,* I told myself, *so let me at least look, without flinching.*

In the next bed, I remember (there were at least a dozen beds crammed into a ward that should have held six), there was an old man so meagre, so cadaverous that his wristbones and the beak of his nose seemed to want to break through his skin. Though he had no visitors, he was always awake at the times when I came.

He would roll his watery blue eyes toward me. *Help me, please,* he seemed to say, *help me to die!* But I could not help him.

Maria Regina never, thank God, visited that place. A psychiatric hospital is not a place for children. On the first Sunday I asked Joana to accompany me to help with the unfamiliar trains. Even Joana came away disturbed, not just by the spectacle of her father but also by things she saw in that hospital, things no girl should have to witness.

Why does he have to be here? I said to the doctor, the one who spoke about doing tricks. He is not mad – why does he have to be among mad people? Because we have the facilities for his kind of case, said the doctor. Because we have the equipment. I should have asked what equipment he meant, but I was too upset. Later I found out. He meant shock equipment, equipment to send my husband's body into convulsions, in the hope of *doing the trick* and bringing him back to life.

If I had been forced to spend an entire Sunday in that crowded ward I swear I would have gone mad myself. I used to take breaks, wander around the hospital grounds. There was a favourite bench I had, under a tree in a secluded corner. One day I arrived at my bench and found a woman sitting there with her baby beside her. In most places – in public gardens and on station platforms and so forth – benches used to be marked *Whites* or *Non-whites*; however, this one was not. I said to the woman *What a pretty baby* or something like that, wanting to be friendly. A frightened look came over her face. *Dankie, mies*, she whispered, which meant *Thank you, miss*, and she picked up her baby and crept away.

I am not one of them, I wanted to call out to her. But of course I did not.

I wanted time to pass and I did not want time to pass. I wanted to be by Mario's side and I wanted to be away, free of him. At the beginning I would bring a book with me, hoping to sit beside him and read. But I could not read in that place, could not concentrate. I thought to myself, *I should take up knitting. I could knit whole bedspreads while I wait for this thick, heavy time to pass.*

When I was young, in Brazil, there was never enough time for all I wanted to do. Now time was my worst enemy, time that would not pass. How I longed for it all to end, this life, this death, this living death! What a fatal mistake when we took the ship to South Africa!

So. That is the story of Mario.

He died in the hospital?

He died there. He could have lived longer, he had a strong constitution, he was like a bull. When they saw their tricks would not work, however, they stopped paying attention to him. Perhaps they stopped feeding him too, I can't say for sure, he always looked the same to me, he did not get thinner. Yet to tell the truth I did not mind, we wanted to be released, all of us, he and I and the doctors too.

We buried him in a cemetery not far from the hospital, I forget the name of the place. So his grave is in Africa. I have never been back, but I think of him sometimes, lying there all alone.

What is the time? I feel so tired, so sad. It always depresses me to be reminded of those days.

Shall we stop?

No, we can go on. There is not much more to say. Let me tell you about my dance classes, because that was where he pursued me, your Mr Coetzee. Then maybe you can answer one question for me. Then we will be finished.

I could not get proper work in those days. There were no professional openings for someone like me, coming from the *balet folclórico*. In South Africa the companies danced nothing but *Swan Lake* and *Giselle*, to prove how European they were. So I took the job I told you about, in a dance studio, teaching Latin American dance. Most of my students were what they called Coloured. By day they worked in shops or offices, then in the evenings they came to the studio to learn the latest Latin American steps. I liked them. They were nice people, friendly, gentle. They had romantic illusions about Latin America, Brazil above all. Lots of palm trees, lots of beaches. In Brazil, they thought, people like themselves would feel at home. I said nothing to disappoint them.

Each month there was a new intake, that was the system at the studio. No one was turned away. As long as a student paid, I had to teach them. One day when I walked in to meet my new class, there he was among the students, and there his name was on the list: *Coetzee, John*.

Well, I cannot tell you how upset I was. It is one thing, if you are a dancer who performs in public, to be pursued by admirers. I was used to that. Now, however, it was different. I was no longer putting myself on show, I was just a teacher now, I had a right not to be harried.

I did not greet him. I wanted him to see at once that he was not welcome. What did he think – that if he danced before me the ice in my heart would melt? How crazy! And all the crazier because he had no feeling for dance, no aptitude. I could see that from the first moment, from the way he walked. He was not at ease in his body. He moved as though his body were a horse that he was riding, a horse that did not like its rider and was resisting. Only in South Africa did I meet men like that, stiff, intractable, unteachable. Why did they ever come to Africa, I wondered – to Africa, the birthplace of dance? They would have been better off staying in Holland, sitting in their counting-houses behind their dykes counting money with cold fingers.

I taught my class as I was paid to do, then when the hour was over left the building at once by the back exit. I did not want to speak to Mr Coetzee. I hoped he would not return.

Yet the next evening there he was again among the students, doggedly following instructions, performing steps for which he had no feel. I could see he was not popular with the other students. They tried to avoid him as a partner. As for me, his presence in the room took away all my pleasure. I tried to ignore him, but he would not be ignored, watching me, devouring my life.

At the end of the class I called to him to stay behind. 'Please stop this,' I said to him. He stared back at me without protest, mute. I could smell the cold sweat on his body. I felt an urge to strike him, lash him across the face. 'Stop this!' I said. 'Stop following me. I do not want to see you here again. And stop looking at me like that. Stop forcing me to humiliate you.'

There was more I could have said, but I was afraid I would lose control and start shouting.

Afterwards I spoke to the man who owned the studio, his name was Mr Anderson. There is a student in my class who is spoiling it for the other students, I said – please give him his money back and tell him to leave. But Mr Anderson would not. If there is a student disrupting your class it is up to you to put a stop to it, he said. This man is not doing anything wrong, I said, he is simply a bad presence. You cannot eject a student because he has a bad presence, said Mr Anderson. Find another solution.

After the next class I called him back. There was nowhere private to go, I had to speak to him in the corridor with people passing all the time. 'This is my work, you are disrupting my work,' I said. 'Go away from here. Leave me alone.'

He did not answer, but reached out a hand and touched my cheek. That was the one and only time he ever touched me. The anger inside me boiled over. I knocked his hand aside. 'This is not a love-game!' I hissed. 'Don't you see I detest you? Leave me alone and leave my child alone too or I will report you to the school!'

It was true: if he had not been filling my daughter's head with dangerous nonsense I would never have summoned him to our flat, and his miserable pursuit of me would never have begun. What was a grown man doing in a girls' school anyway, Saint Bonaventure, that was supposed to be a nuns' school, only there were no nuns?

And it was true too that I detested him. I was not afraid to say so. He forced me to detest him.

When I pronounced that word, *detest,* he just stared back at me in bewilderment, as if he could not believe his ears – that the woman to whom he was offering himself could refuse him. It gave me no pleasure to see such bewilderment, such help-lessness. I did not even like to see him on the dance floor. It was as if he was naked: a man dancing naked, who did not know how to dance. I wanted to shout at him. I wanted to beat him. I wanted to cry.

[Silence.]

This is not the story you wanted to hear, is it? You wanted a different kind of story for your book. You wanted to hear of the romance between your hero and the beautiful foreign ballerina. Well, I am not giving you romance, I am giving you the truth. Maybe too much truth. Maybe so much truth that there will be no place for it in your book. I don't know. I don't care.

Go on. It is not a very dignified picture of Coetzee that emerges from your story, I won't deny that, but I will change nothing, I promise.

Not dignified, you say. Well, that is what you risk when you fall in love. You risk losing your dignity.

[Silence.]

Anyway, I went back to Mr Anderson. Get this man out of my class or I will resign, I said. I will see what I can do, said Mr Anderson. We all have difficult students to cope with, you are not the only one. He is not difficult, I said, he is mad.

Was he mad? I don't know. But he certainly had an *idée fixe* about me.

The next day I went to my daughter's school, as I had warned him I would, and asked to see the principal. The principal was busy, I was told. I will wait, I said. For an hour I waited in the secretary's office. Not one friendly word. No *Would you like a cup of tea, Mrs Nascimento?* Then at last, when it became plain I would not go away, they capitulated and let me see the principal.

'I have come to speak to you about my daughter's English lessons,' I said to her. 'I would like my daughter to go on with her lessons, but I want to her to have a proper English teacher with a proper qualification. If I must pay more I will pay.'

The principal fetched a folder out of a filing cabinet. 'According to Mr Coetzee, Maria Regina is making good progress in English,' she said. 'That is confirmed by her other teachers. So what exactly is the problem?'

'I cannot tell you what is the problem,' I said. 'I just want her to have another teacher.'

This principal was not a fool. When I said I could not tell her what was the problem, she knew at once what was the problem. 'Mrs Nascimento,' she said, 'if I understand what you are saying, you are making a very serious complaint. But I can't act on such a complaint unless you are prepared to be more specific. Are you complaining about Mr Coetzee's actions toward your daughter? Are you telling me there has been something untoward in his behaviour?'

She was not a fool, but I am not a fool either. *Untoward*: what does that mean? Did I want to make an accusation against Mr Coetzee and sign my name to it, and then find myself in a court of law being interrogated by a judge? No. 'I am not making a complaint against Mr Coetzee,' I said, 'I am only asking you, if there is a proper English teacher, can Maria Regina take lessons from her instead.'

The principal did not like that. She shook her head. 'That is not possible,' she said. 'Mr Coetzee is the only teacher, the only person on our staff, who teaches extra English. There is no other class into which Maria Regina can move. We don't have the luxury, Mrs Nascimento, of offering our girls a range of teachers to choose among. And furthermore, with all respect, may I ask you to reflect, are you in the best position to judge Mr Coetzee's teaching, if it is simply the standard of his teaching we are discussing today?'

I know you are an Englishman, Mr Vincent, so don't take this personally, but there is a certain English manner that infuriates me, that infuriates many people, where the insult comes coated in pretty words, like sugar on a pill. *Dago*: you think I don't know that word, Mr Vincent? *You Portugoose dago!* she was saying — *How dare you come here and criticize my school! Go back to the slums where you came from!*

'I am Maria Regina's mother,' I said, 'I alone will say what is good for my daughter and what is not. I do not come to make trouble for you or Mr Coetzee or anyone else, but I tell you now, Maria Regina will not continue in that man's class, that is my word and it is final. I pay for my daughter to attend a good school, a school for girls, I do not want her in a class where the teacher is not a proper teacher, he has no qualification, he is not even English, he is a Boer.'

Maybe I should not have used that word, it was like *dago*, but I was angry, I was provoked. *Boer*: in that little office of hers it was like a bomb. A bomb-word. But not as bad as *mad*. If I had said Maria Regina's teacher, with his incomprehensible poems and his talk of making students burn with an intenser light, was mad, then the room would truly have exploded.

The woman's face grew stiff. 'It is up to me and to the school committee, Mrs Nascimento,' she said, 'to decide who is and who is not qualified to teach in this school. In my judgment and in the judgment of the committee Mr Coetzee, who holds a university degree in English, is adequately qualified for the work he does. You may remove your daughter from his class if you so wish, indeed you may remove her from the school, that is your right. But bear it in mind, it will be your daughter who will suffer in the end.'

'I will remove her from that man's class, I will not remove her from the school,' I replied. 'I want her to have a good education. I will myself find an English teacher for her. Thank you for seeing me. You think I am just some poor refugee woman who doesn't understand anything. You are wrong. If I were to tell you the whole story you would see how wrong you are. Goodbye.'

Refugee. They kept calling me a refugee in that country of theirs, when all I desired was to escape from it.

When Maria Regina came home from school the next day a veritable storm burst over my head. 'How could you do it, *mãe*?' she shouted at me. 'How could you do this behind my back? Why do you always have to interfere in my life?'

For weeks and months, ever since Mr Coetzee made his appearance, relations had been strained between Maria Regina and myself. But never before had my daughter used such words to me. I tried to calm her. We are not like other families, I told her. Other girls do not have a father in hospital and a mother who has to humiliate herself to earn a few pennies so that a child who never lifts a finger in the home, or says thank you, can have extra classes in this and extra classes in that.

It was not true, of course. I could not have wished for better daughters than Joana and Maria Regina, serious, hard-working girls. But sometimes it is necessary to be a little harsh, even with those we love.

Maria Regina heard nothing that I said, she was in such a fury. 'I hate you!' she shouted. 'You think I don't know why you are doing this! It is because you are jealous, because you don't want me to see Mr Coetzee, because you want him for yourself!'

'*I* am jealous of *you*? What nonsense! Why should I want this man for myself, this man who is not even a real man? Yes, I say he is not a real man! What do you know about men, you, a child? Why do you think this man wants to be among young girls? Do you think that is normal? Why do you think he encourages your dreaming, your fantasies? Men like that should not be allowed near a school. And you – you should be thankful I am saving you. But instead you shout abuse and make accusations against me, your mother!'

I saw her lips move soundlessly, as though there were no words bitter enough for what was in her heart. Then she turned and ran out of the room. A moment later she was back, waving the letters that this man, this teacher of hers, had sent me, that I had put away in the bureau for no special reason, I certainly did not treasure them. 'He writes love-letters to you!' she screamed. 'And you write love-letters back to him! It's disgusting! If he is not normal why are you writing love-letters to him?'

Of course what she was saying was untrue. I wrote him no love-letters, not one. But how could I make the poor child believe that? 'How dare you!' I said. 'How dare you pry into my private papers!'

How I wished, at that moment, that I had burnt those letters of his, letters I never asked for!

Maria Regina was crying now. 'I wish I had never listened to you,' she sobbed. 'I wish I had never let you invite him here. You just spoil everything.'

'My poor child!' I said, and took her in my arms. 'I never wrote letters to Mr Coetzee, you must believe me. Yes, he wrote letters to me, I don't know why, but I never wrote back. I am not inter-ested in him in that way, not in the slightest. Don't let him come between us, my darling. I am just trying to protect you. He is not right for you. He is a grown man, you are still a child. I will get you another teacher. I will get you a private teacher who will come here to the flat and help you. We will manage. A teacher is not expensive. We will get someone who has proper qualifi-cations and knows how to prepare you for the examinations. Then we can put this whole unhappy business behind us.'

So that is the story, the full story, of his letters and the trouble his letters caused me.

There were no more letters?

There was one more, but I did not open it. I wrote RETURN TO SENDER on the envelope and left it in the foyer for the postman to pick up. 'See?' I said to Maria Regina. 'See what I think of his letters?'

And what of the dance classes?

He stopped coming. Mr Anderson spoke to him and he stopped coming. Maybe he even gave back his money, I don't know.

Did you find another teacher for Maria Regina?

Yes, I found another teacher, a lady, a retired teacher. It cost money, but what is money when your child's future is at stake?

Was that the end, then, of your dealings with John Coetzee?

Yes. Absolutely.

You never saw him again, never heard from him?

I never saw him. I made sure Maria Regina never saw him. He may have been full of romantic nonsense, but he was too Dutch to be reckless. When he realized I was serious, not playing some love-game with him, he gave up his pursuit. He left us alone. His grand passion turned out to be not so grand after all. Or maybe he found someone else to be in love with.

Maybe. Maybe not. Maybe he kept you alive in his heart. Or the idea of you.

Why do you say that?

[Silence.]

Well, perhaps he did. You are the one who has studied him, you will know better. With some people it does not matter who they are in love with as long as they are in love. Perhaps he was like that.

[Silence.]

In retrospect, how do you see the whole episode? Do you still feel anger toward him?

Anger? No. I can see how a lonely and eccentric young man like Mr Coetzee, who spent his days reading old philosophers and making up poems, could fall for Maria Regina, who was a real beauty and would break many hearts. It is not so easy to see what Maria Regina saw in him; but then, she was young and impressionable, and he flattered her, made her think she was different from the other girls and had a great future.

Then when she brought him home and he laid eyes on me, I can see he might change his mind and decide to make me his true love instead. I am not claiming I was a great beauty, and of course I was not young any more, but Maria Regina and I were the same type: same bones, same hair, same dark eyes. And it is more practical – is it not? – to love a woman than to love a child. More practical, less dangerous.

What did he want from me, from a woman who did not respond to him and gave him no encouragement? Did he hope to sleep with me? What pleasure can there be for a man in sleeping with a woman who does not want him? Because, truly, I did not want this man, for whom I had not the slightest flicker of feeling. And what would it have been like anyway if I had taken up with my daughter's teacher? Could I have kept it secret? Certainly not from Maria Regina. I would have brought shame on myself before my children. Even when I was alone with him I would have been thinking, *It is not me he desires, it is Maria Regina, who is young and beautiful but is forbidden to him*.

But perhaps what he really wanted was both of us, Maria Regina and me, mother and daughter – perhaps that was his fantasy, I can't say, I can't look into his mind.

I remember, in the days when I was a student, existentialism was the fashion, we all had to be existentialists. But to be accepted as an existentialist you had first to prove you were a libertine, an extremist. *Obey no restraints! Be free!* – that was what we were told. But how can I be free, I asked myself, if I am obeying someone else's order to be free?

Coetzee was like that, I think. He had made up his mind to be an existentialist and a romantic and a libertine. The trouble was, it did not come from inside him, therefore he did not know how. Freedom, sensuality, erotic love – it was all just an idea in his head, not an urge rooted in his body. He had no gift for it. He was not a sensual being. And anyway, I suspect he secretly liked it when a woman was cold and distant.

You say you decided not to read his last letter. Do you ever regret that decision?

Why? Why should I regret it?

Because Coetzee was a writer, who knew how to use words. What if the letter you did not read contained words that would have moved you or even changed your feelings about him?

Mr Vincent, to you John Coetzee is a great writer and a hero, I accept that, why else would you be here, why else would you be writing this book? To me, on the other hand – pardon me for saying this, but he is dead, so I cannot hurt his feelings – to me he is nothing. He is nothing, was nothing, just an irritation, an embarrassment. He was nothing and his words were nothing. I can see you are cross because I make him look like a fool. Nevertheless, to me he really was a fool.

As for his letters, writing letters to a woman does not prove you love her. This man was not in love with me, he was in love with some idea of me, some fantasy of a Latin mistress that he made up in his own mind. I wish, instead of me, he had found some other writer, some other fantasist, to fall in love with. Then the two of them could have been happy, making love all day to their ideas of each other.

You think I am cruel when I talk like this, but I am not, I am just a practical person. When my daughter's language teacher, a complete stranger, sends me letters full of his ideas about this and his ideas about that, about music and chemistry and philosophy and angels and gods and I don't know what else, page after page, poems too, I don't read it all and memorize it for future generations, all I want to know is one simple, practical thing, which is, *What is going on between this man and my daughter who is only a child?* Because – forgive me for saying this – beneath all the fine words what a man wants from a woman is usually very basic and very simple.

You say there were poems too?

I did not understand them. Maria Regina was the one who liked poetry.

You recall nothing about them?

They were very modernistic, very intellectual, very obscure. That is why I say it was all a big mistake. He thought I was the kind of woman you lie in bed with in the dark, discussing poetry; but I was not like that at all. I was a wife and mother, the wife of a man locked up in a hospital that might as well have been a prison or a graveyard and the mother of two girls whom I had somehow to keep safe in a world where when people want to steal your money they bring along an axe. I had no time to take pity on this ignorant young man who was throwing himself at my feet and humiliating himself in front of me. And, frankly, if I had wanted a man, it would not be a man like him.

Because, let me assure you – I am keeping you late, I apologize – let me assure you, I was not without feeling, far from it. Do not go away with a false impression of me. I was not dead to the world. In the mornings, when Joana was at work and Maria Regina was at school and the sun shone its rays into that little flat of ours, which was usually so dark and gloomy, I would sometimes stand in the sunlight by the open window listening to the birds and feeling the warmth on my face and my breast; and at times like that I would long to be a woman again. I was not too old, I was just waiting. So. Enough. Thank you for listening.

You said last time that you had a question for me.

Yes, I forgot, I have a question. It is this. I am not usually wrong about people; so tell me, am I wrong about John Coetzee? Because to me, frankly, he was not anybody. He was not a man of substance. Maybe he could write well, maybe had a certain talent for words, I don't know, I never read his books, I was never curious to read them. I know he won a big reputation later; but was he really a great writer? Because to my mind, a talent for words is not enough if you want to be a great writer. You have also to be a great man. And he was not a great man. He was a little man, an unimportant little man. I can't give you a list of reasons A-B-C-D why I say so, but that was my impression from the beginning, from the moment I set eyes on him, and nothing that happened afterwards changed it. So I turn to you. You have studied him deeply, you are writing a book about him. Tell me: What is your estimation of him? Was I wrong?

My estimation of him as a writer or my estimation of him as a human being?

As a human being.

I can't say. I would be reluctant to pronounce a judgment on anyone without ever meeting him face to face. Him or her. But I think that, at the time he met you, Coetzee was lonely, unnaturally lonely. Perhaps that explains certain — what shall I say? — certain extravagances of behaviour.

How do you know that?

From the record he left behind. From putting two and two together. He was a little lonely and a little desperate.

Yes, but we are all a little desperate, that is life. If you are strong you conquer the despair. That is why I ask: how can you be a great writer if you are just an ordinary little man? Surely you must have a certain flame in you that sets you apart from the people in the street. Maybe in his books, if you read them, you can see that flame. But for me, in the times I was with him I never felt any fire. On the contrary, he seemed to me — how shall I express it? — tepid.

To an extent I would agree with you. Fire is not the first word that comes to mind when one thinks of his books. But he had other virtues, other strengths. For instance, I would say he was steady. He had a steady gaze. He was not easily fooled by appearances.

For a man who was not fooled by appearances, he fell in love rather easily, don't you think?

[Laughter.]

But maybe, when he fell in love, he was not fooled. Maybe he saw things that other people do not see.

In the woman?

Yes, in the woman.

[Silence.]

You tell me he was in love with me even after I sent him away, even after I forgot he even existed. Is that what you mean by steadiness? Because to me it just seems stupid.

I think he was dogged. A very English word. Whether there is an equivalent in Portuguese I don't know. Like a bulldog that grips you with his teeth and does not let go.

If you say so, then I must believe you. But being like a dog — is that admirable, in English?

[Laughter.]

You know, in my profession, rather than just listen to words, we like to watch the way people move, the way they carry themselves. That is our way to get to the truth, and it is not a bad way. Your Mr Coetzee may have had a talent for words but, as I told you, he could not dance. He could not dance – here is one of the phrases I remember from South Africa, Maria Regina taught it to me – *he could not dance to save his life.*

[Laughter.]

But seriously, Senhora Nascimento, there have been many great men who were not good dancers. If you must be a good dancer before you can be a great man, then Gandhi was not a great man, Tolstoy was not a great man.

No, you are not listening to what I say. I too am serious. You know the word *disembodied*? This man was disembodied. He was divorced from his body. To him, the body was like one of those wooden puppets that you move with strings. You pull this string and the left arm moves, you pull that string and the right leg moves. And the real self sits up above, where you cannot see him, like the puppet-master pulling the strings.

Now this man comes to me, to the mistress of the dance. *Show me how to dance!* he implores. So I show him, show him how we move in the dance. *So*, I say to him – *move your feet so and then so.* And he listens and tells himself, *Aha, she means pull the red string followed by the blue string!* – *Turn your shoulder so*, I say to him, and he tells himself, *Aha, she means pull the green string!*

But that is not how you dance! That is not how you dance!

Dance is incarnation. In dance it is not the puppet-master in the head that leads and the body that follows, it is the body itself that leads, the body with its soul, its body-soul. Because the body knows! It knows! When the body feels the rhythm inside it, it does not need to think. That is how we are if we are human. That is why the wooden puppet cannot dance. The wood has no soul. The wood cannot feel the rhythm.

So I ask: How could this man of yours be a great man when he was not human? It is a serious question, not a joke any more. Why do you think I, as a woman, could not respond to him? Why do you think I did everything I could to keep my daughter away from him while she was still young, with no experience to guide her? Because from such a man no good can come. Love: how can you be a great writer when you know nothing about love? Do you think I can be a woman and not know in my bones what kind of lover a man will be? I tell you, I shiver with cold when I think of, you know, intimacy with a man like that. I don't know if he ever married, but if he did I shiver for the woman who married him.

Yes. It is getting late, it has been a long afternoon, my colleague and I must be on our way. Thank you, Senhora Nascimento, for the time you have so generously given us. It has been most gracious of you. Senhora Gross will transcribe our conversation and tidy up the translation, after which I will send it to you to see if there is anything you would like to change or add or cut out.

I understand. Of course you offer to me that I can change the record, I can add or cut out. But how much can I change? Can I change the label I wear around my neck that says I was one of Coetzee's women? Will you let me take off that label? Will you let me tear it up? I think not. Because it would destroy your book, and you would not allow that.

But I will be patient. I will wait to see what you send me. Perhaps – who knows? – you will take seriously what I have told you. Also – let me confess – I am curious to see what the other women in this man's life have told you, the other women with labels around their necks – whether they too found this lover of theirs to be made of wood. Because, you know, that is what I think you should call your book: *The Wooden Man*.

[Laughter.]

But tell me, seriously again, did this man who knew nothing about women ever write about women, or did he just write about dogged men like himself? I ask because, as I say, I have not read him.

He wrote about men and he wrote about women too. For example – this may interest you – there is a book named Foe *in which the heroine spends a year shipwrecked on an island off the coast of Brazil. In the final version she is an Englishwoman, but in the first draft he made her a* Brasileira.

And what kind of woman is this *Brasileira* of his?

What shall I say? She has many good qualities. She is attractive, she is resourceful, she has a will of steel. She hunts all over the world to find her young daughter, who has disappeared. That is the substance of the novel: her quest to recover her daughter, which overrides all other concerns. To me she seems an admirable heroine. If I were the original of a character like that, I would feel proud.

I will read this book and see for myself. What is the title again?

Foe, *spelled* F–O–E. *It was translated into Portuguese, but the translation is probably out of print by now. I can send you a copy in English if you like.*

Yes, send it. It is a long time since I read an English book, but I am interested to see what this man of wood made of me.

[Laughter.]

Interview conducted in São Paulo,
Brazil, in December 2007.

Martin

IN ONE OF his late notebooks Coetzee writes an account of his first meeting with you, on the day in 1972 when you were both being interviewed for a job at the University of Cape Town. The account is only a few pages long – I'll read it to you if you like. I suspect it was intended to fit into the third memoir, the one that never saw the light of day. As you will hear, he follows the same convention as in Boyhood *and* Youth, *where the subject is called 'he' rather than 'I'.*

This is what he writes.

'He has had his hair cut for the interview. He has trimmed his beard. He has put on a jacket and tie. If he is not yet Mr Sobersides, at least he no longer looks like the Wild Man of Borneo.

'In the waiting room are the two other candidates for the job. They stand side by side at the window overlooking the gardens, conversing softly. They seem to know each other, or at least to have struck up an acquaintance.'

You don't recall who this third person was, do you?

He was from the University of Stellenbosch, but I don't remember his name.

He goes on: 'This is the British way: to drop the contestants into the pit and wait to see what will happen. He will have to reaccustom himself to British ways of doing things, in all their brutality. A tight little ship, Britain, crammed to the gunwales. Dog eat dog. Dogs snarling and snapping at one another, each guarding its little territory. The American way, by comparison, decorous, even gentle. But then there is more space in America, more room for urbanity.

'The Cape may not be Britain, may be drifting further from Britain every day, yet what is left of British ways it clutches tight to its chest. Without that saving connection, what would the Cape be? A minor landing on the way to nowhere; a place of savage idleness.

'In the order paper pinned to the door, he is Number Two to appear before the committee. Number One, when summoned, rises calmly, taps out his pipe, stores it away in what must be a pipe-case, and passes through the portal. After twenty minutes he re-emerges, his face inscrutable.

'It is his turn. He enters and is waved to a seat at the foot of a long table. At the far end are his inquisitors, five in number, all men. Because the windows are open, because the room is above a street where cars are continually passing by, he has to strain to hear them, and raise his own voice to make himself heard.

'Some polite feints, then the first thrust: If appointed, what authors would he like to teach?

'"I can teach pretty much across the board," he replies. "I am not a specialist. I think of myself as a generalist."

'As an answer it is at least defensible. A small department in a small university might be happy to recruit a jack of all trades. But from the silence that falls he gathers he has not answered well. He has taken the question too literally. That has always been a fault of his: taking questions too literally, responding too briefly. These people don't want brief answers. They want something more leisurely, more expansive, something that will allow them to work out what kind of fellow they have before them, what kind of junior colleague he would make, whether he would fit in in a provincial university that is doing its best to maintain standards in difficult times, to keep the flame of civilization burning.

'In America, where they take job-hunting seriously, people like him, people who don't know how to read the agenda behind a question, can't speak in rounded paragraphs, don't put themselves over with conviction – in short, people deficient in people skills – attend training sessions where they learn to look the interrogator in the eye, smile, respond to questions fully and with every appearance of sincerity. Presentation of the self: that is what they call it in America, without irony.

'What authors would he prefer to teach? What research is he currently engaged in? Would he feel competent to offer tutorials in Middle English? His answers sound more and more hollow. The truth is, he does not really want this job. He does not want it because in his heart he knows he is not cut out to be a teacher. Lacks the temperament. Lacks zeal.

'He emerges from the interview in a state of black dejection. He wants to get away from this place at once, without delay. But no, first there are forms to be filled in, travel expenses to be collected.

'"How did it go?"

'The speaker is the candidate who was interviewed first, the pipe-smoker.' That is you, if I am not mistaken.

Yes. But I have given up the pipe.

'He shrugs. "Who knows?" he says. "Not well."

'"Shall we get a cup of tea?"

'He is taken aback. Are the two of them not supposed to be rivals? Is it permitted for rivals to fraternize?

'It is late afternoon, the campus is deserted. They make for the Student Union in quest of their cup of tea. The Union is closed. MJ' – that is what he calls you – 'takes out his pipe. "Ah well," he says. "Do you smoke?"

'How surprising: he is beginning to like this MJ, with his easy, straightforward manner! His gloom is fading fast. He likes MJ and, unless it is all just an exercise in self-presentation, MJ seems inclined to like him too. And this mutual liking has grown up in a flash!

'Yet should he be surprised? Why have the two of them (or the three of them, if the shadowy third is included) been selected to be interviewed for a lectureship in English literature, if not because they are the same kind of person, with the same formation behind them (formation: not the customary English word, he must remember that); and because both, finally and most obviously, are South Africans, white South Africans.'

That is where the fragment ends. It is undated, but I am pretty sure he wrote it in 1999 or 2000. So . . . a couple of questions relating to it. First question: You were the successful candidate, the one who was awarded the lectureship, while Coetzee was passed over. Why do you think he was passed over? Did you detect any resentment on his part?

None at all. I was from inside the system – the colonial university system as it was in those days – while he was from outside, insofar as he had gone off to America for his graduate education. Given the nature of all systems, namely to reproduce themselves, I was always going to have the edge over him. He understood that, in theory and in practice. He certainly didn't put the blame on me.

Very well. My second question: He suggests that in you he has found a new friend, and goes on to list traits that you and he have in common. But when he gets to your white South Africanness he stops and writes no more. Have you any idea why he should have stopped just there?

Why he raised the topic of white South African identity and then dropped it? There are two explanations I can offer. One is that it might have seemed too complex a topic to be explored in a memoir or diary – too complex or too close to the bone. The other is simpler: that the story of his adventures in the academy was too boring to go on with.

And which explanation do you incline toward?

Probably the first, with an admixture of the second. John left South Africa in the 1960s, came back in the 1970s, for decades hovered between South Africa and the United States, then finally decamped to Australia and died there. I left South Africa in the 1970s and never returned. Broadly speaking, he and I shared an attitude toward South Africa and our continued presence there. Our attitude was that, to put it briefly, our presence there was legal but illegitimate. We had an abstract right to be there, a birthright, but the basis of that right was fraudulent. Our presence was grounded in a crime, namely colonial conquest, perpetuated by apartheid.

Whatever the opposite is of *native* or *rooted*, that was what we felt ourselves to be. We thought of ourselves as sojourners, temporary residents, and to that extent without a home, without a homeland. I don't think I am misrepresenting John. It was something he and I talked about a great deal. I am certainly not misrepresenting myself.

Are you saying that you and he commiserated together?

Commiserated is the wrong word. We had too much going for us to see our fate as a miserable one. We had our youth – I was still in my twenties at the time, he was only slightly older – we had a not-bad education behind us, we even had modest material assets. If we had been whisked away and set down somewhere else in the world – the civilized world, the First World – we would have prospered, flourished. (About the Third World I am not so sure. We were not Robinson Crusoes, either of us.)

Therefore no, I did not regard our fate as tragic, and I am sure he did not either. If anything, it was comic. His ancestors in their way, and my ancestors in theirs, had toiled away, generation after generation, to clear a patch of wild Africa for their descendants, and what was the fruit of all their labours? Doubt in the hearts of those descendants about title to the land; an uneasy sense that it belonged not to them but, inalienably, to its original owners.

Do you think that if he had gone on with the memoir, if he had not stopped writing, that is what he would have said?

More or less. Let me add one further comment on our stance toward South Africa: that we cultivated a certain provisionality in our feelings toward it, he perhaps more so than I. We were reluctant to invest too deeply in the country, since sooner or later our ties to it would have to be cut, our investment in it annulled.

And?

That's all. We had a certain style of mind in common, a style that I attribute to our origins, colonial and South African. Hence the commonality of our outlook.

In his case, would you say that the habit you describe, of treating feelings as provisional, of not committing himself emotionally, extended beyond relations with the land of his birth into personal relations too?

I don't know. You are the biographer. If you find that train of thought worth following up, follow it.

Can we now turn to his teaching? He writes that he was not cut out to be a teacher. Would you agree?

I would say that one teaches best what one knows best and feels most strongly about. John knew a fair amount about a range of things, but not a great deal about anything in particular. I would count that as one strike against him. Second, though there were writers who mattered deeply to him – the nineteenth-century Russian novelists, for instance – the depth of his involvement did not come out in his teaching, not in any obvious way. Something was always being held back. Why? I don't know. All I can suggest is that a strain of secretiveness that seemed to be engrained in him, part of his character, extended to his teaching too.

Do you feel then that he spent his life in a profession for which he had no talent?

That is a little too sweeping. John was a perfectly adequate academic. A perfectly adequate academic but not a notable teacher. Perhaps if he had taught Sanskrit it would have been different, Sanskrit or some other subject in which the conventions permit you to be a little dry and reserved.

He told me once that he had missed his calling, that he should have been a librarian. I can see the sense in that.

I haven't been able to lay my hands on course descriptions from the 1970s — the University of Cape Town doesn't seem to archive material like that — but among Coetzee's papers I did come across an advertisement for a course that you and he offered jointly in 1976, to extramural students. Do you remember that course?

Yes, I do. It was a poetry course. I was working on Hugh McDiarmid at the time, so I used the occasion to give McDiarmid a close reading. John had the students read Pablo Neruda in translation. I had never read Neruda, so I sat in on his sessions.

A strange choice, don't you think, for someone like him: Neruda?

No, not at all. John had a fondness for lush, expansive poetry: Neruda, Whitman, Stevens. You must remember that he was, in his way, a child of the 1960s.

In his way — what do you mean by that?

I mean within the confines of a certain rectitude, a certain rationality. Without being a Dionysian himself, he approved in principle of Dionysianism. Approved in principle of letting oneself go, though I don't think he ever let himself go — would probably not have known how to. He had a need to believe in the resources of the unconscious, in the creative force of unconscious processes. Hence his inclination toward the more vatic poets.

You must have noted how rarely he discussed the sources of his own creativity. In part that came out of the native secretiveness I mentioned. But in part it also suggests a reluctance to probe the sources of his inspiration, as if being too self-aware might cripple him.

Was the course a success — the course you and he taught together?

I certainly learned from it — learned about the history of surrealism in Latin America, for instance. As I said, John knew a little about a lot of things. What our students came away with I don't know. Students, in my experience, soon work out whether what you are teaching matters to you. If it does, then they are prepared to consider letting it matter to them too. But if they conclude, rightly or wrongly, that it doesn't, then, curtains, you may as well go home.

And Neruda didn't matter to him?

No, I'm not saying that. Neruda may have mattered a great deal to him. Neruda may even have been a model – an unattainable model – of how a poet can respond to injustice and repression. But – and this is my point – if you treat your connection with the poet as a personal secret to be closely guarded, and if moreover your classroom manner is somewhat stiff and formal, you are never going to acquire a following.

You are saying he never acquired a following?

Not as far as I am aware. Perhaps he smartened up his act in his later years. I just don't know.

At the time when you met him, in 1972, he had a rather precarious position teaching at a high school. It wasn't until some time later that he was actually offered a position at the University. Even so, for almost all of his working life, from his mid-twenties until his mid-sixties, he was employed as a teacher of one kind or another. I come back to my earlier question: Doesn't it seem strange to you that a man who had no talent as a teacher should have made teaching his career?

Yes and no. The ranks of the teaching profession are, as you must know, full of refugees and misfits.

And which was he: a refugee or a misfit?

He was a misfit. He was also a cautious soul. He liked the security of a monthly salary cheque.

You sound critical.

I am only pointing to the obvious. If he hadn't wasted so much of his life correcting students' grammar and sitting through boring meetings, he might have written more, perhaps even written better. But he was not a child. He knew what he was doing. He made his choice.

On the other hand, being a teacher allowed him contact with a younger generation. Which he might not have had, had he withdrawn from the world and devoted himself solely to writing.

True.

Did he have any special friendships that you know of among students?

Now you sound as if you are angling. What do you mean, special friendships? Do you mean, did he overstep the mark? Even if I knew, which I don't, I would not comment.

Yet the theme of the older man and the younger woman keeps coming back in his fiction.

It would be very, very naive to conclude that because the theme was present in his writing it had to be present in his life.

In his inner life, then.

His inner life. Who can say what goes on in people's inner lives?

Is there any other aspect of him that you would like to bring forward? Any stories worth recounting?

Stories? I don't think so. John and I were colleagues. We were friends. We got on well together. But I can't say I knew him intimately. Why do you ask if I have stories?

Because in biography one has to strike a balance between narrative and opinion. I have no shortage of opinion – people are more than ready to tell me what they think or thought of Coetzee – but one needs more than that to bring a life-story to life.

Sorry, I can't help you. Perhaps your other sources will be more forthcoming. How many people will you be speaking to?

Five. I have cut the list down to five.

Only five? Don't you think that is risky? Who are the lucky five? How did you choose us?

From here I'll be making another trip to South Africa to speak to Coetzee's cousin Margot, with whom he was close. From there to Brazil to see a woman named Adriana Nascimento who lived in Cape Town for some years during the 1970s. And then – the date isn't fixed yet – I will go to Canada to see someone named Julia Frankl, who in the 1970s would have gone under the name Julia Smith. And I also plan to see Sophie Denoël in Paris. Do you or did you know any of them?

Sophie I knew, but not the others. How did you choose us?

Basically I let Coetzee himself do the choosing. I simply followed up on clues he dropped in his notebooks — clues as to who was important to him at the time. The other criterion you had to meet was to be alive. Most of the people who knew him well are, as you must know, dead by now.

It sounds a peculiar way of selecting biographical sources, if you don't mind my saying so.

Perhaps. But I am not interested in coming to a final judgment on Coetzee. I leave that to history. What I am doing is telling the story of a stage in his life, or if we can't have a single story then several stories from several perspectives.

And the sources you have selected have no axes to grind, no ambitions of their own to pronounce final judgment on Coetzee?

[Silence.]

Leaving aside Sophie, leaving aside his cousin, was either of the women you mentioned emotionally involved with Coetzee?

Yes. Both.

Shouldn't that give you pause? Are you not inevitably going to come out with an account that is slanted toward the personal and the intimate at the expense of the man's actual achievements as a writer? Will it amount to anything more than – forgive me for putting it this way – anything more than women's gossip?

Because my informants are women?

Because it is not in the nature of love affairs for the lovers to see each other whole and steady.

[Silence.]

I repeat, it seems to me strange to be doing the biography of a writer while ignoring his writing. But perhaps I am wrong. Perhaps I am out of date. I must go. One final thing: if you are planning to quote me, would you make sure I have a chance to check the text first?

Of course.

Interview conducted in Sheffield, England,
in September 2007.

Sophie

MME DENOËL, TELL me how you came to know John Coetzee.

He and I were for years colleagues at the University of Cape Town. He was in the Department of English, I was in French. We collaborated to offer a course in African literature. This was in 1976. He taught the Anglophone writers, I the Francophone. That was how our acquaintance began.

And how did you yourself come to be in Cape Town?

My husband was sent there to run the Alliance Française. Before that we had been living in Madagascar. During our time in Cape Town our marriage broke up. My husband returned to France, I stayed on. I took a position at the University, a junior position teaching French language.

And in addition you taught this joint course that you mention, in African literature.

Yes. It may seem odd, two whites offering a course in black African literature, but that is how it was in those days. If we had not offered it, no one would have.

Because blacks were excluded from the University?

No, no, by then the system had started to crack. There were black students, though not many; some black lecturers too. But very few specialists in Africa, the wider Africa. That was one of the surprising things I discovered about South Africa: how insular it was. I went back on a visit last year, and it was the same: little or no interest in the rest of Africa. Africa was a dark continent to the north, best left unexplored.

And you? Where did your interest in Africa come from?

From my education. From France. Remember, France had been a major colonial power. Even after the colonial era officially ended, France had other means at its disposal to maintain its influence – economic means, cultural means. *La Francophonie* was the new name we invented for the old empire. Writers from *Francophonie* were promoted, fêted, studied. For my *agrégation* I worked on Aimé Césaire.

And the course you taught in collaboration with Coetzee – was that a success, would you say?

Yes, I believe so. It was just an introductory course, but students found it, as you say in English, an eye-opener.

White students?

White students plus a few black. We did not attract the more radical black students. Our approach would have been too academic for them, not *engagé* enough. We thought it sufficient to give students a glimpse of the riches of the rest of Africa.

And you and Coetzee saw eye to eye on this approach?

I believe so. Yes.

You were a specialist in African literature, he was not. His training was in the literature of the metropolis. How did he come to be teaching African literature?

It is true, he had no formal training in the field. But he had a good general knowledge of Africa, admittedly just book knowledge, not practical knowledge, he had not travelled in Africa, but book knowledge is not worthless – right? He knew the anthropological literature better than I did, including the francophone materials. He had a grasp of the history, the politics. He had read the important writers working in English and in French (of course in those days the body of African literature was not large – things are different now). There were gaps in his knowledge – the Maghreb, Egypt, and so forth. And he didn't know the diaspora, particularly the Caribbean, which I did.

What did you think of him as a teacher?

He was good. Not spectacular but competent. Always well prepared.

Did he get on well with students?

That I can't say. Perhaps if you track down old students of his they will be able to help you.

And yourself? Compared with him, did you get on well with students?

[Laughs.] What is it you want me to say? Yes, I suppose I was the more popular one, the more enthusiastic. I was young, remember, and it was a pleasure for me to be talking about books for a change, after all the language classes. We made a good pair, I thought, he more serious, more reserved, I more open, more flamboyant.

He was considerably older than you.

Ten years. He was ten years older than me.

[Silence]

Is there anything you would like to add on the subject? Other aspects of him you would like to comment on?

We had a liaison. I presume you are aware of that. It did not endure.

Why not?

It was not sustainable.

Would you like to say more?

Would I like to say more for your book? Not before you tell me what kind of book it is. Is it a book of gossip or a serious book? Do you have authorization? Who else are you speaking to besides me?

Does one need authorization to write a book? From whom would one seek it? I certainly don't know. But I can give you my assurance, it is a serious book, a seriously intended biography. I concentrate on the years from Coetzee's return to South Africa in 1971/72 until his first public recognition in 1977. That seems to me an important period of his life, important yet neglected, a period when he was still finding his feet as a writer.

As for whom I have chosen to interview, the answer is not straightforward. I made two trips to South Africa, last year and the year before, to speak to people who had known Coetzee. Those trips were not, on the whole, successful. My informants had less to offer than I had hoped for. In one or two cases people claimed to have known him, but after a little scratching it turned out they had the wrong Coetzee (Coetzee is a not uncommon name there). Of the people he had been closest to, many had left the country or died or both. His whole generation was in fact on the point of dying out. The upshot is, the core of the biography will come from a handful of friends and colleagues who are prepared to share their memories. Including, I would hope, yourself. Is that enough to reassure you?

No. What of his diaries? What of his letters? What of his notebooks? Why so much emphasis on interviews?

Mme Denoël, I have been through the letters and diaries. What Coetzee writes there cannot be trusted, not as a factual record — not because he was a liar but because he was a fictioneer. In his letters he is making up a fiction of himself for his correspondents; in his diaries he is doing much the same for his own eyes, or perhaps for posterity. As documents they are valu-

able, of course; but if you want the truth you have to go behind the fictions they elaborate and hear from people who knew him directly, in the flesh.

But what if we are all fictioneers, as you call Coetzee? What if we all continually make up the stories of our lives? Why should what I tell you about Coetzee be any worthier of credence than what he tells you himself?

Of course we are all fictioneers. I do not deny that. But which would you rather have: a set of independent reports from a range of independent perspectives, from which you can then try to synthesize a whole; or the massive, unitary self-projection comprised by his oeuvre? I know which I would prefer.

Yes, I can see that. There remains the question of discretion. I am not one of those who believe that once a person is dead all restraint falls away. What existed between him and me I am not necessarily prepared to share with the world.

I accept that. It is your privilege, your right. But I ask you to pause and consider. A great writer becomes the property of all of us. You knew Coetzee closely. One of these days you too will no longer be with us. Do you think it good that your memories should pass away with you?

A great writer? How John would laugh if he could hear you! The day of the great writer is gone for ever, he would say.

The day of the writer as oracle — yes, I would agree, that day is past. But would you not accept that a well-known writer — let us call him that instead — a well-known figure in our common cultural life, is to some extent public property?

On that subject my opinion is irrelevant. What is relevant is what he himself believed. And there the answer is clear. He believed our life-stories are ours to construct as we wish, within or even against the constraints imposed by the real world – as you yourself acknowledged a moment ago. That is why I asked about authorization, a question which you brushed aside. It was not the authorization of his family or his executors that I had in mind, it was his own authorization. If you were not authorized by him to expose the private side of his life, then I certainly won't assist you.

He cannot have authorized me for the simple reason that he and I never had any contact. So let us abandon that line of inquiry and return instead to the course you mentioned, the course you and he taught together. One remark that you made intrigues me. You said you and he did not attract the more radical African students. Why do you think that was so?

Because we were not radicals ourselves, not by their standards. We had both, of course, been affected by 1968. In 1968 I was a student at the Sorbonne, and took part in the manifestations, the days in May. John was in the United States at the time, and fell foul of the authorities there, I don't remember the details, but I know it was a turning-point in his life. Yet I stress we were not Marxists, either of us, and certainly not Maoists. I was probably to the left of him, but I could afford that because I was shielded by my status in the French diplomatic enclave. If I had gotten into trouble with the South African police I would have been discreetly put on a plane to Paris, and that would have been the end of the matter. I would not have ended up in a prison cell.

Whereas Coetzee . . .

Coetzee would not have ended up in a prison cell either. He was not a militant. His politics were too idealistic, too Utopian for that. In fact he was not political at all. He looked down on politics. He didn't like political writers, writers who espoused a political programme.

Yet he published some quite left-leaning commentary in the 1970s. I think of his essays on Alex La Guma, for example. He was sympathetic to La Guma, and La Guma was a communist.

La Guma was a special case. He was sympathetic to La Guma because La Guma was from Cape Town, not because he was a communist.

You say he was not political. Do you mean that he was apolitical? Because some people would say that the apolitical is just one variety of the political.

No, not apolitical, I would rather say anti-political. He thought that politics brought out the worst in people. It brought out the worst in people and also brought to the surface the worst types in society. He preferred to have nothing to do with it.

Did he preach this anti-political politics in his classes?

Of course not. He was very scrupulous about not preaching. His political beliefs you discovered only when you got to know him better.

You say his politics were Utopian. Are you implying they were unrealistic?

He looked forward to the day when politics and the state would wither away. I would call that Utopian. On the other hand, he did not invest a great deal of himself in these Utopian longings. He was too much of a Calvinist for that.

Please explain.

You want me to say what lay behind Coetzee's politics? You can best get that from his books. But let me try anyway.

In Coetzee's eyes, we human beings will never abandon politics because politics is too convenient and too attractive as a theatre in which to give play to our baser emotions. Baser emotions meaning hatred and rancour and spite and jealousy and bloodlust and so forth. In other words, politics is a symptom of our fallen state and expresses that fallen state.

Even the politics of liberation?

If you refer to the politics of the South African liberation struggle, the answer is yes. As long as liberation meant national liberation, the liberation of the black nation of South Africa, John had no interest in it.

Was he then hostile to the liberation struggle?

Was he hostile? No, he was not hostile. Hostile, sympathetic — as a biographer you above all ought to be wary of putting people in neat little boxes with labels on them.

I hope I am not putting Coetzee in a box.

Well, that is how it sounds to me. No, he was not hostile to the liberation struggle. If you are a fatalist, as he tended to be, there is no point in being hostile to the course of history, however much you may regret it. To the fatalist, history is fate.

Very well, did he then regret the liberation struggle? Did he regret the form the liberation struggle took?

He accepted that the liberation struggle was just. The struggle was just, but the new South Africa toward which it strove was not Utopian enough for him.

What would have been Utopian enough for him?

The closing down of the mines. The ploughing under of the vineyards. The disbanding of the armed forces. The abolition of the automobile. Universal vegetarianism. Poetry in the streets. That sort of thing.

In other words, poetry and the horse-drawn cart and vegetarianism are worth fighting for, but not liberation from apartheid?

Nothing is worth fighting for. You compel me into the role of defending his position, a position I do not happen to share. Nothing is worth fighting for because fighting only prolongs the cycle of aggression and retaliation. I merely repeat what Coetzee says loud and clear in his writings, which you say you have read.

Was he at ease with his black students – with black people in general?

Was he at ease with anyone? He was not an at-ease person (can you say that in English?). He never relaxed. I witnessed that with my own eyes. So: Was he at ease with black people? No. He was not at ease among people who were at ease. The ease of others made him ill at ease. Which sent him off – in my opinion – in the wrong direction.

What do you mean?

He saw Africa through a romantic haze. He thought of Africans as embodied, in a way that had been lost long ago in Europe. What do I mean? Let me try to explain. In Africa, he used to say, body and soul were indistinguishable, the body was the soul. He had a whole philosophy of the body, of music and dance, which I can't reproduce, but which seemed to me, even then – how shall I say? – unhelpful. Politically unhelpful.

Please continue.

His philosophy ascribed to Africans the role of guardians of the truer, deeper, more primitive being of humankind. He and I argued quite strenuously about this. What his position boiled down to, I said, was old-fashioned Romantic primitivism. In the context of the 1970s, of the liberation struggle and the apartheid state, it was unhelpful to look at Africans in his way. And anyway, it was a role they were no longer prepared to fulfil.

Was this the reason why black students avoided his course, your joint course, in African literature?

It was a viewpoint that he did not openly propagate. He was always very careful in that respect, very correct. But if you listened carefully it must have come across.

There was one further circumstance, one further bias to his thinking, that I must mention. Like many whites, he regarded the Cape, the western Cape and perhaps the northern Cape along with it, as standing apart from the rest of South Africa. The Cape was a country of its own, with its own geography, its own history, its own languages and culture. In this mythical Cape the Coloured people were rooted, and to a lesser extent the Afrikaners too, but Africans were aliens, latecomers, as were the English.

Why do I mention this? Because it suggests how he could justify the rather abstract, rather anthropological attitude he took up toward black South Africa. He had no *feeling* for black South Africans. That was my private conclusion. They might be his fellow citizens but they were not his countrymen. History – or fate, which was to him the same thing – might have cast them in the role of inheritors of the land, but at the back of his mind they continued to be *they* as opposed to *us*.

If Africans were they, *who were* us? *The Afrikaners?*

No. *Us* was principally the Coloured people. It is a term I use only reluctantly, as shorthand. He – Coetzee – avoided it as far as he could. I mentioned his Utopianism. This avoidance was another aspect of his Utopianism. He longed for the day when everyone in South Africa would call themselves nothing, neither African nor European nor white nor black nor anything else, when family histories would have become so tangled and inter-mixed that people would be ethnically indistinguishable, that is to say – I utter the tainted word again – Coloured. He called that the Brazilian future. He approved of Brazil and the Brazilians. He had of course never been to Brazil.

But he had Brazilian friends.

He had met some Brazilian refugees in South Africa.

[Silence.]

You mention an intermixed future. Are we talking here about biological mixture? Are we talking about intermarriage?

Don't ask me. I am just delivering a report.

Then why, instead of contributing to the future by fathering Coloured children – why was he having a liaison with a young white colleague from France?

[Laughs.] Don't ask me.

What did you and he talk about?

About our teaching. About colleagues and students. In other words, we talked shop. We also talked about ourselves.

Go on.

You want me to tell you if we discussed his writing? The answer is no. He never spoke to me about what he was writing, nor did I press him.

This was around the time when he was writing In the Heart of the Country.

He was just completing *In the Heart of the Country.*

Did you know that In the Heart of the Country *would be about madness and parricide and so forth?*

I had absolutely no idea.

Did you read it before it was published?

Yes.

What did you think of it?

[Laughs.] I must tread carefully. I presume you do not mean, what was my considered critical judgment, I presume you mean how did I respond? Frankly, I was at first nervous. I was nervous that I would find myself in the book in some embarrassing guise.

Why did you think that might be so?

Because – so it seemed to me at the time, now I realize how

naive this was – I believed you could not be closely involved with another person and yet exclude her from your imaginative universe.

And did you find yourself in the book?

No.

Were you upset?

What do you mean – was I upset not to find myself in his book?

Were you upset to find yourself excluded from his imaginative universe?

No. It was part of my education. Shall we leave it at that? I think I have given you enough.

Well, I am certainly grateful to you. But, Mme Denoël, let me make one further appeal. Coetzee was never a popular writer. By that I do not simply mean that his books did not sell well. I also mean that the public never took him to their collective heart. There was an image of him in the public realm as a cold and supercilious intellectual, an image he did nothing to dispel. Indeed one might even say he encouraged it.

Now, I don't believe that image does him justice. The conversations I have had with people who knew him well reveal a very different person – not necessarily a warmer person, but someone more uncertain of himself, more confused, more human, if I can use that word.

I wonder if you would be prepared to comment on the human side of him. I value what you have said about his politics, but are there any more personal stories from your time together that you would be prepared to share?

Stories that will reveal him in a warmer light, you mean? Stories of his kindness toward animals – animals and women? No, those stories I will be saving for my own memoirs.

[Laughter.]

All right, I will tell you one story. It may not seem personal, it may again seem to be political, but you must remember, in those days politics pushed its way into everything.

A journalist from *Libération*, the French newspaper, came on an assignment to South Africa, and asked whether I could set up an interview with John. I went back to John and persuaded him to accept: I told him *Libération* was a good paper, I told him French journalists were not like South African journalists, they would never arrive for an interview unprepared. And this was of course in the days before the Internet, so journalists could not simply copy their stories one from another.

We held the interview in my office on the campus. I thought I would assist in case there were language problems, John's French was not good.

Well, it soon became clear that the journalist was not interested in John himself but in what John could tell him about Breyten Breytenbach, who was at the time in trouble with the South African authorities. Because in France there was a lively interest in Breytenbach – he was a romantic figure, he had lived in France for many years, he had connections in the French intellectual world.

John's response was that he could not help: he had read Breytenbach but that was all, he did not know him personally, had never even met him. All of which was true.

But the journalist, who was used to literary life in France, where everything is so much more incestuous, would not believe him. Why would one writer refuse to comment on another writer from the same little tribe, the Afrikaner tribe, unless there was some personal grudge between them, or some political animosity?

So he kept pressing John, and John kept trying to explain how hard it was for an outsider to appreciate Breytenbach's standing as an Afrikaans poet, since his poetry was so deeply rooted in the *volksmond*, the language of the people.

'Are you referring to his dialect poems?' said the journalist. And then, when John failed to understand, he remarked, very disparagingly, 'Surely one cannot write great poetry in dialect.'

That remark really angered John. But, since his way of being angry was, rather than raising his voice, to turn cold and withdraw into silence, the man from *Libération* was simply confused. He had no idea of what was going on.

Afterwards, when John had left, I tried to explain that Afrikaners became very emotional when their language was insulted, that Breytenbach would probably have responded in the same way. But the journalist just shrugged. It made no sense, he said, to write in dialect when one had a world language at one's disposal (actually he didn't say a dialect, he said an obscure dialect, and he didn't say a world language, he said a proper language, *une vraie langue*). At which point it began to dawn on me that he was putting Breytenbach and John in the same category, as vernacular or dialect writers.

Well, of course John did not write in Afrikaans at all, he wrote in English, very good English, and had written in English all his life. Even so, he responded in very prickly fashion to what he saw as an insult to the dignity of Afrikaans.

He did translations from Afrikaans, didn't he? I mean, translated Afrikaans writers.

Yes. He knew Afrikaans well, I would say, though in much the same fashion as he knew French, that is, better on the page than spoken. I was not competent to judge his Afrikaans, of course, but that was the impression I got.

So we have the case of a man who spoke the language only imperfectly, who stood outside the state religion, whose outlook was cosmopolitan, whose politics was – what shall we say? – dissident, yet who was ready to embrace an Afrikaner identity. Why do you think that was so?

My opinion is that under the gaze of history he felt there was no way in which he could separate himself off from the Afrikaners while retaining his self-respect, even if that meant being associated with all that the Afrikaners were responsible for, politically.

Was there nothing that drew him more positively to embrace an Afrikaner identity – nothing at a personal level, for example?

Perhaps there was, I can't say. I never got to meet his family. Perhaps they would provide a clue. But he was by nature very cautious, very much the tortoise. When he sensed danger, he would withdraw into his shell. He had been rebuffed by the Afrikaners too often, rebuffed and humiliated – you have only to read his book of childhood memories to see that. He was not going to take the risk of being rejected again.

So he preferred to remain an outsider.

I think he was happiest in the role of outsider. He was not a joiner.

You say you were never introduced to his family. Do you not find that strange?

No, not at all. His mother had passed away by the time we met, his father was not well, his brother was overseas, he was on strained terms with the wider family. As for me, I was a married woman, so our relationship, as far as it went, had to be clandestine.

But he and I talked, of course, about our families, our origins. What distinguished his family, I would say, is that they were cultural Afrikaners but not political Afrikaners. What do I mean? Reflect on Europe in the nineteenth century. All over the continent you see ethnic or cultural identities being transformed into political identities. The process starts in Greece and spreads through the Balkans and central Europe. Soon that same wave hit the Cape Colony. Dutch-speaking Creoles begin to reinvent themselves as the Afrikaner nation and to agitate for national independence.

Well, somehow or other that wave of nationalist enthusiasm passed John's family by. Or else they decided not to swim with it.

They kept their distance because of the politics associated with nationalist enthusiasm – I mean, the anti-imperialist, anti-English politics?

Yes. First they were disturbed by the whipped-up hostility to everything English, by the mystique of *Blut und Boden*; then later they recoiled from the policies that the nationalists took over from

239

the radical right in Europe: scientific racism, the policing of culture, militarization of the youth, a state religion, and so forth.

So, all in all, you see Coetzee as a conservative, an anti-radical.

A cultural conservative, yes, as many of the modernists were cultural conservatives – I mean the modernist writers from Europe who were his models. He was deeply attached to the South Africa of his youth, a South Africa which by 1976 was starting to look like a never-never land. For proof you have only to turn to the book I mentioned, *Boyhood,* where you find a palpable nostalgia for the old feudal relations between white and Coloured. To people like him, the National Party with its policy of apartheid represented not rural conservatism but on the contrary new-fangled social engineering. He was all in favour of the old, complex, feudal social textures which so offended the tidy minds of the *dirigistes* of apartheid.

Did you ever find yourself at odds with him over questions of politics?

That is a difficult question. Where, after all, does character end and politics begin? At a personal level, I saw him as rather too fatalistic and therefore too passive. Did his mistrust of political activism express itself in passivity in the conduct of his life, or did an innate fatalism express itself in mistrust of political action? I cannot decide. But yes, at a personal level there was a certain tension between us. I wanted our relationship to grow and develop, he wanted it to remain the same, without change. That was what caused the breach, in the end. Because between a man and a woman there is no standing still, in my view. Either you are going up or you are going down.

When did the breach occur?

In 1980. I left Cape Town and came back to France.

Did you and he have no further contact?

For a while he wrote to me. He sent me his books. Then he stopped writing. I presumed he had found someone else.

And when you look back over the relationship, how do you see it?

How do I see our relationship? John was the kind of man who is convinced that supreme felicity will be his if only he can acquire a French mistress who will recite Ronsard to him and play Couperin on the clavecin while simultaneously inducting him into the mysteries of love, French style. I exaggerate, of course. Nevertheless, he was a marked Francophile.

Was I the French mistress of his fantasy? I doubt it very much. Looking back, I now see our relationship as comical in its essence. Comico-sentimental. Based on a comic premise. Yet with a further element that I must not minimize, namely, that he helped me escape from a bad marriage, for which I remain grateful to this day.

Comico-sentimental . . . You make it sound rather light. Did Coetzee not leave a deeper imprint on you, and you on him?

As to what imprint I may have left on him, that I am not in a position to judge. But in general I would say that unless you have a strong presence you do not leave a deep imprint; and John did not have a strong presence. I don't mean to sound flippant.

241

I know he had many admirers; he was not awarded the Nobel Prize for nothing; and of course you would not be here today, doing these researches, if you did not think he was important as a writer. But – to be serious for a moment – in all the time I was with him I never had the feeling I was with an exceptional person, a truly exceptional human being. It is a harsh thing to say, I know, but regrettably it is true. I experienced no flash of lightning from him that suddenly illuminated the world. Or if there were flashes, I was blind to them.

I found John clever, I found him knowledgeable, I admired him in many ways. As a writer he knew what he was doing, he had a certain style, and style is the beginning of distinction. But he had no special sensitivity that I could detect, no original insight into the human condition. He was just a man, a man of his time, talented, maybe even gifted, but, frankly, not a giant. I am sorry if I disappoint you. From other people who knew him you will get a different picture, I am sure.

Turning to his writings: speaking objectively, as a critic, what is your estimation of his books?

I did not read all of them. After *Disgrace* I lost interest. In general I would say that his work lacks ambition. The control of the elements is too tight. Nowhere do you get a feeling of a writer deforming his medium in order to say what has never been said before, which is to me the mark of great writing. Too cool, too neat, I would say. Too easy. Too lacking in passion. That's all.

Interview conducted in Paris in January 2008.

Notebooks: undated fragments

Undated fragment

IT IS A Saturday afternoon in winter, ritual time for the game of rugby. With his father he catches a train to Newlands in time for the 2.15 curtain-raiser. The curtain-raiser will be followed at 4.00 by the main match. After the main match they will catch a train home again.

He goes with his father to Newlands because sport – rugby in winter, cricket in summer – is the strongest surviving bond between them, and because it went through his heart like a knife, the first Saturday after his return to the country, to see his father put on his coat and without a word go off to Newlands like a lonely child.

His father has no friends. Nor has he, though for a different reason. He had friends when he was younger; but these old friends are by now dispersed all over the world, and he seems to have lost the knack, or perhaps the will, to make new ones. So he is cast back on his father, as his father is cast back on him. As they live together, so on Saturdays they take their pleasure together. That is the law of the family.

It surprised him, when he came back, to discover that his

father knew no one. He had always thought of his father as a convivial man. But either he was wrong about that or his father has changed. Or perhaps it is simply one of the things that happen to men as they grow older: they withdraw into themselves. On Saturdays the stands at Newlands are full of them, solitary men in grey gabardine raincoats in the twilight of their lives, keeping to themselves as if their loneliness were a shameful disease.

He and his father sit side by side on the north stand, watching the curtain-raiser. Over the day's proceedings hangs an air of melancholy. This is the last season when the stadium will be used for club rugby. With the belated arrival of television in the country, interest in club rugby has dwindled away. Men who used to spend their Saturday afternoons at Newlands now prefer to stay at home and watch the game of the week. Of the thousands of seats in the north stand no more than a dozen are occupied. The railway stand is entirely empty. In the south stand there is still a bloc of diehard Coloured spectators who come to cheer for UCT and Villagers and boo Stellenbosch and Van der Stel. Only the grandstand holds a respectable number, perhaps a thousand.

A quarter of a century ago, when he was a child, it was different. On a big day in the club competition – the day when Hamiltons played Villagers, say, or UCT played Stellenbosch – one would struggle to find standing-room. Within an hour of the final whistle *Argus* vans would be racing through the streets dropping off bundles of the Sports Edition for the vendors on the street corners, with eyewitness accounts of all the first-league games, even the games played in far-off Stellenbosch and Somerset West, together with scores from the lesser leagues, 2A and 2B, 3A and 3B.

Those days are gone. Club rugby is on its last legs. One can sense it today not just in the stands but on the field itself. Depressed by the booming space of the empty stadium, the players seem merely to be going through the motions. A ritual is dying out before their eyes, an authentic petit-bourgeois South African ritual. Its last devotees are gathered here today: sad old men like his father; dull, dutiful sons like himself.

A light rain begins to fall. Over the two of them he raises an umbrella. On the field thirty half-hearted young men blunder about, groping for the wet ball.

The curtain-raiser is between Union, in sky-blue, and Gardens, in maroon and black. Union and Gardens are at the bottom of the first-league table and in danger of relegation. It used not to be like that. Once upon a time Gardens was a force in Western Province rugby. At home there is a framed photograph of the Gardens third team as it was in 1938, with his father seated in the front row in his freshly laundered hooped jersey with its Gardens crest and its collar turned up fashionably around his ears. But for certain unforeseen events, World War II in particular, his father might even – who knows? – have made it into the second team.

If old allegiances counted, his father would cheer for Gardens over Union. But the truth is, his father does not care who wins, Gardens or Union or the man in the moon. In fact he finds it hard to detect what his father cares about, in rugby or anything else. If he could solve the mystery of what in the world his father wants, he might perhaps be a better son.

The whole of his father's family is like that – without any passion that he can put a finger on. They do not even seem to care about money. All they want is to get along with everyone and have a bit of a laugh in the process.

In the laughing department he is the last companion his father needs. In laughing he comes bottom of the class. A gloomy fellow: that must be how the world sees him, when it sees him at all. A gloomy fellow; a wet blanket; a stick in the mud.

And then there is the matter of his father's music. After Mussolini capitulated in 1944 and the Germans were driven north, the Allied troops occupying Italy, including the South Africans, were allowed to relax briefly and enjoy themselves. Among the recreations mounted for them were free performances in the big opera houses. Young men from America, Britain, and the far-flung British dominions across the seas, wholly innocent of Italian opera, were plunged into the drama of *Tosca* or *The Barber of Seville* or *Lucia di Lammermoor*. Only a handful took to it, but his father was among that handful. Brought up on sentimental Irish and English ballads, he was entranced by the lush new music and overwhelmed by the spectacle. Day after day he went back for more.

So when Corporal Coetzee returned to South Africa at the end of hostilities, it was with a newfound passion for opera. '*La donna è mobile,*' he would sing in the bath. '*Figaro here, Figaro there,*' he would sing, '*Figaro, Figaro, Feeegaro!*' He went out and bought a gramophone, their family's first; over and over again he would play a 78 rpm recording of Caruso singing 'Your tiny hand is frozen.' When long-playing records were invented he acquired a new and better gramophone, together with an album of Renata Tebaldi singing well-loved arias.

Thus in his adolescent years there were two schools of vocal music at war with each other in the house: an Italian school, his father's, manifested by Tebaldi and Tito Gobbi in full cry; and a German school, his own, founded on Bach. All of Sunday afternoon the household would drown in choruses from the B-minor Mass; then in the evenings, with Bach at last silenced, his father would pour himself a glass of brandy, put on Renata Tebaldi, and sit down to listen to real melodies, real singing.

For its sensuality and decadence – that was how, at the age of sixteen, he saw it – he resolved he would for ever hate and despise Italian opera. That he might despise it simply because his father loved it, that he would have resolved to hate and despise anything in the world that his father loved, was a possibility he would not admit.

One day, while no one was around, he took the Tebaldi record out of its sleeve and with a razor blade drew a deep score across its surface.

On Sunday evening his father put on the record. With each revolution the needle jumped. 'Who has done this?' he demanded. But no one, it seemed, had done it. It had just happened.

Thus ended Tebaldi; now Bach could reign unchallenged.

For that mean and petty deed of his he has for the past twenty years felt the bitterest remorse, remorse that has not receded with the passage of time but on the contrary grown keener. One of his first actions when he returned to the country was to scour the music shops for the Tebaldi record. Though he failed to find it, he did come upon a compilation in which she sang some of the same arias. He brought it home and played it through from beginning to end, hoping to lure his father out of his room as a hunter might lure a bird with his pipes. But his father showed no interest.

'Don't you recognize the voice?' he asked.

His father shook his head.

'It's Renata Tebaldi. Don't you remember how you used to love Tebaldi in the old days?'

He refused to accept defeat. He continued to hope that one day, when he was out of the house, his father would put the new, unblemished record on the player, pour himself a glass of brandy, sit down in his armchair, and allow himself to be transported to Rome or Milan or wherever it was that as a young man his ears were first opened to the sensual beauties of the human voice. He wanted his father's breast to swell with that old joy; if only for an hour, he wanted him to relive that lost youth, forget his present crushed and humiliated existence. Above all he wanted his father to forgive him. *Forgive me!* he wanted to say to his father. *Forgive you? Heavens, what is there to forgive?* he wanted to hear his father reply. Upon which, if he could summon up the courage, he would at last make full confession: *Forgive me for deliberately and with malice aforethought scratching your Tebaldi record. And for more besides, so much more that the recital would take all day. For countless acts of meanness. For the meanness of heart in which those acts originated. In sum, for all I have done since the day I was born, and with such success, to make your life a misery.*

But no, there was no indication, not the faintest, that during his absences from the house Tebaldi was being set free to sing. Tebaldi had, it seemed, lost her charms; or else his father was playing a terrible game with him. *My life a misery? What makes you think my life has been a misery? What makes you think you have ever had it in your power to make my life a misery?*

Intermittently he plays the Tebaldi record for himself; and as he listens the beginnings of some kind of transformation seem to take place inside him. As it must have been with his father in 1944, his heart too begins to throb in time with Mimi's. As the great rising arc of her voice must have called out his father's soul, so it now calls out his soul too, urging it to join hers in passionate, soaring flight.

What has been wrong with him all these years? Why has he not been listening to Verdi, to Puccini? Has he been deaf? Or is the truth worse than that: did he, even as a youth, hear and recognize perfectly well the call of Tebaldi, and then with tight-lipped primness ('I won't!') refuse to heed it? *Down with Tebaldi, down with Italy, down with the flesh!* And if his father must go down too in the general wreck, so be it!

Of what is going on inside his father he has no idea. His father does not talk about himself, does not keep a diary or write letters. Only once, by accident, has the door opened a chink. In the Lifestyle supplement to the weekend *Argus* he has come upon a Yes–No quiz that his father has filled in and left lying around, a quiz titled 'Your Personal Satisfaction Index'. Next to the third question – 'Have you known many members of the opposite sex?' – his father has ticked the box No. 'Have relations with the opposite sex been a source of satisfaction to you?' reads the fourth. No, is the answer again.

Out of a possible twenty, his father scores six. A score of fifteen or above, says the creator of the Index, one Ray Schwarz, MD, PhD, author of *How to Succeed in Life and Love*, a best-selling guide to personal development, means that the respondent has lived a fulfilled life. A score of less than ten, on the other hand, suggests that he or she needs to cultivate a more positive outlook, to which end joining a social club or taking up dancing might be a first step.

Theme to carry further: his father and why he lives with him. The reaction of the women in his life (bafflement).

Undated fragment

Over the airwaves come denunciations of the communist terrorists, together with their dupes and cronies in the World Council of Churches. The terms of the denunciations may change from day to day, but their hectoring tone does not. It is a tone familiar to him from the Worcester of his schooldays, where once a week all the children, from youngest to oldest, were herded into the school hall to have their brains washed. So familiar is it that at its first breath a visceral loathing rises in him and he dives for the off switch.

He is the product of a damaged childhood, that he long ago worked out; what surprises him is that the worst damage was done not in the seclusion of the home but out in the open, at school.

He has been reading here and there in educational theory, and in the writings of the Dutch Calvinist school he begins to recognize what underlay the form of schooling that was administered to him. The purpose of education, say Abraham Kuyper and his disciples, is to form the child as congregant, as citizen, and as parent to be. It is the word *form* that gives him pause. During his years at school in Worcester, his teachers, themselves formed by followers of Kuyper, had all the time been labouring to form him and the other little boys in their charge – form them as a craftsman forms a clay pot; and he, using what pathetic, inarticulate means he had at his disposal, had been resisting them – had resisted them then as he resists them now.

But why had he so doggedly resisted? Where did that resistance of his come from, that refusal to accept that the end goal of education should be to form him in some predetermined image, who would otherwise have no form but wallow instead in a state of nature, unsaved, savage? There can be only one answer: the kernel of his resistance, his counter-theory to their Kuyperism, must have come from his mother. Somehow or other, either from her own upbringing as the daughter of the daughter of an Evangelical missionary, or more likely from her sole year in college, a year from which she emerged with nothing but a diploma licensing her to teach in primary schools, she must have picked up an alternative ideal of the educator and the educator's task, and then somehow impressed that ideal on her children. The task of the educator, according to his mother, should be to identify and foster the natural talents of the child, the talents with which the child is born and which make the child unique. If the child is to be pictured as a plant, then the educator should feed the roots of the plant and watch over its growth, rather than – as the Kuyperists preached – prune its branches and shape it.

But what grounds does he have for thinking that in bringing him up – him and his brother – his mother followed any theory at all? Why should the truth not be that his mother let the two of them grow up wallowing in savagery simply because she herself had grown up savage – she and her brothers and sisters on the farm in the Eastern Cape where they were born? The answer is given in names he dredges up from the recesses of memory: Montessori; Rudolf Steiner. The names meant nothing when he heard them as a child. But now, in his readings in education, he comes across them again. Montessori, the Montessori Method: so that is why he was given blocks to play with, wooden blocks that he would at first fling hither and thither across the room, thinking that was what they were for, then later pile one on top of the other until the tower (always a tower!) came crashing down and he would howl with frustration.

Blocks to make castles with, and plasticine to make animals with (plasticine which, at first, he would try to chew); and then, before he was ready for it, a Meccano set with plates and rods and bolts and pulleys and cranks.

My little architect; my little engineer. His mother departed the world before it became incontrovertibly clear that he was going to become neither of these, and therefore that the blocks and the Meccano set had not worked their magic, perhaps not the plasticine either (*my little sculptor*). Did his mother wonder: *Was it all a big mistake, the Montessori Method?* Did she even, in darker moments, think to herself: *I should have let them form him, those Calvinists, I should never have backed him in his resistance?*

If they had succeeded in forming him, those Worcester school-teachers, he would more than likely have become one of them himself, patrolling rows of silent children with a ruler in his hand, rapping on their desks as he passed to remind them who was boss. And at the end of the day he would have had a Kuyperian family of his own to go home to, a well-formed, obedient wife and well-formed, obedient children – a family and a home within a community within a homeland. Instead of which he has – what? A father to look after, a father not very good at looking after himself, smoking a little in secret, drinking a little in secret, with a view of their joint domestic situation no doubt at variance with his own: for instance, that it has fallen to him, the unlucky father, to look after him, the grown-up son, since he, the son, is not very good at looking after himself, as is all too evident from his recent history.

To be developed: his own, home-grown theory of education, its roots in (a) Plato and (b) Freud, its elements (a) discipleship (the student aspiring to be like the teacher) and (b) ethical idealism (the teacher striving to be worthy of the student), its perils (a) vanity (the teacher basking in the student's worship) and (b) sex (sex as shortcut to knowledge).

His attested incompetence in matters of the heart; transference in the classroom and his repeated failures to manage it.

Undated fragment

His father works as a bookkeeper for a firm that imports and sells components for Japanese cars. Because most of these components are made not in Japan but in Taiwan, South Korea, or even Thailand, they cannot be called authentic parts. On the other hand, because they do not come in forged manufacturers' packaging but proclaim (in small print) their country of origin, they are not pirate parts either.

The owners of the firm are two brothers, now in late middle age, who speak English with eastern European inflections and pretend to be innocent of Afrikaans though in fact they were born in Port Elizabeth and understand street Afrikaans perfectly well. They employ a staff of five: three counter hands, a bookkeeper, and a bookkeeper's assistant. The bookkeeper and his assistant have a little wood and glass cubicle of their own to insulate them from the activities around them. As for the hands, they spend their time bustling back and forth between the counter and the racks of auto parts that stretch into the shadowy recesses of the store. The chief counter hand, Cedric, had been with them from the start. No matter how obscure a part may be – a fan housing for a 1968 Suzuki three-wheeler, a kingpin bush for an Impact five-ton truck – Cedric will know where it is.

Once a year the firm does a stocktaking during which every part bought or sold, down to the last nut and bolt, is accounted for. It is a major undertaking: most dealers would shut their doors for the duration. But Acme Auto Parts has got where it has got, say the brothers, by staying open from eight a.m. until five p.m. five days of the week, plus eight a.m. until one p.m. on Saturdays, come hell or high water, fifty-two weeks of the year, Christmas and New Year excepted. Therefore the stock-taking has to be done after hours.

As bookkeeper his father is at the centre of operations. During the stocktaking he sacrifices his lunch hour and works late into the evening. He works alone, without help: working overtime, and therefore catching a late train home, is something that neither Mrs Noerdien, his father's assistant, nor even the counter hands is prepared to do. Riding the trains after dark has become too dangerous, they say: too many commuters are being attacked and robbed. So after closing time it is only the brothers, in their office, and his father, in his cubicle, who stay behind, poring over documents and ledgers.

'If I had Mrs Noerdien for just one extra hour a day,' says his father, 'we could be finished in no time. I could call out the figures and she could check. Doing it by myself is hopeless.'

His father is not a qualified bookkeeper; but during the years he spent running his own legal practice he picked up at least the rudiments. He has been the brothers' bookkeeper for twelve years, ever since he gave up the law. The brothers, it must be presumed – Cape Town is not a big city – are aware of his chequered past in the legal profession. They are aware of it and therefore – it must be presumed – keep a close watch on him, in case, even so close to retirement, he should think of trying to diddle them.

'If you could bring the ledgers home with you,' he suggests to his father, 'I could give you a hand with the checking.'

His father shakes his head, and he can guess why. When his father refers to the ledgers, he does so in hushed tones, as though they were holy books, as though keeping them were a priestly function. There is more to keeping books, his attitude would seem to suggest, than applying elementary arithmetic to columns of figures.

'I don't think I can bring the ledgers home,' his father says at last. 'Not on the train. The brothers would never allow it.'

He can appreciate that. What would become of Acme if his father were mugged and the sacred books stolen?

'Then let me come in to the city at closing time and take over from Mrs Noerdien. You and I could work together from five till eight, say.'

His father is silent.

'I'll just help with the checking,' he says. 'If anything confidential comes up, I promise I won't look.'

By the time he arrives for his first stint, Mrs Noerdien and the counter hands have gone home. He is introduced to the brothers. 'My son John,' says his father, 'who has offered to help with the checking.'

He shakes their hands: Mr Rodney Silverman, Mr Barrett Silverman.

'I'm not sure we can afford you on the payroll, John,' says Mr Rodney. He turns to his brother. 'Which do you think is more expensive, Barrett, a PhD or a CA? We may have to take out a loan.'

They all laugh together at the joke. Then they offer him a rate. It is precisely the same rate he earned as a student, sixteen years ago, for copying household data onto cards for the municipal census.

With his father he settles down in the bookkeepers' glass cubicle. The task that faces them is simple. They have to go through file after file of invoices, confirming that the figures have been transcribed correctly to the books and to the bank ledger, ticking them off one by one in red pencil, checking the addition at the foot of the page.

They set to work and make steady progress. Once every thousand entries they come across an error, a piddling five cents one way or the other. For the rest the books are in exemplary order. As defrocked clergymen make the best proofreaders, so debarred lawyers seem to make good bookkeepers – debarred lawyers assisted if need be by their overeducated, underemployed sons.

The next day, on his way to Acme, he is caught in a rainshower. He arrives sodden. The glass of the cubicle is fogged; he enters without knocking. His father is hunched over his desk. There is a second presence in the cubicle, a woman, young, gazelle-eyed, softly curved, in the act of putting on her raincoat.

He halts in his tracks, transfixed.

His father rises from his seat. 'Mrs Noerdien, this is my son John.'

Mrs Noerdien averts her gaze, does not offer a hand. 'I'll go now,' she says in a low voice, addressing not him but his father.

An hour later the brothers too take their leave. His father boils the kettle and makes them coffee. Page after page, column after column they press on with the work, until ten o'clock, until his father is blinking with exhaustion.

The rain has stopped. Down a deserted Riebeeck Street they head for the station: two men, able-bodied more or less, safer at night than a single man, many times safer than a single woman.

'How long has Mrs Noerdien been working for you?' he asks.

'She came last February.'

He waits for more. There is no more. There is plenty he could ask. For instance: How does it happen that Mrs Noerdien, who wears a headscarf and is presumably Muslim, comes to be working for a Jewish firm, one where there is no male relative to keep a protective eye on her?

'Is she good at her job? Is she efficient?'

'Very good. Very meticulous.'

Again he waits for more. Again, that is the end of it.

The question he cannot ask is: What does it do to the heart of a lonely man like yourself to be sitting side by side, day after day, in a cubicle no larger than many prison cells, with a woman who is not only as good at her job and as meticulous as Mrs Noerdien, but also as feminine?

For that is the chief impression he carries away from his brush with her. He calls her feminine because he has no better word: the feminine, a higher rarefaction of the female, to the point of becoming spirit. With Mrs Noerdien, how would a man, how even would Mr Noerdien, traverse the space from the exalted heights of the feminine to the earthly body of the female? To sleep with a being like that, to embrace such a body, to smell and taste it – what would it do to a man? And to be beside her all day, conscious of her slightest stirring: did his father's sad response to Dr Schwarz's lifestyle quiz – 'Have relations with the opposite sex been a source of satisfaction to you?' – 'No' – have something to do with coming face to face, in the wintertime of his life, with beauty such as he has not known before and can never hope to possess?

Query: Why say that his father is in love with Mrs Noerdien when he has so obviously fallen for her himself?

Undated fragment.
Idea for a story.

A man, a writer, keeps a diary. In it he notes down thoughts, ideas, significant occurrences.

Things take a turn for the worse in his life. 'Bad day,' he writes in his diary, without elaboration. 'Bad day,' he writes, day after day.

Tiring of calling each day a bad day, he decides to simply mark bad days with an asterisk, as some people (women) mark with a red cross days when they will bleed, or as other people (men, womanizers) mark with an X days when they have notched up a success.

The bad days pile up; the asterisks multiply like a plague of flies.

Poetry, if he could write poetry, might take him to the root of his malaise, this malaise that blossoms in the form of asterisks. But the spring of poetry in him seems to have dried up.

There is prose to fall back on. In theory prose can perform the same cleansing trick as poetry. But he has doubts about that. Prose, in his experience, calls for many more words than poetry. There is no point in embarking on prose if one lacks confidence that one will be alive the next day to carry on with the task.

He plays with thoughts like these – the thought of poetry, the thought of prose – as a way of not writing.

In the back pages of his diary he makes lists. One of them is headed *Ways of Doing Away with Oneself*. In the left-hand column he lists *Methods,* in the right-hand column *Drawbacks.*

Of the ways of doing away with oneself he has listed, the one he favours, on mature consideration, is drowning, that is to say, driving to Fish Hoek at night, parking near the deserted end of the beach, undressing in the car, putting on swimming trunks (why?), crossing the sand and entering the water (it will have to be a moonlit night), breasting the waves, striking out into the dark, swimming to the limit of physical endurance, then letting fate take its course.

All of his intercourse with the world seems to take place through a membrane. Because the membrane is there, fertilization will not take place. It is an interesting metaphor, full of potential, but it does not take him anywhere that he can see.

Undated fragment

His father grew up on a farm in the Karoo drinking artesian water high in fluoride. The fluoride turned the enamel of his teeth brown and hard as stone. His boast used to be that he never needed to see a dentist. Then in mid-life his teeth began to go rotten, one after another, and he had to have them all extracted.

Now, in his mid-sixties, his gums are giving him trouble. Abscesses are forming that will not heal. His throat becomes infected. He finds it painful to swallow, to speak.

He goes first to a dentist, then to a doctor, an ear, nose and throat specialist, who sends him for X-rays. The X-rays reveal a cancerous tumour on the larynx. He is advised to submit to surgery urgently.

He visits his father in the male ward at Groote Schuur Hospital. He is wearing general-issue pyjamas and his eyes are frightened. Inside the too-large jacket he is like a bird, all skin and bone.

'It is a routine operation,' he reassures his father. 'You will be out in a few days.'

'Will you explain to the brothers?' his father whispers with painful slowness.

'I will phone them.'

'Mrs Noerdien is very capable.'

'I am sure Mrs Noerdien is very capable. I am sure she will manage until you come back.'

There is nothing more to say. He could stretch out and take his father's hand and hold it, to comfort him, to convey to him that he is not alone, that he is loved and cherished. But he does no such thing. Save in the case of small children, children not yet old enough to be formed, it is not the practice in their family for one person to reach out and touch another. Nor is that all. If on this one extreme occasion he were to ignore family practice and grasp his father's hand, would what that gesture implied be true? Is his father truly loved and cherished? Is his father truly not alone?

He takes a long walk, from the hospital to the Main Road, then along the Main Road as far as Newlands. The south-easter is howling, whipping up trash from the gutters. He walks fast, conscious of the vigour of his limbs, the steadiness of his heart-beat. The air of the hospital is still in his lungs; he must expel it, get rid of it.

When he arrives in the ward the next day, his father is flat on his back, his chest and throat swathed in a dressing with tubes running out of it. He looks like a corpse, the corpse of an old man.

He has been prepared for the spectacle. The larynx, which was tumorous, had to be excised, says the surgeon, there was no avoiding that. His father will no longer be able to speak in the normal way. However, in due course, after the wound has healed, he will be fitted with a prosthesis that will permit vocal communication of a kind. A more urgent task is to ensure the cancer has not spread, which will mean further tests, plus radiotherapy.

'Does my father know that?' he asks the surgeon. 'Does he know what he is in for?'

'I tried to fill him in,' says the surgeon, 'but I am not sure how much he absorbed. He is in a state of shock. Which is to be expected, of course.'

He stands over the figure in the bed. 'I phoned Acme,' he says. 'I spoke to the brothers and explained the situation.'

His father opens his eyes. Generally he is sceptical about the capacity of the ocular orbs to express complex feelings, but this time he is shaken. The look his father gives him speaks of utter indifference: indifference to him, indifference to Acme Auto, indifference to everything but the fate of his own soul in the prospect of eternity.

'The brothers send their best wishes,' he continues. 'For a speedy recovery. They say not to worry, Mrs Noerdien will hold the fort until you are ready to come back.'

It is true. The brothers, or whichever of the brothers he spoke to, could not be more solicitous. Their bookkeeper may not be of the faith, but the brothers are not cold people. 'A jewel' – that is what the brother in question called his father. 'Your father is a jewel, his job will always be open for him.'

It is of course a fiction, all of it. His father will never go back to work. In a week or two or three he will be sent home, cured or part cured, to commence the next and final phase of his life, during which he will depend for his daily bread on the charity of the Automotive Industry Benefit Fund, of the South African state through its Department of Pensions, and of his surviving family.

'Is there anything I can bring you?' he inquires.

His father makes tiny scrabbling motions with his left hand, whose fingernails, he notes, are not clean. 'Do you want to write?' he says. He brings out his pocket diary, opens it to the page headed *Telephone Numbers*, and proffers it together with a pen.

The fingers cease moving, the eyes lose focus.

'I don't know what you mean,' he says. 'Try again to tell me what you mean.'

Slowly his father shakes his head, left to right.

On the stands beside the other beds in the ward there are vases of flowers, magazines, in some cases framed photographs. The stand beside his father's bed is bare save for a glass of water.

'I must go now,' he says. 'I have a class to teach.'

At a kiosk near the front entrance he buys a packet of sucking sweets and returns to his father's bedside. 'I got these for you,' he says. 'To hold in your mouth if your mouth gets dry.'

Two weeks later his father comes home in an ambulance. He is able to walk in a shuffling way with the aid of a stick. He makes his way from the front door to his bedroom and shuts himself up.

One of the ambulancemen hands him a cyclostyled sheet of instructions titled *Laryngectomy – Care of Patients*, and a card with a schedule of times when the clinic is open. He glances over the sheet. There is an outline sketch of a human head with a dark circle low in the throat. *Care of Wound*, it says.

He draws back. 'I can't do this,' he says. The ambulancemen exchange glances, shrug. It is not their business, taking care of the wound, taking care of the patient. Their business is to convey the patient to his or her place of residence. After that it is the patient's business, or the patient's family's business, or else no one's business.

It used to be that he, John, had too little employment. Now that is about to change. Now he will have as much employment as he can handle, as much and more. He is going to have to abandon some of his personal projects and be a nurse.

265

Alternatively, if he will not be a nurse, he must announce to his father: *I cannot face the prospect of ministering to you day and night. I am going to abandon you. Goodbye.* One or the other: there is no third way.